D. M. THOMAS

D. M. Thomas lives in Truro, Cornwall, the county where he was born and grew up. FLYING IN TO LOVE is his ninth novel. He has also published several volumes of poetry and translations of Russian poets, including THE PUBERTY TREE (Poems 1960–90). His third novel, THE WHITE HOTEL, was short-listed for the Booker Prize and has been translated into twenty languages.

'The book has moments of great poetic power . . . he has succeeded in releasing Kennedy the saint from the circumstances surrounding his canonisation'

The Independent on Sunday

'The power of Thomas's writing is beyond doubt'

The Spectator

'He presents simultaneously all the contradictory faces of Jack Kennedy and recaptures with extraordinary intensity the rarified atmosphere of the 1960s'

Glasgow Herald

'Absorbing . . . creates a brilliant picture of the Kennedy entourage in action . . . his most successful novel since THE WHITE HOTEL'

Today

'Thomas brings home the magnitude of the event, presenting it in timeless, unashamedly mythic terms . . . With a few sentences he wrenches you out of comfortable, recurring acquiescence and confronts you with shared psychic trauma. Yet he is hypnotic and irresistible'

San Diego Tribune

'Thomas' portrayal of our mass psyche rings intimately true . . . He has fixed his penetrating gaze on America's deepest public shame and created a haunting, caustic novel . . . a dark view of America from a writer who defies taboos of sensibility to probe a profound cultural mystery'

Chicago Tribune

D. M. Thomas

FLYING IN TO LOVE

First published in Great Britain in 1992 by Bloomsbury Publishing Ltd

Sceptre edition 1993

Sceptre is an imprint of Hodder and Stoughton Paperbacks, a division of Hodder and Stoughton Ltd

The lines from 'Time and Again' by Rainer Maria Rilke, from *Selected Poems*, translated by J. B. Leichmann, are reprinted by permission of the Hogarth Press.

The lines from 'Birches' by Robert Frost, from *The Poetry of Robert Frost*, edited by Edward Connery Latham, are reprinted by permission of the Estate of Robert Frost and Jonathan Cape.

British Library C.I.P.

A CIP catalogue record is available

ISBN 0-340-57903-X

Printed and bound in Great Britain for Hodder and Stoughton Paperbacks, a division of Hodder and Stoughton Ltd, Mill Road, Dunton Green, Sevenoaks, Kent TN13 2YA. (Editorial Office: 47 Bedford Square, London WC1B 3DP) by Clays Ltd, St Ives plc.

ACKNOWLEDGEMENT

Among numerous works consulted for background information and speculation some of the most valuable have been: Peter Collier & David Horowitz's *The Kennedys*; Henry Hurt's *Reasonable Doubt*; Mark Lane's *Rush to Judgement*; David S. Lifton's *Best Evidence*; Jim Marrs' *Crossfire*; William Manchester's *Death of a President*; Priscilla Johnson McMillan's *Marina and Lee*; the Warren Commission Report; and Bryan Woolley's *November 22*. Only the last of these, a fine novel, is openly a work of fiction; but every book about the assassination of John F. Kennedy has mingled reality and fiction, and mine is no different.

FOR ALEX

We dance round in a ring and suppose,
But the Secret sits in the middle and knows.

– Robert Frost

O Captain! my Captain! our fearful trip is done.

– Walt Whitman

I

Through the Underpass

1

'Ten thousand dreams a night,' a Dallas psychologist told me, when I dined with her and her black lover, 'are dreamt about Kennedy's assassination.' Since dreams begin anywhere, and since fiction is a kind of dream, and history is a kind of dream, and this is both, we could begin with the shots in Dealey Plaza; or, a few seconds and an eternity later, the screaming cars and motor cycles through the triple underpass, the nightmare of blood and brain, heading not for the Trade Mart but Parkland Hospital, so conveniently close by. Or we could start with Sister Agnes, at home with her elderly, sick father, painfully going through *Tom Sawyer* with him; he is in bed, tired because last night he'd stayed up later, watching with liberal horror the eye-witness reports of missiles raining on Baghdad; she was very conscious of an empty armchair, her mother having died of a stroke before Christmas. But let's begin with the soul, Kennedy's soul, and the priest. The priest, who has come as quickly as possible through the traffic-jam, has seen the gaping exit wound at the back of the skull. This priest knows entry wounds and exit wounds, Dallas is violent. His faith shivered as he gave conditional absolution. He is also full of guilt because, when asked to say some prayers, he started to kneel, then thought better of it, seeing all the blood on the trauma room floor.

But now he steps tentatively towards the widow in her stained clothes, her back turned to him, and touches her shoulder. 'I am convinced,' he whispers, 'that the soul . . . you know . . .'

3

'I know.'

She comforted the distraught priest by allowing him to offer her his few words of comfort. She had had to rest her forehead against the wall because her head was spinning. In her mind it was Jack she was resting against. It was a relief to escape back, for a few moments. They'd just arrived at the Hotel Texas in Fort Worth and were in his bedroom of the presidential suite. It was late and they were swaying together like boxers in the last round, Jack had joked. He'd kissed her on the forehead and she on his cheek, leaving a faint red mark.

Sleep well, honey, he'd murmured.

And you.

He thanked her for coming on this trip and she said she was enjoying it. He complimented her on how she'd looked, told her she'd stunned all the crowds. He kissed her again on the brow, releasing her, and she opened the door into her bedroom. She saw the pink suit hung up. She wondered if it was the right choice for Dallas tomorrow. She heard the rain rustling against the high window.

After Jackie had gone, closing the connecting door gently, he unscrewed a thermos of iced water, poured some into a glass, and drank. He went to the bathroom and bathed his hands, which were bruised from so many handshakes. The iced water and the bathing soothed him; he felt less tired. Picking up the phone from a bedside table, he dialled Johnson's suite. Connally answered, and behind his Texan voice Jack could hear the sounds of a party. Yes, Lyndon was right here; and the next moment Lyndon was on the line.

'Mr President?'

'How's the party?'

'Oh, we're havin' ourselves a great time.'

'Good! You deserve it. Any decent broads?'

'Not unless you count Bird, Mr President. Everyone but Bird here has a dangler. Leastways I'd guess they do. You and Jackie wanna come up?'

'Thanks, Lyndon, but no. Jackie's hit the sack already, and

I guess I should call it a day too. I just wanted to thank you and Lady Bird for all you've done today.'

'It's been a pleasure, Mr President; but we ain't done nothin'. It's you and Jackie – the Texans love you.'

They said their good-nights. Jack broke the connection and redialled. 'Can we have the air-conditioning off, please?' he requested. 'It's mighty cold . . . Thank you.'

He sat down on the bed, hunching forward, his hands loosely clasped. He reflected on how little power a president had to get things moving. The night-porter he'd spoken to was a Negro: scared to death, awed. Happy to be a night-porter in such a luxurious hotel. Would a Negro ever be manager of this hotel? And the trouble was, you were so used to speaking to them in a certain way, polite but superior. The Civil Rights Bill, if it could get passed, would be a start; they'd be able to drink in the same bars, eat in the same restaurants, as whites. Above all, more of them would get a decent education.

But shit, there was so much hypocrisy! Look at that poll in California. Among so-called liberals. Weren't in favour of desegregation in *their* areas. Just everywhere else. And George Wallace, who hates violence; but it's strange how little black girls get killed in their Sunday schools. And nobody ever gets caught.

It could cost me the election. If it was this year I'd lose it for sure. It's important to take it at a measured pace. We've had some successes. King's demonstration was a triumph. Meredith got his degree. The problem is, a lot of them want it all at once; they're their own worst enemies. Malcolm X. Dangerous. The so-called fucking intellectuals, like that writer, Baldwin. Don't know how hard it is. If I only had Khrushchev's power.

We have to get bipartisan support. Can't they see it's inevitable, that you can't keep a whole race down for ever? Dying seven years earlier, earning half as much. Eisenhower should do more. He didn't ask the colour of their skin before sending them on to the beaches on D-Day. He's not a bigot, but he's cautious. And Johnson – where does he stand on it, in his heart? Of course, he has to go carefully, as a Southerner; but

I can never figure out what he believes in. He lies even when he doesn't need to.

The whine of the air-conditioning had stopped. Complete silence, a shade unnerving.

He pulled himself to his feet and took two uncertain steps. Those damn crutches, he should have brought them. But it was bad enough wanting justice for Negroes without also being seen to need crutches. He stood for a moment, his shoulders hunched, a hand in his coat-pocket, then moved quickly, gaining confidence and strength. He walked into an entrance-hallway and threw open the door. Outside, in the silent, plush-carpeted corridor, a man was sitting on a hard chair, reading a magazine. He laid it aside and stood up, buttoning his suit-jacket.

'I feel kinda hungry, Jim. Can you rustle me up something?'

'Sure, Mr President. I can offer you a Mexican hotpot, or best Texan beef.'

'Which should I go for?'

'The beef. Very tender, perfect.'

'Prime rump?'

'And prime topside. *Filet mignon*. It'll melt in your mouth, sir.'

'Sounds great!' He smiled and clasped Jim's shoulder. 'Take me to it.'

'It's down one floor, sir. Follow me, please.'

'I want you to know I don't make a practice of this.'

'I don't give a damn whether you do or not.' He stretched forward, slid his hand up her thigh under her cream skirt. She flinched away slightly. 'You're wearing a pantie girdle!' he exclaimed.

'Is there anything wrong with that?'

'No. It just kind of limits the foreplay!'

'Can't we have some of that in bed?'

Pulling off his tie, he smiled and said, 'I'm afraid not! Coolidge brought in a law against presidential foreplay in bed. President Harding had done too much of it, wasted too much time.'

The young woman ran her fingers under her long blonde hair to unclasp her pearls. 'Are you in so much hurry, Mr President?'

'I *have* to be in a hurry, Catherine. I've had a busy day and tomorrow – today – will be busier. I've no time to waste.'

She stood up, stubbing her cigarette. 'If I'd known, I'd have just worn my mink. I hope we can talk a little?'

He was naked except for his back-brace. 'Of course.'

As she removed her jacket and laid it carefully on a chair back she turned away from him, towards the window. 'I'm glad it's raining; I hope it goes on. I didn't come here just to offer you sex, Mr President, though I can't say this isn't a dream come true. I'm worried about Dallas. People like my husband hate your guts. Anything could happen there.' Her skirt, unhooked, slid slowly to the floor. 'I guess if it's raining you'll have to have a top on your car?'

'I guess so. Mrs Kennedy hates to get her hair mussed.'

'Well, that's a relief!' She turned to him again, sat down, unclipping her stockings. 'I was so worried you might take the risk, in view of what the press will make of it – you must know the *News* will say you were chicken.'

'Really?'

'Oh, of course! Even if a tornado was blowing, they'd say you had a top on for security reasons and nobody got a good look at you.'

'Well, screw them.'

'Yes, screw them!' Her anxious frown cleared into a smile as she put her hand on his knee. 'I really came here to say please be careful. We need you.'

'Not as much as I need *you* right now, as you can see.'

2

Jackie drifted awake. Despite her exhaustion the spirit of her dead baby would not let her sleep through the night but seemed to want to remind her of his absence, his presence. She heard him in the fine rain rustling at the window. She turned on to her side and curled up small, as if this would reduce the sorrow. There was silence from Jack's room; nothing ever interrupted his sleep.

3

Impatient and irritated, delayed on the way to business meetings, lunch dates, motel liaisons, drivers fume and honk their horns. They wonder, vaguely, why Dealey Plaza shows abnormal activity; why there are cops swarming over the grassy knoll and around the Book Depository; why there are people looking dazed, and a few in tears. One or two drivers wind down their windows and shout, 'What's happened?'

'Someone shot the President.'

'Jesus Christ! You're kidding!'

Other drivers are jolted by announcements, breaking into pop music on their car radios; and they feel anguished or thrilled as their politics dictate. But most drivers and their passengers, at this early stage, are merely annoyed at the traffic chaos. They light up cigarettes, drum their fingers on steering-wheels, scratch themselves, mutter to the car ahead, 'Move, you sonofabitch.'

Time has stopped. It can only be a few minutes after the gunshots as the first held-up cars are allowed through, driving over bloodstains and bullet-marks. The President has just been pulled from his wife's lap outside Parkland Hospital and laid on a stretcher. A policeman has dashed into the Book Depository and accosted a young worker quietly drinking a Coke on the second floor; but his boss has vouched for him. A high-powered Mauser rifle has been found on the sixth floor. All across the world radio and TV programmes are broken into, and people feel suddenly drained of life and

9

hope; they burst into sobs as though they have lost a wife or husband.

A young deaf-mute on the grassy knoll, where police are swarming and an acrid smell hangs in the air, tries to explain in gestures that he has seen a man running with a rifle through the parking-lot. He can't get through to them. He jumps into his van and drives to FBI headquarters, where he writes down on a memo pad what he has seen. The female clerk, chewing gum, filing her nails, drops his report into a drawer. Outside, the deaf-mute sees people huddled weeping over a transistor radio. He sees two tall men leap high and throw their Stetsons into the air. Tears spring to his eyes too; for the first time in his life he is glad he has never truly joined the world.

The worker accosted in the textbook warehouse, Lee Harvey Oswald, leaves the building and takes a bus then a taxi to his lodging-house. Or he jumps into a station wagon driven by a thick-set Hispanic. It is only reasonably certain that he reaches his lodging-house.

He is in his mid-twenties, slightly built, sharp-featured, narrow-eyed. He stands now at a bus-stop in the quiet suburb of Oak Cliff, his mind in a turmoil. There is a .38 under his zip-up windbreaker, and the police-car has come by his lodging-house, giving him the signal. He should walk to Tenth and Patton, pull a gun on the cop who would be parked there, Tippit, and give him a flesh-wound; then nip around the corner to meet up with the second, cruising patrol-car. They'd drive him at high speed to an out-of-the-way airfield, where Ferrie would be waiting to fly him off to Cuba and fame. But something's gone disastrously wrong – it's the President who's been shot, not Governor Connally; the President's gravely wounded; Lee caught those words in passing on his housekeeper's distorted TV as he dashed to get his .38 and change his jacket.

Feeling wounded to the heart himself, he doesn't know what to do. Hell, he likes the President. He has that *Life* magazine, with smiling pictures of the President and Mrs Kennedy, and now the cops will think he has brought him Death.

How will Castro react, if Kennedy dies? Could it have been

an accident, a shot that went astray? Or has he been made a fool of? Did they think they could make a fool of Lee Harvey Oswald? Of O.H. Lee? Of A.J. Hidell? Well, he is nobody's fool. He's not going to take the rap for this.

His first thought, after he heard about Kennedy's condition, was to go to Ruby's flat and have it out with him. He could walk there in a few minutes. He would threaten him with the gun into telling him the truth. Was it a set-up or had the shooting gone terribly wrong? If it was the first, he would kill Ruby probably; if the second, he would ask him what the fuck they intended doing about it to get him off the hook. That Mannlicher-Carcano they'd planted on the sixth floor, and the bullet-cases – they'd have to fucking pick them up before the police or FBI found them.

But now, standing irresolutely at the bus-stop, he's not so sure. Ruby won't be in, or there'll be someone with him: he would be establishing an alibi. It will waste precious time. Better to take a bus to Irving; Marina will know what to do. He can rely on Marina, she's resourceful, she's been trained to be, she'll take care of him. Hide him. Or somehow work things out.

Impulsively, hands in pockets, he sets off walking, in the opposite direction from the way the bus would have taken him. It's no good hiding behind a woman's skirts. It's best to sort this out for himself. He's an ex-Marine, he works for the CIA and FBI. Shit, at twenty, when other green kids were in college, he was sailing to England, flying to Finland in a military plane; staying overnight in the best hotel in Helsinki before going to Moscow. There are no flies on him; just because he has no formal education. He'll walk to meet this patrolman hovering along Tenth, but he won't shoot him. He'll tell him all bets are off; just a small-time cop making an extra buck, he'll probably be shit-scared himself. Just take me to an honest cop, he'll tell Tippit; you can have the honour of arresting me; I'll leave you in the clear. You just saw me acting suspiciously. You can still be a hero but without a sore arm.

Then Lee would spill what he knew. At worst he'd get a

couple of years in jail; but jail's not so bad, you can think in jail, work on your ideological viewpoint, read Nietzsche and Marx while the other guys are reading the comics. And he'll be pretty famous, there'll be court appearances, and everyone will think he was misled for a while but really he's a great patriot, coming forward like that.

He feels patriotic; he's proud of the American and Texan flags fluttering outside quiet homes as he strides along. He never did nothing to do down America. Even the information about the U2, they wanted him to give that information, wanted Gary Powers shot down, to scupper the peace plans, keep America strong.

His feet don't seem to be touching the pavement; he doesn't feel in control of what he's doing, where he's going. He is leaning back as he walks, as if his body is protesting at the direction in which it is being carried. Unreality has taken hold of him too. The blood pounds in his ears; his breath rasps. The warm afternoon appears to be so normal. Why, just an hour ago he was drinking a Coke, a decent, law-abiding citizen. Life can't change so much in just an hour. The sky would look different; but it's still the same throbbing blue, and there's the same hum of distant traffic.

4

At the Sacred Heart Convent, a century-old, red-brick building surrounded by tall pecan trees, it is the first lesson of the afternoon. The girls in Sister Agnes's seventh-grade history class are hard at work, writing. The young sister had planned a more active lesson, but she can't wait to write home about the great event of the morning. She is scribbling her letter in a notebook; she will tear the sheets out later and stuff them in an envelope.

'Dear Mom and Dad,' she writes. 'I have seen the President and spoken to him! Less than an hour ago! I still can't believe it's happened to me, and I just had to tell you right away, even though I have a class. (They are doing a test.) I know that you, Dad, will be very envious.

'You probably heard they were visiting Dallas. Well, because he is our first Catholic President, we were given an early lunch-recess so we could go and see the motorcade. Not everyone in Dallas – as you can imagine – likes him, and it was thought he should find out that he has people here who love him. So along we went, to stand by the route. That was exciting enough; there were lots of people and the atmosphere was surprisingly friendly. We heard the police sirens, and then the first car came in sight – I think the police chief was in that one. Then, with police on motor cycles alongside, *they* were in sight! Mrs Kennedy looked wonderful, in a pink suit and a matching pill-box hat; she really is stunning. And the President – well, I can't find the words! He looked tremendously young and powerful and boyish, he was smiling very happily and waving. He's much handsomer than in that snap on our cabinet; he was quite skinny then, wasn't he? Photographs don't do justice to him, the sun was glinting on his chestnut hair . . .'

A girl with her hand up caught her eye. 'All right, Jane: be quick.' She shouldn't allow visits to the bathroom during a test, but what the heck? And the girl was on edge, her Mom ill in hospital.

The hint of red in the President's hair showed the Celt in him. Jean, her sister, had it too, inherited from Mom. Her own was jet-black, and wonderfully curly when it had flowed down over her shoulders. Now it was well hidden and too short for curls – but in other ways she had the maternal Scottish strain, she felt. It was a tough stock; she thought of Great-aunt Mabel – well, really she was a great-great-aunt – still alive, incredibly, in a rest home near Boston. Well over the century; one of the oldest people in Massachusetts. Sister Agnes didn't want to live that long.

The girl came back and nodded at her gratefully; smoothed her grey skirt under her as she sat and focused at once on her papers. They were nice, hardworking girls on the whole. Catholics, and therefore outsiders in Texas.

Immigration was the theme of the test. Sister Agnes was glad to have mixed blood and no fixed family roots, her parents having moved about a great deal before settling in Louisiana. For rootedness often meant dogmatism. Her mom and dad weren't intolerant; they could have made a much greater fuss – a heck of a bigger fuss – when she'd announced she was becoming a Catholic. Friends and neighbours were horrified; but they'd stuck up for her. She hadn't been at home but away at college when she'd announced the second, far worse, blow: that she was to become a nun. There were hysterical letters from Mom; yet they had forgiven her, in time. She saw with affection their blurred images, almost as powerful as those of the Kennedys: Dad spare-framed in his white three-piece suit, very elegant; Mom plump and bouncy and floral, with that wide-brimmed straw hat. They would be coming to see her next summer.

'He seemed to be looking straight at us, smiling broadly. I know everyone thinks that, on such occasions, but in our case it was true! – because we saw him give an order to the driver and the car stopped, right next to us! He jumped out and ran around to us! My hand was being shaken by his; I felt dithery and there was a roaring in my ears. I told him how proud we were – ' (Sister Agnes crossed out the last four words; it would hardly be tactful, admitting she'd told him of her pride in having a Catholic President.) 'I told him you'd been instructed by him, and he remembers you well! He said you were one of the finest recruits – wasn't that nice?'

It was also totally untrue. It was clear he hadn't remembered him and was just being polite. But it was a well-intentioned white lie. Dad had always felt bad because they hadn't sent him to the war-zone after all that training. It was probably because he was older and had a young family; and also they'd needed his skill and experience in dealing with illiteracy.

Turning her thoughts back to the President she wrote: 'He seemed immeasurably kind and gentle and *interested*. We're very lucky to have him as our President. I look at my hand, and think that an hour ago it held the hand of President Kennedy!! I thought of Great-aunt Mabel. She was so proud of having perched on Lincoln's shoulder! I shall tell her about this on my Christmas card – though I don't know if she takes anything in.'

Hearing a sound she glanced up. Martha and Helen were having a small fight over their ruler, which one should have it; she fixed them with a mock-severe look and they gave an embarrassed grin and stopped poking each other.

'Excuse the lined paper; but it's rather apt because I know I've been writing like a gushing schoolgirl. Well, I don't care, everyone in the world should have just one day like this, don't you agree? What was your great, memorable day? The day you were married? I bet it was.

'I'm glad your hand isn't so painful, Dad. Thank God it was the left. I was so pleased to get your letter, explaining just what happened – Mom and Jean were too upset, understandably, to make much sense. Of *course* I'll write to Jean, telling her it's stupid to blame herself. It was one of those situations where everyone was trying to be helpful – Jean to spare Mark while he was so busy with his first Thanksgiving sermon; you trying to spare *her*; and little Bernard, bless his heart, seeing the switch was not pressed down and thinking he'd help his Mommy. But it really was very stupid of you to grab hold of the hedge-trimmer by the blade. When Mom's letter came it was like my own fingers were being cut – horrible! And I felt so useless, being so far away.'

She paused in the flow of her pen and lifted her head. Not only useless, but a little malicious – according to Father O'Conlan. Because there'd been another reaction, swiftly following horror: a strange thrill, just for a moment, almost like satisfaction. And it had tormented her until Father O'Conlan explained it, and then she'd felt a little better though still troubled. It was natural, he'd said, for young nuns to feel envious when hearing about family get-togethers. The accident, though shocking, hadn't done very great damage, and so she'd had a little demon in her saying: *That's* spoiled their cosy holiday at my sister's home! He had given her penance; and she would keep praying to be more worthy of God's grace.

Her pen hovered; she'd been guilty of another untruth; she *did* blame Jean, irrationally perhaps. She should have taken her finger from the start-button as soon as her father came anywhere near; she was careless and trigger-happy, always had been; Sister Agnes herself had scars to prove it. And what about the little puppy of theirs she'd run over while learning to drive? She shuddered at the memory of the poor writhing creature. Vivacious: oh yes, vivacious! The boys queuing up for her; open-mouthed kisses at fifteen; but trigger-happy.

'Anyway,' she continued, 'it's clear you haven't lost your sense of humour; I'm sure Mom wouldn't *let* you do that. And there are two great comforts. We must thank God Jean lives next door to a nurse, and that she was off-duty. Also that the shock doesn't seem to have affected the pregnancy, as it might easily have done. Like you said, it could have been much worse.

'I must close now – it's almost time to end the test. God bless you both!

                                    Love, Tessa'

Blotting the page, she screwed up her Parker pen. A girl in the front row was doing the same, with a look of satisfaction. Rachel was a good student. The teacher's and the pupil's eyes met, and a shy smile was exchanged.

That was good too, Sister Agnes reflected. A moment of intimate contact, friendly, affectionate. It was a day of miracles.

She tells the pupils there's five minutes to go. Several of them groan, and their pens rush.

But she will not make a god of the President. The true God is there, hanging on the cross.

Glancing out, she catches sight of a grey squirrel leaping from a high branch of one pecan tree to another, and she marvels at life's intricacy and beauty. The fullness, harmony, joy of existence gushes into her and she has to close her eyes for a moment, dazed by it.

When the bell rang, and the girls filed quietly out, Jane lingered behind, wanting a word with her. 'Sister Agnes, do you think, with immigration, the USA should be governed more by idealistic or phlegmatic motives?'

Don't you mean pragmatic? she asked the tall and gawky girl – who blushed to the roots of her sandy, ponytailed hair. She was intelligent, yet continually overstretched herself, and was very conscious of having an important political father. But she looked lovable when she blushed so, and the nun put her arm round her shoulders and led her out of the classroom, while answering her question. Then, strolling with her along the corridor, Sister Agnes discovered that what Jane had *really* wanted to tell her was that she would be cooking dinner tonight for her dad and three brothers. It was Conchita's night off; the teenager felt terribly proud and suddenly grown-up.

Sister Agnes felt warm affection towards her, and all the girls who flitted by, smiling at her. Despite a touch of sadness that she would never have a child of her own, the world was really a beautiful place.

David Ferrie has dashed in to the tiny clapboard house, kicked off muddy shoes, stripped himself naked, downed most of a quarter of Scotch, and thrown himself on the bed. All without a word to his host, a slender, girlish youth wearing shorts and a pair of earrings. The middle-aged man with the extraordinary red wig and painted-on eyebrows looks exhausted and overwrought. His eyes are almost as red as his hair.

The youth, who is a ballet student, looks down on him with compassion and something approaching awe. An extraordinary man. Knows all about theology and gun-running, flying and fist-fucking. Slightly crazy: but who wouldn't be, in this crazy world?

'Would you like me to give you a massage, David?' the youth asks.

Ferrie grunts a yes. He stretches out luxuriously, placing a hand under the back of his head.

He feels his toes being pinched, separated and rubbed; and then the whole foot vigorously caressed. It is soothing. His passionate excitement at seeing Kennedy's head explode in a burst of blood and brain is settling down a little, to become a permanent and always conscious memory. He will never be able to come off in some guy's ass or mouth without seeing the head jerk back and explode so colourfully. That cunt who was too chicken to deal with Castro, who left the Cubans to die in the Bay of Pigs. That Commie-lover.

Youthful, tender hands are stroking, with long downward movements, his smooth leg that would be girlish were it not for a varicose vein. Ferrie's body is entirely hairless. Soothed and calmed, he reflects how unbelievably well it's gone. Everything worked. The Secret Service men were there, doing their job. Already a description has gone out that matches Oswald. Oswaldsky. It's been like taking candy from a baby. Oswald would pull a gun on Tippit and Tippit would blow him away, in self-defence.

There are two kinds of conspiracy, he reflects. There's the kind that is kept to two or three reliable people; it appears to be impenetrable; but if someone finds just one clue the whole thing unravels. The other kind involves dozens of people, most of whom don't know each other and don't know *of* each other. They know only the small part they've been asked to play. The whole thing is messy, there seem to be innumerable clues; but almost all of them turn out to be red herrings, and they simply draw people deeper into a maze that has no exit. This conspiracy is of that kind.

From what he can gather, in the melting-pot of New Orleans, about half a dozen organisations think they are the lynchpin of the conspiracy. The CIA, the FBI, the Mafia, the anti-Castro Cubans, the Dallas oil-men. There is even a rumour that Castro is paying for it; that he's been duped into believing Kennedy has a perfect execution-plan prepared for him, his fate is sealed with Kennedy in power, but that Johnson would be more accommodating. Ferrie grins at the possibility of Castro paying to kill that cunt.

'Does it feel good?' He has moved to the other leg.

Ferrie grunts his satisfaction. Now it is his thigh being pummelled and stroked, and the young man's fingers have become even more sensually aware. They rise to within a whisper of the hairless genitals.

'Do you like me, David? Do I make you feel good?'

'Uh-huh.'

'You should visit Dallas more often.'

Marcello will be over the moon. No more trouble from

Bobby Kennedy. He sees the thick-jowled godfather at his farm outside New Orleans place the head of the gripped, writhing lizard in his mouth, and bite. Spit the head out. 'Dat's de way you gotta do it, Dave. Ain't enough to bite off de tail – de head might grow anudder tail.' And he throws the headless lizard into the green swamp, the morning mist swirling. 'Dey's a lot of human lizards in dat swamp. De snakes here grow fat, dey's fond of me, I give 'em plenty food, y'know, I look after 'em.'

The jury should be bringing in the verdict any time now. Marcello's not afraid; he owns New Orleans. Dallas too. It'll be the greatest day of his life.

'We could spend Christmas together, David.'

'Maybe.'

What puzzles Ferrie is why, when they clearly want Oswald to take the rap, they'd arranged for crossfire. It hadn't been strictly necessary; one first-class marksman behind the fence, or high up in a building, would have sufficed. The crossfire could confuse the issue, the autopsy could suggest or even prove a conspiracy. Still, it isn't for him to worry about that. They presumably know what they're doing.

And whether it comes out as the work of a lone pro-Castro nut, or a conspiracy involving Castro forces, Ferrie predicts there'll be an invasion of Cuba by Christmas. And if that leads to Russia's involvement, Johnson won't be chicken like Kennedy.

'Did you get to see the motorcade?'

'Uh-huh.'

'Is Kennedy as handsome as he looks on TV?'

Ferrie doesn't answer. His balls are being lightly stroked; he tingles with tired pleasure.

'Rim me,' he orders, pulling his legs up and opening them.

There are some who think that Hoover, even Johnson himself, are involved. Hoover is a patriot; so is Johnson, despite being a Democrat. It's possible. Someone claimed they saw Hoover in Dallas yesterday, climbing into a car with one of the big oil-men. Hoover could double for Marcello; the same thick jowls, same turned-down lips and small, piercing eyes. They're really on the same side.

If anyone says anything – what little they know – they'll get what's coming to them.

'That feels fucking good.'

'Fuck me, David.'

A phone rings in the next room. The youth is prepared to ignore it, but Ferrie says he should answer it. The probing, delicate tongue withdraws.

The youth comes back. 'It's for you, darling.'

Ferrie pulls himself from the bed and pads into the next room. He picks up the phone. A flat voice says, 'Tippit's been killed.'

'Shit. I thought Ruby said Tippit was quick on the draw? How'd he let that little fucker get him?'

'Oswald didn't shoot him. We don't think so.'

'Then who the fuck did?'

'We don't know.'

'Where's Oswald?'

'Fuck knows.'

Ferrie's mind races. 'It'll be OK. He'll show up. He can be nailed for this.'

The caller sounds relieved. 'I guess you're right.' Then astonished, joyful: 'It *worked*!'

'You're fucking right it worked!'

He put the phone down and padded slowly back to the bedroom. The young man was sitting cross-legged on the floor, smoking. That sweet marijuana smell. 'A problem?' he asked.

'No.'

He stretched out on the bed and opened his legs. 'Again,' he said. 'Only this time go deeper.'

6

'You were right, Jim – she was quite a dish. Thanks for bringing my robe, by the way.'

The agent looked embarrassed. 'I thought I heard you call come in, Mr President: I'm sorry!'

'That's OK! I *did* say come in. I reckoned you've got a raw deal, having to sit here all night while your colleagues are out on the town. Don't try to tell me they're not! She had a sweet ass, didn't you think?'

'One helluva sweet ass.'

'How about you – you getting much?'

'Can't complain!'

'Glad to hear it!' Jack opened the door to their suite. 'Well, good-night!'

'Good-night, sir. Sleep well.'

Entering his bedroom Jack pulled off the blue silk robe, poured and drank some more iced water from the thermos, then knelt by the bed, composing his hands in prayer. He prayed for John and Caroline, for little Patrick and the other dead – Joe Junior and Kathleen; for all the living family. For Jackie, for himself and for America. He rose stiffly, went to the window and drew back the curtain. Looking down through the rain, he saw, eight floors below, neon signs for a launderette, a snack bar, a gas-station; some of the letters were blanked out. There was a dreariness about it. The American dream. He moved back to the bed, climbed in and switched off the bedside lamp.

He hoped and believed sleep would come quickly, as it

usually did after sex. But his back was painful, preventing him from settling, and he felt a touch of panic as that other, mental pain took over. Not pain precisely but loneliness, from a turning inwards to a space inside his head, empty as the cosmos. He only felt it when he was trying to sleep. That was why, if Jackie and the kids were away and he was alone high up in the White House, he often sent for Fiddle or Faddle. It wasn't so much the fuck he was after as someone's presence while he fell asleep. He thought of the woman – what was her name? Carol? No, Catherine – driving back to Dallas. It would have been nicer if she could have been here in this room with him.

Inga. Yes, a touch like her. He saw her image. Dad had had her. Dad, lining the boys up very serious. Something to say to you. Some advice. And they'd expected a homily about being true to themselves, or whatever, but instead he'd said, Get laid as often as you can! And then the huge grin! And no doubt he lined the girls up and told them it was their duty to provide lays for their brothers and him.

Dad would have gone for Catherine. She'd been damned good in bed. For a moment it had been Brendan after the long voyage, it had been Leif the Lucky sailing into Vinland, into Martha's Vineyard. But they always wanted to prolong it, when there were important things to do or think about, like what to say to Lodge on Sunday about the Vietnam situation. That was a fucking awful problem. To throw in troops would be fatal; to do nothing would also be fatal.

A thousand advisers home by Christmas. The rest next year, after the election. He hoped it would stick.

Well, he wasn't going to solve the world's problems tonight. He must sleep, must turn again into that blankness, that inner space. There was no moon in there to send astronauts towards. It wasn't entirely black; his family were there, but they were no longer warm and tangible but rather they were like the phantoms of an early silent film.

It had grown worse as he had risen in the political heaven. Now, at the zenith, there was a great loneliness. But only at night. Only when he was on his own at night.

7

Sister Agnes was at her old home, in Slidell, Louisiana, when Neil Armstrong set foot on the moon, fulfilling JFK's promise. She was at home when Mary Jo Kopechne, a young attractive Democratic helper, died in a car on Chappaquiddick Island, and Edward Kennedy left the scene of the tragedy and didn't report it. It was July 1969. She was home for her father's fiftieth birthday. There was a big party in his honour: relations and neighbours, colleagues and ex-pupils. When they had all left, Sister Agnes helped her mother clear up the mess. They didn't talk much; her mother was tired. The nun guessed that she also felt a little hurt that their elder daughter hadn't come home for such an occasion. She and Mark and the boys could go to Bermuda but they couldn't come south.

It was unspoken. Sister Agnes guessed it in her mother's silence, and in her lack of enthusiasm when their present to him had been unwrapped.

'Well, dear, I think I'll turn in,' her mother said, switching the hoover off, straightening stiffly and yawning. 'Why don't you go out and talk to your dad for a while? Like you used to do?' She smiled. 'He'd appreciate it.'

'I'll do that. Good-night, Mom. It was a wonderful party.' She put her arms rather awkwardly round her mother's plump waist.

'Good-night, honey. Have some more pie before you go to bed – you're too skinny.'

'OK! I can't resist it!'

'Good-night, sweetheart.'

Sister Agnes took off her mother's apron, then opened the front door and filled her lungs with the cool fresh air. She saw her father leaning on the fence, in the glow of a streetlight, looking out at the quiet midnight road. Hoisting her robe, she walked barefoot across the grass. He didn't hear her; she rested her hand on his shoulder. 'Howya doin', old-timer?' she said in the gravelly accent of one of her cousins, not seen till tonight for over ten years.

The check-shirted figure half turned; he placed his hand on hers. 'I'm doin' OK. I'm doin' OK.'

She felt the familiar tug of love and sadness, looking into his glimmering, gaunt face. There was a twitch of a smile under the neat moustache, yet he too looked tired and rather sad. He nodded at the vague verandas of the houses opposite. 'I've been thinking, does this define my life? Do I end up as an elementary teacher in Slidell, Louisiana? Is this all there is?'

'You're greatly loved,' she said. 'I was thinking that at the party. All those people you've taught so well. White and black.'

'Yeah.' He sighed. Fished in his pants-pocket for cigarettes and matches. He cupped his hands and the match flared.

He was also thinking of Edward Kennedy, he said. Robert was gone – and now this. It was the end of the Kennedys, end of the dream they'd stood for. They'd have eight years of Nixon, and then – who could tell? – maybe Spiro Agnew.

'Spiro Agnew!' He chuckled bitterly. He placed his forearms on the fence and gazed at nowhere, his cigarette brightening and fading. 'Did you hear about his library burning down?'

'No.'

Her father nodded. 'Burnt both his books.' She started to chuckle. 'And one of them he hadn't even coloured yet.'

Laughing, she heard her father's gruff, cheerful laugh burst out, and she hugged his arm. But soon he grew morose again. The black kids at the party – what chance did they have in life? Louisiana was corrupt through and through. The Longs. Marcello. Marcello had spread his poison over everything.

And, from cradle to grave, the blacks suffered most. Almost all the black kids at his party had left school illiterate, because their schools were so bad. He tried to help, he coached them, and they were making great strides, it wasn't that they were stupid. But the problem was just immense.

He made an effort to be cheerful; took her into his arms. 'It's good to have you here, Tessa.'

'It's good to be here, Dad. I wish Jean had come.'

'Oh well, she can come quite often. What's a birthday? She has to work hard in the Church; if you're a minister's wife you got to be a kind of social worker too, these days.'

Holding her at arm's length, he gazed warmly into her eyes, then murmured, 'How about you? Are you happy?'

'Very.'

He nodded. He'd thought, he said, her seeing Jake Hammond tonight, with his wife and little baby, she might have had some regrets. No, she said firmly; none. He was a nice man, but she couldn't imagine living with him.

'Well, you could be right.' He let go of her shoulders, stared across the street again. 'It doesn't bother you . . . your vows?'

'No. I guess what you don't have you don't miss.'

'That's true, Tessa. I think your Mom might have done very well in a convent.'

He chuckled, but it was a grim chuckle. She didn't know what to say. She didn't have to say anything, as he added, stubbing the cigarette-end underfoot, 'Your Mom's a wonderful woman. Nobody's perfect . . . I think you know that.' He gazed at her, his mouth tightening, and he sighed again. 'There are things I wish had been different, things I regret. Ah, well . . . Shall we go in?' She nodded and they turned to walk towards the door. 'Do you really have to go back tomorrow?'

'I must. I wish I didn't.'

They entered the silent lounge that had been filled with music and conversation an hour ago. He threw himself into the armchair, next to the yellow-keyed piano, and she perched on the piano stool. She looked around: emptied out, the room looked shabby, like the whole house; the carpet was the same one they'd had when she'd been at home, the walls could do with freshening up. She knew they had a hard job surviving on his small salary. She stood up, and plucked from the piano-top the framed photo of her father and other trainees with the young Kennedy in Miami, '44. Sitting back down, she gazed at it. JFK in the centre, skinny, the bright, boyish smile above the scraggy neck. Glancing from her young father in black-and-white to the man sprawled before her, she said with a smile, 'You've got handsomer, Dad!'

He took the photo away from her. 'No way.' Again the sad half-smile. 'I goofed there too, didn't I?'

'You didn't goof. They just needed your skill somewhere else. Half the recruits were illiterate, you told me that. You taught them to read. There must be a lot of guys, all over America, who are very grateful you didn't get to serve on a PT-boat.'

He dropped his head, took off his thick-framed glasses. 'Ah, well . . . Maybe.'

'I know it.' She moved to perch on the arm of his chair; leaned down and brushed her mouth against his stiff hair, upcombed to hide a bald spot. He squeezed her hand, and reached into his pants-pocket for a handkerchief to dab at his eyes. 'You're a terrific father,' she said.

'And you're a wonderful daughter.' Then he laughed, jumped up, said enough of this mutual admiration, and plumped himself down on the piano stool. He plunged into *Softly, as in a morning sunrise*, the two fingers and thumb of his left hand spanning the keys effortlessly.

'I'd forgotten that tune,' she said.

His eyes were closed. 'Music's the greatest consolation, Tessa. I'm sorry you stopped playing.'

'So am I. I regret it.'

Lying in bed in her old room, Sister Agnes thought about what her father had said, out in the garden. The strong hint of sexual unfulfilment in their marriage. She was asking herself why she'd had a feeling of relief as well as shock. And then it came to her. Those magazines. She'd stumbled across them in her student days, on vacation. She'd been hunting in her father's study for some local history journals. And had found, beneath them in a cupboard, some well-thumbed – sex magazines, she guessed you'd have to call them. They'd made her nape prickle. Of course they'd had an airbrushed innocence compared with the magazines you saw on newsstands today – the one for instance that Becky Smith had been caught circulating under the desks, her brother's, she said. But the 'stories' had been shocking, and she couldn't align the magazine with her cultured father. She'd left the local history magazines where they were.

But now she understood. Or caught a hint of a possible explanation. But how terrible – having to find solace in that sordid way.

In the morning they drove her to the airport, and they hugged and kissed goodbye. They promised a visit to Dallas next year. Sister Agnes bought a paper and went to the departure lounge. The passengers were already boarding. She settled herself in the half-empty plane and pored over the paper. Chappaquiddick. The lunar dust.

After the seatbelt light had gone off, the plane cruising gently, she heard a soft girlish voice say, 'Hello, Sister Agnes!' She glanced aside, and at first couldn't place the tall, thin girl, brightly smiling. Then – glimpsing familiar features above the smocklike, floor-length hippy dress and the beads, and under the fair hair spread out like Dory Previn's on the LP the Hammonds had given to her father – she greeted her warmly.

'Why, hello! This is a surprise!'

'May I join you?'

'Please do.'

Jane Pulman sat beside her, bangles spinning and jingling on her slim brown arm. It was always – well, almost always – a pleasure to meet a former student. And Jane was bright. Though she couldn't settle on her major, she said; she'd moved from art to Oriental religions, but was now considering sociology and psychology. She was also planning to get married. To a fellow student. She sounded embarrassed about it, and the nun wondered if it might be a shotgun wedding. Her parents were powerful in Dallas politics, and very religious people.

They discussed, over their plastic coffee, the political situation. The running sore of Vietnam, which had seen off LBJ. Jane's father was mortified that Humphrey had lost. And now this Kennedy business. It led naturally to memories of that horrific day. Jane said, blushing, 'Actually I've got something to confess to you, sister! I've always wanted to get it off my chest. Well, this is it!'

It was the only time she'd cheated. Sister Agnes had set them a test, which was unusual for a Friday afternoon, but they guessed she wanted to write home about having met the President. Jane had panicked; she couldn't answer the questions. So she'd asked to go to the bathroom and Sister Agnes had said yes.

'But I went straight to the library. Sister Anita was on duty there. I told her you'd asked me to look up some references and she let me go ahead. Poor dear Sister Anita! Afterwards I felt awful. I felt God had punished me by killing President Kennedy.'

'That would have been an excessive reaction,' the nun said, smiling.

'I guess so!'

'And he was already dead.'

'Yeah!' She gave a wry chuckle. 'That didn't occur to me. I guess because we didn't hear till later. When Sister Bernadette rushed into Sister Angelica's Latin class.'

The girl then asked after her old teachers, and the nun enquired about her parents and brothers. She screwed her face up; the atmosphere was pretty tense at home. The marriage was as rocky as Ted Kennedy's, and it was just her parents there – the boys had all scattered too, desperate to escape the rows.

'I'm sorry to hear that.'

'Well – and, to be frank, to avoid being drafted, in Tom's case.' Jane dreaded going home; had taken a summer waitressing job in New Orleans, to delay it as long as possible and because Gary was there. She found everything depressing at the moment. Would the guys in body-bags be still alive if Oswald hadn't shot Kennedy?

'I think they would be. But who can ever tell?' The road not taken, she mused.

'I think Dad's been in a depression ever since. Of course he would have been talking to him at the lunch. Instead of which, this guy comes on and says something terrible has happened, the President's been shot. He says he still can't grasp it; he has the feeling he turned up and everything was normal, just because he wanted it to be like that so badly.'

She'd had an interesting discussion with one of her religious professors. If a sudden violent death occurred – it was in relation to Robert Kennedy's assassination – did the unrealised future of that dead person exist potentially, or did it not? 'He thinks if you crush a flower underfoot, there's another dimension in which the flower lives on unharmed, until maybe it's plucked by some boy to give to his girl. This guy's a bit way out.'

Sister Agnes, trying to glimpse Jane through her long and spiky hair, said, 'Yes, I can see that.'

'It was dreadful, wasn't it – Bobby's death?' And Jackie: what did she think of her marrying Onassis? That was a shock too. Well, Sister Agnes murmured, life had to go on; and she ccould understand her wanting to take the children away from this violent country.

'Yeah. But Onassis! He's old!'

They fell silent. Sister Agnes gazed out at the blue dazzle. We're flying in to Love, she thought. Flying in to Love. The President and Jackie are five minutes late at the Trade Mart, and the waiters are beginning to serve the steaks.

8

Nell Connally turned in her jump-seat and smiled at him: 'You can't say Dallas doesn't love you, Mr President!'

'I sure can't!'

The Governor's wife turned again to the front, smiling. They were travelling slowly; Jack saw, among the crowd who were on a grassy mound, a plump girl in a red dress, waving at him. She pushed her way forward and for a moment he thought she was going to get to the car – he imagined reaching out and enfolding one of her watermelon breasts. But she passed; the pleasant, friendly plaza passed. In the alternative, the rightful, reality, the unviolent world, they were rumbling through the triple underpass. Jackie closed her eyes the better to appreciate the coolness and privacy. Then sunlight hit them again, they were travelling at some speed along the Stemmons Freeway. The crowd here was much thinner but still enthusiastic. Jack was still waving as they pulled in to the Trade Mart entrance. He glanced at his watch; they were only five minutes behind schedule. It seemed no time at all since their arrival at Love Field, Dallas.

The American and the Texan flags fluttered. Police armed with sticks stood shoulder to shoulder all the way around. Their faces were stern; if they were sneaking a glimpse at the presidential party through their mirrored sunglasses it was not apparent. The car door was opened for Jackie and she stepped out. Her skirt was sticking to her at the back; she smoothed herself. Buttoning his coat, stooping slightly, Jack came up beside her and put out his arm to usher her into the building. The rest of the motorcade was piling in; doors were being opened and slammed.

Jack stood in the men's room with O'Donnell and two Secret Service men, staring at white tiles.

'What did you think, Ken?'

'It could have been worse, Mr President.'

'Could have been worse! Hell, it was great!'

'Yeah, I guess that's true. Every Democrat in Dallas must have been out.'

'There's an exceptionally beautiful Democrat nun in Dallas,' Jack said, zipping himself up. 'I want you to get her on the phone. I'd say about twenty-two, twenty-three, grey eyes, very fair complexion. Her birth name is Mason; she's at the Sacred Heart Convent.'

O'Donnell looked terrified. 'Not a nun, Mr President!'

'For Chrissake, Ken, her father was one of my PT-boat recruits in Miami.'

The aide, reassured, nodded. Jack washed his hands and combed his hair, then went out into the lobby. He waited for Jackie. He could hear an expectant, excited hum. His back was hurting badly. He longed to be able to lie out flat. She came out of the ladies' room, refreshed, beautiful, and he took her hand. 'I'm not hungry,' she said.

'I'm not either, but we'll eat. Otherwise some cooks are going to feel mighty hurt and they may not vote for me next year!'

They entered the hall together, and with a rumble of feet and chairs all the guests stood up. Jack, his eyes darting around as he gave a wave, saw that about half the people weren't clapping. 'Gosh, what a hall!' he exclaimed; then straightaway was clasping the hand of a burly, red-faced man, about Jackie's age. 'Henry! It's good to see you again!'

The man's shyness and awkwardness vanished, and he beamed, pumping the President's hand. Jack could feel the guy's relief that he still remembered him, four years after a two-minute conversation at the Convention. The Texan Democrat, one of the few liberal Yarborough supporters, led the President to a table overflowing with yellow roses. The hall rumbled again as everyone sat, and there was a clinking of plates and glasses. The hum of conversation resumed.

Gritting his teeth, trying to ignore the pain, Jack eased himself into a leather chair. Out of the corner of his eye he saw Jackie being manoeuvred between two large Texan men, further up the table. He could see they were already captivated. He extended his hand to others near him, remembering two by name and being introduced to another he had never met. He gave himself to each one, for a moment, gazing into the eyes. That was important: to let them know that, for however short a time, his mind was solely on them.

There was loud clapping as Johnson and Lady Bird came in.

'I hear the motorcade was terrific, Mr President?' Henry remarked as the applause died away and waiters started gliding around.

'Yes, Henry, it touched us both very much. I think all Dallas was out there, hanging from windows . . . Thank you, yes, the swordfish . . . We shall never forget our welcome.'

'That's wonderful!'

'I was worried,' said a mousy-haired woman. 'After Mr Stevenson, that horrible episode, we didn't know how you'd be received.'

'Well, we were a little worried too, but it turned out one of our best motorcades ever, Helen.' He gulped iced water, and glanced around. 'I was saying to Mrs Kennedy, it's an amazing hall. What do you mostly sell here?'

'Women's fashions.'

'Oh my God! Don't tell my wife!'

A fountain leapt, almost as high as the enormous glass roof. Trees spread their greenery around the fountain, and parrots perched in them, squawking.

'We're proud of it,' Henry said, leaning aside to let the waiter fill his wine-glass. 'People have a bad image of our town, and a lot of it is deserved, but we're also capable of good things.'

'Speaking of bad images, did you see Nixon's been visiting us, Mr President?' the mousy woman asked.

'No! What was he doing here?'

'Well, it's a little mysterious . . .' she began.

Henry stepped in quickly, a shade discourteously. Jack recalled his reputation for acting first, thinking after. 'He said in this morning's *News* he was here to attend a board meeting of Pepsi-Cola. He's their attorney. But there hasn't been a board meeting of Pepsi-Cola! I did some business this morning with one of their directors, and he didn't know anything about any board meeting!'

Jack chuckled. 'Tricky Dick!'

'It sure sounds mysterious!' he said, smiling at Helen; and she nodded, grateful.

Still, he didn't contest the election. That was decent of him. I kind of like him.

'He was here with Joan Crawford, who part-owns Pepsi. They flew out this morning,' Henry continued.

Another lunch-guest, straining to get into the conversation, said he thought it was bad taste of Nixon to say he didn't need masses of Secret Service protection the way the President did. That's true, Helen said; it was snide; and saying he thought the President might drop Johnson from the ticket next year was deliberately provocative.

'He said that?' said Jack, chewing his fish slowly. 'He said that to a reporter?'

They nodded. Jack threw his head back in a laugh, attracting glances. What a manipulator! what a trouble-maker! his laugh implied; and they smiled too, relieved. Obviously he had no intention of dropping LBJ.

He changed the subject. The airport. Love Field. Mrs Kennedy and he had been wondering how it got its name. None of them was sure. And he was thinking: I've got to drop the compliments to Johnson from my speech. It would sound like I was calling attention to Nixon's comments, and it would embarrass Lyndon. He does a good job. It's not easy being Vice President. I can't stand too much of him and Jackie hates him because he's so crude; like the way he just belched; but you can't help respecting him, he has dignity in his queer way. But that means I mustn't mention Connally and Yarborough either.

'I was wondering, Helen, if maybe it used to be a trysting-place for lovers.' He glanced intently, warmly, at the mousy-haired Democrat and she blushed, dropped her eyes to her wine-glass. She would remember this always, he thought; yet it wasn't entirely calculated, he did feel warm towards her, a spinster, a lonely woman. He knew what it must feel like to be in her skin.

'How are your children, Mr President?' she asked.

'Oh, they're wonderful!'

'They look real sweet in their pictures.'

'I didn't say they were sweet! They're wonderfully naughty.' He turned to Henry. 'How are your kids, Henry? And Beth – how is she?'

Henry lowered his gaze sadly, yet felt a pleasurable surprise that the President remembered his wife's name. It was quite incredible: a thousand wives to shake hands with in San Francisco – and he remembered his wife's name. 'Oh, the kids are fine, Mr President, doing well in school; but we're all a little upset at the moment.' He looked up into the President's eyes. 'Beth's just had a mastectomy.'

'Hell, I'm sorry!' He put his hand on Henry's shoulder. 'Is she OK?'

Physically she was in good shape. Already, in two weeks, she had got her strength back and was busting to get out. But of course, mentally . . .

'It's hard for women,' Helen said, crossing her arms protectively over her scrawny bosom, wine-glass in hand.

'You must give her my best regards, Henry.'

'I will. Thank you! She's at Parkland. I'm going to see her after this lunch.'

'Is that far?'

'No, no. It's just a couple minutes away.'

Jack nodded, was silent for a while, eating; then addressed

a remark to a woman just within talking distance who had been straining forward for several minutes, trying to attract his attention.

Blue sunlight poured through the glass roof, sparkling off the fountain, making the foliage of the trees blaze.

9

'"Something there is that doesn't love a wall,/That sends the frozen ground swell under it . . ." I have no doubt that one day the Berlin Wall will come down, that the spirit of freedom will be reborn in Eastern Europe and will insist on the Wall coming down. We in this hall may not live to see it but it will happen.'

Even many of the Republicans and Connally Democrats were clapping. He leaned his fists on the table, trying to take some of the weight from his back. He hoped the colour hadn't drained from his face.

'Nevertheless, there are walls in our own country. There is a wall still between whites and blacks, between management and labour, rich and poor. I'd like to see those walls breached too. It can't be done violently; there is no easy nor quick solution. But we have to do our best to help along the frozen ground swell. We can start by each of us trying to reach across in our minds and understand how the other side is feeling. If I have somebody I've got used to thinking of as an enemy I try to imagine what it feels like to be him; to have his problems, his background, his vision of the world. And sometimes he looks at the end of it a little less like an enemy.

'I am reminded of the Texan rancher visiting Ireland, who puts up for the night at a cottage in Connemara, where his host keeps a few sheep on an acre of stony ground. The Texan tells him that he could be driving all day in his car and still not reach the boundaries of his ranch. His Irish host replies, "Sure, and I had a car like that once!"' Jack grinned, and waited for the chuckles to die down. 'It shows there are always at least two ways of looking at everything. We should be staunch for freedom, everywhere in the world, but we should beware of thinking that the American way of life is everywhere desirable or desired. Let us avoid self-righteousness. When we look back at most wars, over the decades and the centuries, we find that the dead are on the same side; and the enemy in one war is often the friend in the next.

'War, in our time, with our weaponry, is already an acknowledgement of defeat, an acceptance of tragedy. If war again comes to American soil, there can be no Gettysburg Address. The ground will not be consecrated by the blood of the fallen, but poisoned for decades after. The fallen will be numbered in millions, and there will be no one to mourn them or bury them. The President, standing on that field of battle, will himself sicken and fall. Therefore I make no apologies for the Nuclear Test Ban Treaty. I look at my children, Caroline and John, and I want them to grow up; I want them, if God grant, to live the normal span of human life. I want that for all American children and all the children of the world.

'If I may conclude by quoting Robert Frost again:

> When I see birches bend to left and right
> Along the line of straighter, darker trees,
> I like to think some boy's been swinging them . . .

I want there to be healthy birches growing in America after I am gone; and I want healthy boys and girls to swing on their branches. I can't think of a much better image of human happiness.

'Let us never lose the integrity, the sense of values, that caused General Lee to cross the river into Virginia. Like him, let us combine our strength and skill with chivalry and honour. Like Lincoln, let us seek for the most just, rather than the easiest and most popular, solution to our problems. Let us bind up the wounds. Our visit to Texas has brought us to a state that is second to none both in its strength and its code of chivalry and honour. We shall never forget the wonderful hospitality you have shown to us. Thank you.'

He sank into the leather chair, drained. His eyes closed briefly and the applause broke over him. When he opened his eyes he saw that rather more than half the audience had got to their feet. The proportion that sat with arms folded was a little less than when he'd come into the room. It was a small victory.

Henry, Helen, and others near him were clapping frantically and leaning to tell him it had been wonderful, it needed saying, and they were glad he had chosen Dallas to say it.

'Thank you! Thank you!'

The clapping died away; guests sat to finish their coffee, or stood to stretch. Jack pushed his chair back and stood up. At that signal everyone at the high table rose. In turn Johnson, Yarborough and Connally came up to shake his hand and offer their congratulations. Cameras flashed at each handshake.

O'Donnell came up to him. 'That was great, Mr President.'

'Thanks, Ken. By the way – that nun.'

'You want me to get hold of her now?'

'It's probably their lunch-break too. I might catch her between prayers.'

'OK. What was the name?'

'Mason.'

O'Donnell vanished. Jack was surrounded by lesser Democrats jostling to meet his eyes, exchange a few words with him, brush against his sleeve. He got into a discussion of the oil depletion allowance and tried to justify his position. The oil industry couldn't expect special privileges.

Gratefully he let O'Donnell draw him away. 'She's on the line,' he said. 'Her name now is Sister Agnes. She teaches; it's a convent high school.'

'Lamb of God. OK, lead me to the phone.'

In a private room behind the hall he found a rocking-chair by a white phone. He sat down and picked up the phone.

'Sister Agnes? Hello: this is the President. Our brief meeting made a big impression on me. I want to thank you and the other sisters for coming out on the streets to support Mrs Kennedy and myself. Meeting you was one of the highlights of our motorcade.'

He waited for her to respond, but there was only silence. She could not have been more tongue-tied, Jack thought, if she had been talking to Christ. At length she managed to stammer something about the honour of his having stopped to speak to them. 'No, you honoured us,' he said. 'We work in different ways, the churches and the executive, but I like to think our ultimate values are the same.' Then he lightened the tone. 'Ask your father if he remembers playing and singing *Yes sir, that's my baby.*'

'Oh, I will!' She sounded thrilled and surprised; so he *did* remember her father, he wasn't lying!

'June or July, '44 – could it have been your birthday?'

'Yes!'

And a few weeks later, at Hyannis, the news of Joe's death. That shattering blow. Jack's stomach contracted at the painful memory. 'Is he still teaching?'

'Yes. In Louisiana.'

'Ah! A fine state. I had fifty point four per cent of its vote – a majority over all parties.' He chuckled. 'Well, I'd better release you to your students.'

'Yes, of course. Thank you – Mr President. Goodbye.'

'Goodbye, sister.'

He put down the phone. It hadn't gone quite as he'd intended. But a nun was a nun. There were limits. Yet her voice was as lovely as her face. Dammit.

When he returned to the hall, he was once again besieged. Taking the hand of a delicious, mink-coated honey-blonde, he caressed her palm with his index finger. She looked startled, her brown eyes widened in shock. Vigorously he pumped her husband's hand.

He turned politely as a tentative hand touched his arm. He saw a permed and pearled lady, sixtyish, in a sequined white dress. He smiled down at her. 'Mr President,' she said, 'I'd like to give you something to remember Dallas by.'

'Oh! That's kind of you.'

'It's this . . .' She raised her white-gloved hand and struck him with full force on the cheek. He reeled from the blow; a camera flashed. A Secret Service man grabbed the woman. 'You've sold us out to the niggers and Communists!' she screamed. Amid cries of 'Oh no!' and 'What's happened?' Jack was scrummaged away by his guards. She shouted over the hubbub, 'My son died in Korea. He didn't die for his country so it could be sold out by you! He didn't die so you could say he's on the same side as the yellow-bellied Communists that killed him! You've insulted my boy, you traitor!'

Taking their signal from the uproar, parrots flew squawking around.

10

The children have left the classroom. Sister Agnes can hear their distant homegoing cries. She takes off her reading glasses and blinks. It's another reminder of age to have to wear them, but they have cured her headaches. She gets up and moves slowly about the room. However hard you try to make them clean up, there is always something left to be tidied. In her class, anyway, for she has never been an effective disciplinarian like Sister Rosa. After twenty years of teaching she's still prone to be played up by the occasional awkward girl.

She stoops painfully again to pick up Marilyn's bible, then dusts it off and slips it into her desk. No wonder the girl was forever losing books. She thinks of the lost bible of Kennedy, taken by someone at Love Field. His family must grieve for it, such a precious reminder of him.

She has got the children to pray for him, on this anniversary day as on all the others since that terrible day. Yet what did it mean to them? What did it mean to eleven-year-old Alyson, who shut her eyes so tight, trying to imagine this long-gone president? Daughter of a woman who had been in that ninth-grade class of '63 – Gloria – who'd become hysterical when the news broke, just before home-time. It could mean very little; it was like, when she was in high school, some ageing teacher asking her to pray for President Harding.

Jane Pulman, Marilyn's mother, though she was now an ardent student of the assassination, remembered the actual day as much for having cheated in a test as for the news of

42

Kennedy's death. Her lapse weighed on her still; she'd brought it up yet again at her daughter's induction meeting – describing for Marilyn's benefit how Sister Agnes had been writing a letter; they'd guessed it, but forgave her because they were fond of her – and how she'd cheated for the first and only time in her life. She'd wanted to stress to her daughter how wrong it was to take advantage of a teacher's good nature, and how lucky she was to have Sister Agnes; yet somehow it seemed more than that. Sister Ursula, who was standing with them, said afterwards, 'I'd say she's cheating on her husband; she feels guilty.' Which was a terrible thing to say, just on the basis of a few rumours.

And now here was her daughter, writing a love-letter to her boyfriend in Sister Agnes's class on November 22. Marilyn had gone bright-red, just like her mother if she'd got something foolishly wrong; but she'd given her the letter back at the end of the lesson, telling her not to do it again. It was life. The living boyfriend, some spotty teenager, was more important than a historic president.

Hadn't she done much the same thing herself? Trembling with first love, the page hidden in her lap behind the desk? When was that? '55, '56?

The leaves are falling on another year. The sky outside is dark-grey, hinting at a storm, though the low sun occasionally gleams through. Her country is still shell-shocked from Vietnam, the Watergate scandal, the hostages in Iran. The Israelis have invaded Lebanon. Where have all the hopes and dreams gone?

A leaden weight rests on her heart. It seems only three hours since, to their incredulous joy, a miracle happened: the President ordered his driver to stop and he got out to speak with them. She felt the pressure of his warm hand; he gazed into her eyes. It is perhaps the sin of pride, but she thought there was a special warmth in his gaze when he turned to her.

And then, just at the end of afternoon school, Sister Bernadette rushed into her class without knocking; she seemed to be gasping for breath in an asthmatic attack, all the nerves of her face were twitching. She came up to her and whispered in a choking voice, 'The President, he's . . .' and she could say no more, but burst into sobs. And then Sister Beatrice appeared in the doorway, her face so white it made the huge birthmark disfiguring her stand out like blood.

All the joy died in Sister Agnes's soul. And almost all the faith. The convent bells started pealing. She told the children what had happened and they got down on their knees. Sister Agnes addressed the crucifix on the wall, but at that moment she hated Him for allowing this to happen.

She had that almost universal experience of knowing it had happened yet refusing to allow it. If Jesus had been willing to permit it, she did not.

Lifting her skirt she settles on to the floor, towards the crucifix. Rosary in hand, she prays for Kennedy.

She prays afterwards that the truth will emerge. But her thoughts veer from God into meditation about truth and lies. At first she believed the Warren Commission, like almost everyone else. A lone, crazy left-winger. All her rage was concentrated on Oswald; she scarcely repented of her savage glee when she saw, on the school television set, Oswald gunned down by Jack Ruby. But then, as the years passed, she read other books and articles suggesting that Oswald probably did not act alone; perhaps did not even fire at the President. She has learned how the Commission, the CIA and the FBI covered up and lied. That Warren, a man she admired, refused Ruby's desperate plea that he be allowed to give evidence in Washington. And that sickened her. Having almost stopped believing in God, she now did not believe at all in her government.

Nor in people. For everyone told a different story, and often the stories contradicted each other. Why, there was even a young man who swore, swore blind, that the man the police arrested in the Texas theatre – Oswald – had been sitting next to him since before one o'clock. Which was impossible; yet he was just as sure of it as Oswald's housekeeper was that he'd dashed in just before one. Whether for or against a conspiracy, people told lies; or at best did not see the same things. Where is truth? Sister Agnes pleaded; and the answer came, Truth is nowhere to be found.

And now, dear God, we have a B-movie president. The Church is changing too; they are to have fashionable new clothes, short skirts. But it is not her long, heavy habit that weighs on her.

As usually happens on the anniversary of her loss of innocence and faith, a host of later events jumbles into her mind. The assassinations of Robert Kennedy and Martin Luther King. The drowning of Mary Jo Kopechne at Chappaquiddick. The Mylai Massacre, and Nixon's pardon of Calley, a man involved in mass murder and rape. The flames streaming up from Jan Palach. Somehow they all seem to fuse with the events in Dealey Plaza, to have happened concurrently. After the first death there is no other.

She tries to pray for all the victims.

Then, resting her arm on a desk, she struggles to her feet. Lately her hip has been troubling her; a touch of rheumatism or arthritis. She has read that shock can bring on such ills, and remembers that after the assassination she suffered a long feverish illness.

Sitting down at her desk, she pulls a pile of work-books towards her, and begins to mark some history essays.

After a period of silence, she can again hear shouts, and a recurrent whistle. It is Father O'Conlan, taking the boys for football. The noises bring back one of the most hateful experiences of that devilish day: the nuns had been walking at night to a church service; they had passed one of the high schools where the floodlights were on and they could hear roars of excitement. A football match . . .

Sister Agnes moves to a pinboard where, alongside a photo of Princess Grace, who died in a car-crash recently, she has pinned up one of President Kennedy. She thinks it is right to tell the children about him – not although but *because* it is ancient history, as distant and unreal to them as the Wall Street Crash is to her. He is smiling as warmly as he smiled at her; she feels now his sweaty palm, the thumb rubbing her knuckle.

Yes, she had felt his sexual magnetism. And had responded to it. If he had not died, she would have been forced to confess it. Almost more painful than the lies relating to the assassination have been the revelations about his affairs. Some of these have made her dizzy, made her almost fall from her chair. She has had to struggle to forgive him; but she has managed to. She quarrels sometimes with Sister Beatrice, who has turned completely against him because he used women. She is angry with all men, with the possible exception of Jesus. Sister Agnes believes the President knew his life would be short, and therefore needed to tear as much experience from it as he possibly could. It did not excuse but it mitigated the offence.

And what he had done was only, she had come to think, what everyone did in their corrupt hearts. In hers also. When, washing her face or cleaning her teeth, she looks in the mirror and sees the wrinkles around her fading eyes, she knows she has had just as many sinful desires as the President had.

She folds up the picture and puts it in the bottom drawer of her desk. She is momentarily distracted from Kennedy by an old photograph nestling there: one she has shown the children on November 11. It is a photo of a young man in First World War officer's uniform, handsome, trim-moustached, arms folded proudly. She has no idea who he is; only that he is probably somewhere or other in her mother's family. Her mother doesn't know either. One of Sister Agnes's great-great-aunts had sent it to her: the great-great-aunt who had been the oldest woman in Massachusetts. Her mother's family lived long.

The nun takes out the sepia photo and turns it over. They had always exchanged Christmas cards, she and Aunt Mabel, though they had never met. This had come the Christmas after the assassination; the old lady must have mistaken it for a card. She had died not long after. On the back she had scrawled some words. First, her name, almost indecipherably – at a quick glance it looked like 'LTME' rather than 'Mabel'. Then, more clearly though wavily, 'Love, Texas'. She had often puzzled what the words meant. Was it short for 'I love Texas'? Was she commanding Sister Agnes to love it?

Where you couldn't solve a simple family message, what chance of solving the events of November 22, 1963? She heaves a sigh, and turns the photo face-up again. Who is he? Did he perish in that war, or does he linger on somewhere in an institution? Her instinct told her he had been cut down. We all go into the darkness: this unknown soldier; Kennedy; Sister Bernadette (she sees the emotional old nun pressing Kennedy's hand to her lips); Princess Grace . . . What does it all mean?

She shuts the desk-drawer and returns to her marking. This is truly history, for both her and the children. The Battle of Gettysburg. She supposes people saw Lincoln's death in the same way as Kennedy's. That train ride across the nation, mournful muffled drums at every stop. O Captain, my Captain. Yet he had fulfilled his task, whereas Kennedy was only a brilliant meteor.

How, suddenly, it had become cold in Dallas that evening, after the hot afternoon. Cold and gusty, and sheet lightning without rain. The first really cold night. The cold had pierced their cloaks, going to Mass.

Father O'Conlan's whistle and loud, critical voice. Cloudy sunlight pouring in, dust-motes dancing. The roars of the high school spectators. Nausea.

11

'I'm OK, really,' Jack said, rubbing his cheek. 'It's the first time I've had my face slapped since my second date with Mrs Kennedy!' He grinned at her. 'Do you remember, sweetheart?' She stroked his sleeve, smiled weakly.

The hysterical woman had been led away; the hubbub in the Trade Mart was dying down. Helen and Henry were wringing their hands and saying Dallas had been disgraced yet again. Ken O'Donnell asked his boss if he wanted to cancel his fifteen-minute meeting with the veterans. He was sure they'd understand.

'As a matter of fact I'd like to do that,' he responded. 'It's Mrs Kennedy they want to see anyway. You and Ken can talk to them, hey, honey?'

She nodded. 'Of course.'

'I have something I need to do.' He put his arm on Henry's shoulder while addressing Jackie. 'Darling, you remember Henry's wife Beth? She's had a mastectomy.'

'Oh, I'm so sorry to hear that, Mr Pulman! How is she?'

'She's doing well, Mrs Kennedy, thank you. Coming home from hospital tomorrow, we hope.'

'That's good! Give her our love and best wishes.'

'We're going to do better than that,' Jack said. 'Henry and I are going to visit her, while you and Ken are with the vets. The hospital's only two minutes away.'

Henry flushed. 'Mr President, she'd be so thrilled! I can't thank you enough.'

It was nothing, compared with Henry's efforts for the Democratic Party, Jack said. He asked O'Donnell to ring Parkland, warning them he'd be calling. No fuss. And just the Lincoln and a couple of agents. O'Donnell scurried off. Jack kissed his wife's cheek, saying he'd see her in fifteen minutes.

Four minutes later Jack and Henry, preceded and followed by alert agents, were walking through the corridors of Parkland Hospital. Flustered, awestruck nurses, doctors, patients, were craning out of doorways and the President was saying, Hi! Howareya? in passing. 'Henry,' he said as they strode, 'give me five minutes alone with her. I know how women feel when they've lost a breast; they start to doubt their attractiveness and the strength of their husband's love. I want to tell her some pretty nice things about you, and I'd be embarrassed if you were there. Do you mind?'

'Of course not. You're right. She's very depressed and I can't seem to get through to her. I'd be very grateful if you'd talk to her.' He stopped, indicating a door. 'This is it.'

'Go and have a coffee, Henry. One of these guys will come and get you.'

'OK, Mr President. Thank you.'

He turned and walked back towards a visitors' lounge. Jack said to the agents, 'Ben, Greg, don't let anybody in. *Anybody.*'

They nodded. He opened the door. Henry's wife, a full-fleshed brunette in her late thirties, was sitting up in bed, in a nightgown and blue housecoat. She hurriedly laid aside a lipstick as she saw the President. He strode forward and leaned down to kiss her scarlet lips. 'How are you, honey?'

'I'm OK. The better for seeing you, Mr President, though it almost finished me off, when they told me you were coming!'

'I had to come.'

He sat on the bed and held her hands. He gazed down compassionately into her wan but excited face. The fresh powder and paint didn't disguise the pain she had suffered, yet she was still almost as attractive as that livewire woman in

San Francisco. Her beautiful blue eyes were only a shade faded, a shade more wrinkled at the corners. Her teeth still sparkled when she smiled, her black hair, though probably tinted, still fell in the same luxuriant curls. He bent and kissed her again, his mouth lingering.

She took a deep breath when he had drawn back. 'God!' she said. 'You're still one helluva kisser!'

He peeled off his coat. 'I've come to give you some post-op therapy,' he said. 'Are you up to it?'

Her pale cheeks flushed, and her eyes darted fearfully towards the door. 'Don't worry,' he assured her, 'nobody's coming in.'

She rested a hand on his arm, gazed into his eyes wistfully. 'I'm maimed,' she said, 'you know that. You said you liked my breasts. I'm not the woman I was.'

'You're not maimed.' He stood up and unfastened his belt. 'You're an Amazon! You're so pretty I can't damn well resist you! I couldn't at the Convention and I can't now.'

'Be gentle,' she said, catching hold of his hand.

'I will.'

He helped her ease off the housecoat and slide down the straps of her nightdress. She turned her head aside and closed her eyes as he saw the bright scar. 'It's fine, honey,' he murmured, climbing in beside her, fondling the healthy breast. 'Henry won't be any different. He's one lucky guy and he knows it.'

Her legs parted for him. 'We've got three minutes,' he said. 'Now, doesn't this feel good?'

'Oh, it's good! It's so good!' She began moving under him more strenuously, confidently; then froze. 'There's a problem. It's a risky time of the month.'

'You want me to put on a rubber?'

'God, no. We're Catholics.'

'Oh yes! I'd forgotten. It's OK, I'll pull out.'

They started moving again, and as they quickened she said breathlessly, 'Don't pull out! What's meant to be *will* be, as my mom always says.'

Henry was adding cream and sugar to his coffee when an

agent tapped him on the arm. 'The President says you can come now, sir.'

When Henry entered his wife's room, the President was sitting at the bedside, chuckling, holding Beth's hand. She looked more cheerful than she had for weeks – since the bad news came. He walked to the other side of her bed and she let go Jack's hand to draw Henry into an embrace. 'Hello, honey!' she said.

'Hello, sweetheart. Howya doin'?'

'I'm fine. This is the best therapy I could have had!' She squeezed Jack's hand again briefly.

'It sure is!' Henry said huskily, overcome by emotion. 'Mr President, you're one hell of a fine man!'

'Thanks, Henry, but anyone would have done it. Beth's a wonderful woman. And you two are going to be fine, and in nine months you're going to have another baby, that's an order!'

Henry, her hands in his, gazed down at her lovingly. 'How about that, sweetheart?'

'Well, we can't disobey a presidential order, can we?' she said, with a brave smile.

He smiled seraphically. 'We sure can't!'

12

A lean, grey-haired woman in her fifties, her face and part of her neck disfigured by a reddish-coloured stain which had been with her since birth, sat in her room at the Sacred Heart Convent in front of a manual typewriter. She was wearing blue tracksuit bottoms, a white T-shirt and sneakers. On the wall above her desk were poster-sized pictures of Sylvia Plath and Angela Davis. She stared through her glasses at the blank sheet in the typewriter. Then, tapping one-fingered, she typed:

JOHN F. KENNEDY AT 70

by Shirley Jansen

Had John F. Kennedy not been shot in Dallas, he would today as I write this (May 29, 1987) be seventy years old. Unless his medical problems had proved debilitating, we can imagine him a hale and still handsome man. We cannot begin to imagine what role he would have, this president at least nineteen years out of office. But certainly he would be a very distinguished elder statesman. Almost as certainly, his grave moral defects would still be unknown. There would on this day be tributes from around the world; probably a White House reception for him and Mrs Kennedy – in the unlikely event they were still together.

Instead, no notice that I am aware of has been taken of his birthday. I would not have known of it had not a friend devoted to his memory mentioned it to me. I should like to mark the occasion with a few reflections on the tragic events of November 22, 1963. First I should declare a very peripheral involvement: I believe I was the last person he spoke to, with the exception of Mrs Connally and perhaps his wife. I was then, and am still, a nun at the Sacred Heart Convent School in Dallas. With the friend I have mentioned and a few others I stood at the roadside to greet the motorcade. Very unexpectedly, as has been recorded, the President asked that the car be stopped and he got out to greet us. I happened to be the last person in our group to exchange a few words with him.

His assassination, therefore, struck me with even more force than it struck almost all Americans and indeed people throughout the world. I experienced that feeling so common at the time – that it could not have happened, it could not be allowed to happen. For at least a day I half-believed he still lived. And still, twenty-four years later, if I watch the Zapruder film of the tragic event, I find myself thinking, as the Lincoln draws near the fateful place: It will be different this time; there will be no shots . . . But there are always the shots.

One might compare the persistent rumours of the survival of the Grand Duchess Anastasia. When persons of a certain charisma die violently, in our lifetime or so close to it that the effects palpably persist, we don't want them to die. As a teacher of literature and a feminist I still wish, for instance, to break into Sylvia Plath's apartment in London on the morning of her suicide, in time to save her. It still seems almost possible to do so. I do not quite understand the psychology of this.

In the case of John F. Kennedy, however, I no longer have that feeling. It is partly because the myth of the 'brief, shining hour' has been so thoroughly exposed. Kennedy was, to put it simply, a rotten apple, a man without principles. But it is also because I am aware that the raw, bleeding and chaotic violence of that moment in my city has become almost a literary 'plot', the characters involved forming a certain aesthetic symmetry; and so one is inclined to feel that the event was fated, it could not have been otherwise.

Let me explore and explain this point. There is a symmetry that a playwright might create, out of both inspiration and laborious craft, in the two 'couples' involved: the Kennedys, the Oswalds. Both with two young children. Both couples 'outsiders' to different degrees. Kennedy, Irish Catholic; Jacqueline, French Catholic. Oswald, a malcontent, a deserter of his country; Marina, a rootless Russian. Kennedy, though in one sense close to his father, felt cut off from him because of his money-making obsession and womanising, which necessitated long absences. Oswald's father died before he was born: indeed, there may well have been an Oedipal motive in his murderous assault. (I am assuming that Oswald was the main, if not the sole, assassin; an assumption which few rational people could doubt.) Marina never saw her father; Jacqueline's father was another womaniser, another absentee from his daughter's life.

The role of the mother, in every case, is somewhat more complex; but again there are interesting parallels – or sometimes contrasts. Contrast is of course as important as similarity in literary symmetry.

Jacqueline could not speak her husband's language, politics; Marina could not speak her husband's language, American English.

All four characters were emotionally deprived. Two were immensely rich and privileged; two were poor and underprivileged.

There is an added dimension to the hierarchy of power revealed. Jacqueline languished under her husband's rule: cast in a pale, derisory role, bringing up the children and refurbishing the White House; above all, being paraded as an icon of glamour and beauty. In the incomparably meaner circumstances of the Oswalds, he too ruled the roost. He sometimes beat her; denied her assistance from her Russian *émigré* friends; stopped her from learning English.

All this would be meat and drink to the dramatist, whether

Classical, Shakespearian or perhaps Racinian. Kennedy was blind to his own faults, like Oedipus or Lear, and travelled recklessly in an open car through the most dangerous city in America – again like Oedipus, who drove on recklessly, relentlessly, to the truth that would be fatal to him. Oswald was an envious, devilish Iago. For the women, naturally, there is only a shadowy, decorative role. There is even, as in Shakespearian drama frequently, a sub-plot, involving the unfortunate policeman, Tippit. There is, too, in the background, the enigmatic pretender to the throne, Lyndon B. Johnson . . .

Eschewing the overt violence, transferring these lives to a musty nineteenth-century Norwegian town, Ibsen could have made a wonderful domestic tragedy out of this material. We can imagine an energetic, womanising, hypocritical town-councillor and his high-spending wife; a sly, malicious male servant and *his* wife, a humbler domestic of foreign origins; a brash and frequent visitor, perhaps a newspaper editor (Johnson), nominally radical but essentially self-seeking, with designs on the councillor's status and property. We can easily imagine some of the plot details: the female servant would have a child of whom her master was secretly the father; the affable editor would pay court to the master's wife, like Judge Brack with Hedda . . .

Finally we may recall the notorious and rather eerie echoes, often remarked on, of Lincoln's assassination in Kennedy's.

As a result, examining these symmetrical *quasi*-literary patterns, who can now imagine as we did at the time – except in rare moments – that John F. Kennedy's assassination in Dealey Plaza was avoidable? No author could have hit upon such a complex pattern on the spur of the moment.

No such pattern is visible in the murders of Robert Kennedy and Martin Luther King; although it might be argued that the train of violence (and we should include Chappaquiddick) also shows a certain symmetry. Spectacular events are said to occur in threes: so, the two Kennedys and King, dying; or the three Kennedys, linked in tragic misfortune. Now,

with the unsuccessful attempts on the lives of Ford and
Reagan, American history would seem to have 'let go' of
this particular plot-line, as if considering it worked out. But
returning to the much richer 'texture' of John Kennedy's
death, are we to say that his death was more inevitable, more
absolute, more 'willed', than those later deaths? That would
seem to be the case. But this raises profound religious and
philosophical questions . . .

13

The plane was stiflingly hot. Entering their bedroom, Jackie kicked off her shoes, took off her jacket, and sank into a chair. Jack too made himself comfortable, loosening his tie and unbuttoning his collar. He threw himself with a sigh on to the bed. 'Thank God that's over!'

'It was fine, until . . .'

'Until an old lady hit me. That's all they'll focus on.'

'Well, it's done. And you made a lot of friends, Jack. Your visit to the hospital after you'd been attacked like that – that was terrific, and *someone* will have reported it.'

'Well, maybe. I didn't do it for that. *You* were terrific, honey.'

'I'm glad I could help a little. I'm going to take a shower – excuse me.'

He lay peacefully. The pain in his back was ebbing into its normal, bearable tooth-like ache. He saw George had laid out a lightweight blue suit for Austin; also slacks and a casual sweater for the ranch. Jesus, that woman from the Fort Worth breakfast, that Mrs Roberts, he'd invited her to the ranch. He'd have to explain it to the Johnsons and Jackie somehow. He wasn't sure he wanted her any more. And it wasn't because he'd unexpectedly satisfied his sexual need; evening was a long way off; no, it was just too predictable that she would yield to him. And as a result she was far-distant in his mind. He ought never to make commitments several hours ahead. Far better to act on impulse, as he'd done with Beth Pulman – that sudden outrageous thought as he strode along the corridor with Henry. It had been fun. It had done her a lot of good.

He heard the shower-water splashing. The man with the umbrella. That had been weird, a black umbrella being pumped up and down, in glorious weather. He smiled. An eccentric. Jackie's book was lying on her bed. Her book of symbols. He reached for it, and took from the pocket of his coat, abandoned on the floor, his glasses-case. Putting on the reading glasses, he opened the book and flipped through it. Umbrella. 'This symbol is invariably related to the sunshade, which is a solar emblem of the monarchs of certain peoples. But its mechanism has tended to lend it a phallic significance. It is a father-symbol for this reason and because of its implication of protection and of mourning.'

The shower had stopped running. He saw in his memory the guy with the umbrella; there had been a Cuban or Mexican – no, he was sure he was Cuban – with him. Suddenly it struck him what the strange act might have signified. Jackie came into the room, towelling herself. 'Jackie, that man with the umbrella, pumping it up and down . . .'

'What man? I didn't see anyone with an umbrella.'

'There was a guy with a black umbrella, in Dealey Plaza. Of course, you were looking the other way. As we were passing, the guy pumped the umbrella up and down. He was white, but with a Cuban. I thought at first he was just some eccentric, but I now think there was more to it.'

He removed his glasses, thoughtful; chewed an ear-piece. 'I think they were telling me something about the Bay of Pigs. I promised an umbrella of support in the air. I used that very word in a speech. I didn't give them it and they died.'

'But it wasn't your fault, Jack. The CIA weren't straight with you, you know that.'

From the corner of his eye he saw her stepping into a white dress.

'There was nothing I could do. We'd have been slaughtered for invading a foreign country. But we sure fouled it up.'

Protection and mourning. Yes, that was the black umbrella.

A symbol of the father, too. There seemed very little protection; I didn't have a room I could call my own. From one enormous house to another. Dad forever away, screwing. Mom unable to touch us, much. With her little memo notes pinned to her dress. I didn't find out the meaning of Love Field.

But he would be an umbrella to Caroline and John, and other children who might come. He'd make damn sure of it. And Jackie was a good mother, you had to give her that.

He would shower. They wouldn't take off yet, as they had to give Johnson time to get to Austin ahead of him. Pulling himself upright, wincing. 'That's a swell dress.' Stripping off his shirt.

'It'll be cooler than my suit. My, wasn't it sweltering in the car? I thought I'd faint. Though I guess in Austin the sun will be going. I should have worn the pink suit there and this dress here.'

He unstrapped his back-brace. The frailties of the flesh. Of his, especially. Would he still be able to walk at sixty? What would he be doing? The height, the zenith, was now. To be President of Harvard, or some bank, was hardly comparable. And then, decline. Poor Dad, drooling his food, able to say 'no' and 'shit', nothing else. His only sentence, 'NO SHIT.'

Stepping into the shower, feeling the healing water drench him, he thought of an answer he'd given to someone who'd asked him his philosophy of life. He had used a quote: 'Let its report be short and round like a rifle, so that it may hear its own echo in the surrounding silence.'

He liked that. You didn't need to be a man of action. It fitted the Bird-man of Alcatraz. Someone you could sum up in a resonant phrase or image.

The plane started to taxi. He'd survived. He'd survived Dallas. It seemed foolish now, all the scaremongering about it.

14

'Time is like a richly spreading pecan tree,' Sister Beatrice writes, 'whose beauty and complexity dazzle us into the impression that it could not have been shaped otherwise. Yet we know this is not true; every one of its massive, twisting brranches could have formed themselves differently; and that difference would have affected the subordinate branches, twigs, foliage. Still, it is just *this* tree that we see; the apparently random has become the inevitable, the intended: at least it is so if we believe in God. Our dazzled impression, though apparently irrational, is proven to be right after all. We may wish, from too close a view, that this branch, or this, had grown differently, as we may wish – I certainly wished it at the time – that President Kennedy had not been shot in Dallas; but if we stand back we know that the tree could not have been otherwise. And the name of the field in which the tree stands is Love.'

She stops typing and leans back in her chair. She is pleased with the essay. Of course it will need revising and polishing. She will try it with the *Southern Texas Review*, who have taken a chapter of her book-in-progress about Sylvia Plath. Unless Sister Agnes wants it for *November 22*, the Kennedy quarterly of which she's taken over the editing. But Sister Beatrice can't imagine her accepting the criticisms of JFK.

It is a truthful essay, she feels; yet it is not the whole truth. Had she been entirely truthful she would have explained just why she had wished that Kennedy had not been shot. Oh, she had loved him at the time, like all the sisters; but beyond that, his assassination had put a stop to her own plans. She had been in a state of suicidal despair at the time of his visit. Not only was it close to the anniversary of the deepest, cruellest betrayal in her life, but she had simultaneously discovered the poetry and the suicide of Sylvia Plath. The discovery had had a great effect on her. It had both deepened her depression and given her the inspiration to follow Plath's example.

Going through with seeing the motorcade had been a great agony. She'd gone back to the convent and read Plath's 'Lady Lazarus' with her senior class: as a secret goodbye. They would see it as such on Monday morning, and be touched by it. She also planned to show it to Sister Agnes, for the same reason.

But Kennedy, even as she read the poem to the girls, was lying dead. And she'd had to comfort Sister Agnes, who was totally distraught. She would never forget the Saturday morning; she'd gone to Sister Agnes's room to see how she was, and had found her hysterical with grief. By a macabre coincidence, the younger sisters had been given as a text for study and meditation the sayings of Dame Juliana of Norwich: 'Sin is Behovely, and all shall be well and all manner of thing shall be well.' Sister Agnes had her head resting on the open book and was sobbing her heart out. And her own empty and bitter heart had gone out in love to her; she had persuaded her to join her in reading aloud 'When Lilacs Last in the Dooryard Bloom'd'. The desolate yet beautiful cadences had helped.

Kennedy's fate changed hers. For she could not add to the grief of so many people dear to her: her sisters, the students.

Though life had picked up, and been bearable on the whole, it would have been better had she joined Sylvia. She assumed, however, God in Her wisdom thought differently. She even wondered, from time to time, if She had seen that only something awful like Kennedy's death could persuade her not to die.

If she'd been wholly truthful, she would have written all that down. She looks out of the window at a blossoming pecan, and sees that Sister Agnes has sat beneath it with a senior student, on the bench dedicated to the memory of

Sister Bernadette. Even after so many years, and even though Sister Agnes now walks awkwardly and her frame is heavier – a thickening accentuated by the modern habit – Sister Beatrice's heart still quickens at the sight of her. She has loved her through twenty-four blossomings and fadings of the lilac. Yet they have never touched, rarely spoken of anything personal. She's never told Sister Agnes about *him*, for instance, whose betrayal of her had sent her into this death-in-life.

It was easier now, in middle age; but sometimes, earlier, if they were kneeling close beside each other in the small chapel, it had been hard to keep her mind on her prayers, on that marble icon of the Virgin gazing compassionately down at them. She would feel herself begin to tremble.

Sister Agnes and the girl had stood up and moved away. Returning to her essay, Sister Beatrice crossed out and inserted. God ought to have revised the world. She was a lazy artist.

Her fingers sore, she leans back on her chair and gazes up at the portrait of Plath. The familiar agony over her fate overwhelms her. Alone in London, in winter; two babies to look after; rising in the middle of the night to write those brilliant, bitterly angry poems. February '63; the *real* tragedy of that violent year. 'Out of the ash / I rise with my red hair / And I eat men like air.' But they'd eaten her. Betrayed, abandoned.

. . . To be brutaly honest, she is infinately more disfigured than you, having suffered first degree burns in a car-crash. And with equal honesty and shame, I am forced to admit that appeals to me. I don't know why. I swear I didn't know this unfortunate aspect of my character till I met Susan. I've told her I'm attracted by her scarring and she accepts that. I've let you down very badly, Shirley darling, I know, but please don't think I didn't like you a lot, and that it was only your birthmark that attracted me to you. That's not so at all. I am sure you will meet someone else who will love you more sincerely than I was able to do, because I was ignorant of my unusual but imperitive needs . . .

She remembers every word of that letter, even to the misspellings, although its pieces were scattered the same day to the Gulf of Mexico. November 23, 1958. A couple of days later they were to have announced their engagement over Thanksgiving dinner with her mother and stepfather. And it's the phrase 'Shirley darling' that has gnawed at her the most over the years in which she has forced herself to pray for him every day.

The days and nights of added torture as, her period late, she waited with dread yet a kind of sick hope. That something might bloom on her poisoned tree.

She slips a fresh sheet in and types. She breaks off once to go to eat supper with her sisters, who have the usual more relaxed Friday-evening air; then she returns to her desk. The light has lost its brilliance. One more thing she takes out – a reference to the Easter suicide, three years before, of David Kennedy, Robert's son. It had seemed relevant, for he had been a Kennedy victim, unable to live up to his family history or to escape from it except into drugs and alcohol. But now it appears to her that she had mentioned his suicide for her own secret reasons and therefore it would be dishonest to keep it in.

Yet, when the paragraph is omitted, it is the image of a Palm Beach hotel door with a 'DO NOT DISTURB' sign on it that goes on haunting her. That pure, clean break from everyone, that leap into freedom.

Sister Beatrice could imagine how he'd felt as he'd made his secret preparations. If the state of his mind had been anything like hers in November '63, he would have experienced an almost sexual thrill. There'd been no doubts in her mind. As Sylvia's friend and fellow-suicide, Anne Sexton, had put it, the question for a determined suicide is not *Why build?* but only *Which tools?* She had planned her death so well. On the Saturday morning she would visit the three or four sisters she really cared for, saying goodbye. Then she would write a short letter to her mother, saying she forgave her for having married such a brutal man, so soon after her father's death, and she should not blame herself. Then she would walk out into the city.

One Saturday afternoon, the previous winter, Sister Beatrice had caught sight of her former fiancé at the corner of Main and Market, waiting for a bus. An electric current had shot through her. She went back the next Saturday, and again he was there. Evidently he had moved from Galveston, Sister Beatrice's home town, to Dallas. He carried a sports bag; she knew he played football. This fall again he haunted the bus-stop, Saturday afternoons. He never saw her. Once or twice, he'd stared right through her. He didn't know she'd become a nun; didn't care.

She was going to post her letter home, then go to that bus-stop. As soon as he arrived, she was going to throw herself in front of a passing vehicle. If he liked disfigured women, he should find out that Shirley Jansen could play in the top league.

15

The plane lifts and they see placards, welcoming them to Dallas or cursing them, lift off the ground and whirl. Jackie lights a Salem as the plane levels off. It shudders, turning south-west into a fierce wind. Dull-grey clouds are scudding swiftly just beneath the wing; the earth looks murkier. The weather has really turned, and she wonders if she's going to be warm enough in the white dress, even with a coat.

She is aware of her deep underlying sorrow, the baby's face, and feels guilty that for a couple of hectic hours in Dallas she has not thought of him.

In the distraction of her grief, Jack's remark catches her by surprise. 'I wish we were going home,' he murmurs. He is stretched out on the bed, his shoes off.

'Home?'

'To Washington.'

'I can't think of the White House as home. But why?'

'I guess that incident at the Trade Mart upset me. Such naked hate.'

But they have also encountered love, she points out. It could have been worse. But I know what you mean.

'I've just had enough of Texas. Austin is one place too many. And Lyndon and Lady Bird are very hospitable, but – well, I could do without the ranch.'

'I guess I could too,' she says. 'Oh, I almost forgot. The Veterans asked me especially to give you a message.'

'What was that?'

'You're to wup the Communists in Vietnam.'

'Well, that sounds great, so long as you're not the poor eighteen-year-old kid who finds his guts spilling out. We should draft the men over fifty to fight down there.' He sighs, and covers his eyes with an arm. There is a knock on the door. 'I'm tired, Jackie; I think I'll pack it in after one term. Come in!'

O'Donnell's glasses and ascetic face appear round the door. 'There's some soup on – like some?'

Not for me, says Jackie: but Jack says, Yes, that would be great; and with an inrush of energy rises from the bed. He needs to eat often and little. Soup would be good. Soup is suddenly the most desirable thing in the world.

'Coming right up!'

As the plane fights turbulence he feels the approach of Hill Country, Johnson country. Land of pioneers, who thought it would be lush and rich, but they didn't know how little it rained. So they had remained poor; Lyndon never tired of telling everyone just how poor. The wives old at forty from overwork. It made him feel guilty. Hyannis, Palm Beach, all that wealth.

His father's whimsical, bespectacled face. The umbrella. It wouldn't do to go too deeply into how he made his money. Bootleg liquor, that was for sure. Costello claimed he worked with Dad. How closely crime and respectable wealth were linked in America. Sinatra with his Mafia buddies. There was that awful story, he hoped it wasn't true but so many people swore to it. At a fund-raising gala organised by Sinatra a prostitute got drunk and made a nuisance of herself. And Frank said to his toughs, get rid of her, meaning throw her out. But they had bundled the drunken woman into a car, driven her somewhere lonely, and left her with a bullet in her head. It curdled the blood.

Politics is a dirty game. It doesn't have much to do with Love Field.

Rosemary's well off, perhaps, in her dim mental world. It

keeps her innocent. The Inauguration, Rosemary sitting in a car, hardly knowing what's going on. That glassy look when she came home after the lobotomy. Heart-breaking.

'I'm glad it happened to me, and not you, Jack,' she said on the beach at Hyannis, on a lucid morning. 'I'm used to it.' I was too choked up to say anything, just gave her a big hug. The world is just so crammed with beauty and heart-break. Religion is about the only thing that makes any sense, and even that doesn't make too much.

Precisely at three-fifteen Air Force One came in to land at Bergstrom Air Force Base. As they taxied towards the terminal, Jack saw Lyndon and Lady Bird at the head of a welcoming committee, all stiffly at attention. The wind was tugging at Lyndon's coat-tails and flattening his grey pants against his legs. Lady Bird was clutching on to her wide-brimmed blue hat. The plane did a turn on the runway, losing the people who were waiting; at the next sighting Johnson was much clearer and taller. It seemed to Jack that he was a kind of shadow, appearing always before him wherever he went.

Jackie decided to go hatless. Let the wind tousle her hair; it was better than having to clutch on to a hat.

'Do I look OK?'

'You look terrific.'

He let her go before him. A cold blast of air struck her; she clutched at her galing skirt. Jack, one hand in the pocket of his lightweight blue suit, waved to the distant crowd. He heard claps and hurrahs. He stepped down after his wife, and his hand was being engulfed by Lyndon's. 'Welcome to Austin, Mr President!'

'It's good to be here, Lyndon!'

'The weather's turned unkind. This wind's like a Comanche's tomahawk.'

'So long as it's the only axe we'll meet in Austin we won't mind.'

'Oh, Austin's a friendly city. I promise there ain't gonna be any crazies here.'

After Johnson had led him along the line of welcomers –

one of whom presented Jack with a baseball cap in Texan colours – they strode together towards the host of mainly friendly placards near the terminal. 'Lyndon,' Jack said, 'I'd like you to do me a favour.'

'Say away.'

'That lady I was talking to at the Fort Worth breakfast – a redhead, Mrs Roberts – you know who I mean?'

'I know her.'

'I got kind of carried away. I invited her to the ranch, which I shouldn't have done without asking you and Bird . . .'

'No, that's fine. Swell tits.'

'But I don't want her there any more. It wouldn't be fair on Jackie. It might be embarrassing for Bird too. Would you have someone call her? Tell her – I don't know, make up some excuse?'

'No problem, Mr President.'

'Thanks. I appreciate it.' A weight dropped from his shoulders. 'She was going to fly in by helicopter,' he said, his breath rasping in the wind. 'WE LOVE YOU, JACK AND JACKIE!' loomed close, over excited faces.

'That might have been a little conspicuous. You can't be too careful when you're in politics. I've had a relationship with a real lovely Virginian for twenty-five years, and no one's ever suspected. Her former husband was my best friend, in fact. Bird never found out, at least I don't think so. Of course it cools off over the years; it's not the same, but I still see her now and then.'

'ALL THE WAY WITH JFK AND LBJ!'

Jack put on his grin; Lyndon thrust out his hand. Good to seeya again! How's the farm? You all keepin' well? When was it we last shook hands? – when I was up for the Senate? You look real good!

'GO HOME, NIGGER LOVER.'

Faces, outthrust hands, the press of bodies. America. I speak the pass-word primeval, I give the sign of democracy. Jack Kennedy, a kosmos, of Boston the son, Turbulent, fleshy, sensual, eating, drinking and breeding . . .

16

Sister Beatrice couldn't sleep. It often happened; she'd been an insomniac all her convent nights. She couldn't untense herself.

In earlier years she would have got out of bed, put on her tracksuit over her pyjamas, and gone for an after-midnight jog to use up her energy; but now it was too risky, there had been several muggings and rapes in the area during the past few months.

She might have worked on Plath, exploring the feelings of that deep-suffering poet, alone in frozen London with her two babies. Sister Beatrice kept trying to imagine what it was like to kiss your sleeping babes goodbye, place bread and milk by their cots, then put your head in a gas-oven.

But tonight she crept through the silent convent to her English Room. Having switched on the lights, she unlocked a cupboard and took out a video; then she took it next door to the Media Room where she slotted it into a recorder.

The video was a recording of a TV programme investigating the assassination. It belonged to Sister Agnes. Sister Beatrice kept it for her in her private cupboard because the video was supposed to have been destroyed. There'd been problems with a student, Jackie Greenwald; she'd had a breakdown, and her parents had stupidly blamed it on Sister Agnes for showing her this video. There'd been a great fuss. At first they were going to discipline the nun severely, setting constraints on what she taught and on her research; but there had been protests from Sister Beatrice and a few others, demanding academic freedom.

It felt peaceful in the Media Room, to the drowsy chirp of cicadas. Sister Beatrice switched the machine on and sat in a comfortable chair to watch. As the programme explored various lies and cover-ups, she thought: so what? Didn't everyone cover up? It didn't imply anything sinister. Hadn't she, herself, walked to the bus-stop on Main that Saturday afternoon, fully intending to die – despite Sister Agnes's grief? She'd waited, and waited; buses came and went. Until she realised her ex-fiancé wasn't going to come; and she realised why: his team must be one of the few that had cancelled their games.

Next week! she'd thought. But then, day by day, she'd started to feel needed by Sister Agnes, and saw her pupils' distress too. But it wasn't the instant virtue she usually pretended to herself. We all covered up.

She fast-forwarded the video till she came to the crucial moment, an enhancement of the Zapruder film. She watched in fascination as the Lincoln turned the corner into Elm. This time it won't happen, I don't want it to happen, she thought. There'll be a miracle. Yet, at the moment when it did happen, she had that familiar mixture of repulsion and fascination; her head jerked back as if in sympathetic motion, matter spraying from his head like a nimbus, and she had that feeling: God, what a shot! that was almost admiration. It was something you could never confess.

Her head thumping as if it were in a clamp, she decided to run back the video and to go with it. Her skin tingled with excitement; she breathed quickly. The sensations brought back the sick, shivery expectation she'd felt as she stood in the Saturday afternoon street of shocked Dallas. She would take revenge for Sylvia, through something quite unspeakable. She spread herself more comfortably on the chair; and as the Lincoln approached she lightly rubbed the remote control against her tracksuited groin. As the shot struck home, she allowed her head to jerk back without restraint or guilt and her mouth to cry out in pleasure.

Then she clicked off the recorder and rocked back and forth, hugging herself tight. She knew that must never, never be repeated. She would forget it had happened.

Outside, a mocking-bird started up. It had been around the convent all day.

II

Morning Glory

1

On the day that should have been Kennedy's seventieth birthday, the day of Sister Beatrice's memorial essay, her friend Sister Agnes was persuading a senior girl to write her semester paper on the President's last morning. The girl, Emily, had been fired by her teacher's enthusiasm and was gifted. 'You'll need Manchester's *Death of a President*,' the nun told her, as they sat in the shade of the pecans; 'but you can go beyond that, Emily. A lot's been discovered since, mainly from Dallas gossip. One can't *trust* gossip, of course, but then, a lot of history is little more than gossip. You can indicate whether you think the information trustworthy. How about it?'

'I don't know, Sister Agnes. I don't think I'm capable of it.'

A pleasant breeze had risen, late in the afternoon, after all the other children had gone home, and it fanned through Emily's mass of wheaten hair. She had to keep flicking strands from her eyes.

'You know that's nonsense, Emily! You just lack confidence.'

Sister Agnes watched her face in silhouette, the slim neck, its adam's apple gently curved, rising from the open-necked white blouse, her brow furrowed anxiously. 'OK!' Emily said at last. 'If you think I'm capable of it, I'd like to try.'

'Good!' She laid her pale hand encouragingly on the girl's sunburnt hand resting on the memorial seat. 'I can put you on to several people who might be willing to talk to you.'

There was Elizabeth Austin Rawlings, for example, wife of Tom Rawlings the big oil-man. Sister Agnes had met her at a charitable function, and not cared for her much, she'd seemed terribly snobby and right-wing – even for Dallas; but she'd told the nun she'd talked to Kennedy during the Fort Worth breakfast. She claimed the President had made advances, and it was not inconceivable; she was still quite an attractive woman, though she'd probably had a face-lift.

Back in her own room, Sister Agnes paused with a drawer half-opened, wondering at her own motives. There was some deep psychological need to make him live again, almost to breathe the air he breathed. She longed to turn history into reality; to go beyond Manchester's elegant phrases to the actual words used by Kennedy. And not only what he said but what he was thinking. She longed for the impossible.

Well, it was still a good test of Emily's ability and initiative. She pulled the drawer fully open and took out a notebook. She found Mrs Rawlings' number and other numbers and addresses. A businessman who'd been with a group of Jefferson High School boys at Love, waving anti-Kennedy placards; the elderly daughter of an old lady who'd shaken hands with the President before he spoke to blue-collar workers in Forth Worth; three or four others present at the breakfast. Then there was Pancho, a Cuban labourer, who'd turned up once at an assassination class meeting, and spoken about an odd encounter outside the Hotel Texas. Looking back, he and his workmates were sure they'd talked with President Kennedy; but since that was very unlikely, Pancho thought Kennedy had sent a double to Dallas. He thought the double had been killed, and the real JFK had been kidnapped and taken to Russia so the Soviets could worm vital secrets out of him. It was an even crazier theory than the one that had Kennedy decerebrate, drooling in a New Mexico monastery, but Emily should certainly write to Pancho.

'I thought you guys could do with a drink.'

He holds out a bottle. The hand is fine, pampered; it doesn't often hold out a bottle in a drizzly, gusty street before dawn.

Pancho, a squat and heavy-moustached Mexican, stares at the bottle for a moment, then accepts it. 'Thanks. You here with the President by any chance?'

'That's right.'

'The President? He's here in Fort Worth?' A giant crewcut Negro, jigging on the spot, was incredulous.

'Yep!' said the benevolent stranger, his face masked by the raincoat over his head and the just-lightening darkness. 'Up there on the eighth floor.' His coat-tails billowed as a gust took them.

'Don't you ever read a paper or watch the news, Three-Balls?' asked Pancho.

'I watch the sport. Jackie too? She's here?'

'Right up there with him.'

The workmen, passing the bourbon from hand to hand, agreed Jackie was a classy lady. 'So what's he like to work for?' asked Juan, huddling into his parka after passing on the bottle.

'Oh, he's OK. He likes you to work hard but he's fair, he'll have a joke with you.'

'It was no fuckin' joke when our boys were dying at the Bay of Pigs,' Pancho said; and Juan nodded agreement. 'Too fuckin' right.'

'Well, there were problems,' the clipped Northern voice said. 'It wasn't entirely his fault; but I know he feels bad about it.'

'Feelin' bad about it ain't goin' to bring those guys back to life.'

The fourth man there, another Negro, said, 'I reckon he's OK. Look how he kicked ass when the steel bosses put up their prices. He's on our side.'

'How can a rich guy be on our side?' asked Juan. 'Unless he sells all he has and gives it to the poor.'

'Where the fuck is Shorty?' The tall Negro craned to look down the rain-slicked road with its steady stream of lit-up traffic.

'Drugged up to the eyes. That bastard Hudson'll get rid of us if we keep turnin' up late.'

'Are you going to vote for Kennedy next time?' the stranger asked.

They glanced at one another; one said, Yeah, firmly, two others just shrugged. Juan shook his head. No way would he vote for a murderer.

A mud-coloured jalopy drew in to the kerb with a screech of brakes and wet tyres. 'Keep it,' the stranger said to Three-Balls as he offered him the bottle back. Hands wrenched at door handles. 'Shorty, you cunt! You sonofabitch . . .' They roared off before the doors were shut. Winding down a window frantically Juan leaned out and shouted back, 'Tell him to screw Castro!'

'Good luck, you guys! Nice talking to you!'

He watched the van screech round the corner and vanish. Then he watched himself walk back to the hotel in the rain. Wasn't that the last sentence of some novel? Fitzgerald? Hemingway? Anyway it was a sad ending. He felt pretty sad himself.

2

The heavy drizzle was falling in Irving, a suburb of Dallas, where a young woman was just drifting awake.

She had been in an American car – she thought it was called a Lincoln – but the landscape was Russian: alternate birch-forest and steppe. Lee was in the back seat lying down, curled up very small like a snake or a large worm; sitting beside him was her Uncle Ilya, wearing a black uniform – the dress-uniform of the KGB. Of course that was silly, she reflected drowsily, because really he was in the MVD. She was in the passenger-seat, and beside her, driving, was that old man from ZAGS, the registration bureau in Minsk, who had married her and Lee.

The old man was driving fast, one-handed; they were late for the movie. With his free hand he was offering her the book to sign, to register her marriage. And he was mumbling more or less the same words he had used to them in the actual marriage ceremony: 'Don't expect it to be easy. There's give and take in any marriage. Come back next year to register a baby but I don't want you back for a divorce.'

He fell silent. Just like at the ceremony, when she had expected more, perhaps a solemn religious vow in words of dignity and splendour. In the dream again there was nothing; he just waggled the book for her to sign. At last she did so, after which he handed the book over her shoulder – not to Lee, but to Uncle Ilya, who signed with a flourish. She knew she ought to protest; this was a mistake. She kept quiet, however, not altogether displeased. Uncle Ilya was a handsome man.

As Marina lay considering her dream, she realised Lee hadn't been woken by the alarm. She nudged him. 'Alik!'

He mumbled.

'It's time you got up.'

He mumbled again. A few moments later she felt the bedsprings ease as he got out of bed. She heard him leave the room; the bathroom door bang shut.

What was the rest of the dream? Ah, yes: we reached the movie theatre but the parking-lot was full. There was one space, but our American car was too long to park it there. So we drove it straight into the foyer. I told the ticket-collector my father was the star of the movie, so she let us drive right down the aisle and park in front of the screen. Marina had been breathless with excitement waiting for her father to appear; but at that instant the alarm had gone off, waking her – and still she had never seen that mysterious father of hers.

All her life she had pined for him, longed to meet him; or at least to know who he was. Her mother had seemed on the verge of telling her when she was dying in the hospital. She hadn't got round to it. Had he died in the war? In a camp? He was the key that might have unlocked her sadness, her loneliness.

That brought me close, she thought, to Lee. He too had never seen his father, dead while Lee was still in the womb. They were like babes in the wood, orphaned. Lee, her Alik, became her father. Almost she didn't mind his striking her, because it was good to feel possessed by somebody.

A gust of rain and wind rattled the window. Curled up warm, she could imagine she was in Russia. That drizzle was piling in from the Arctic; the ships were riding out the storm in the harbour. Or it was blowing along the Neva. On the Neva's banks was where she constantly thought she glimpsed her father, like the ghost in Gogol's *Overcoat*. If they ever did go back, they must live in Leningrad. But Lee refused; it had to be Moscow.

He was back in the room, quietly dressing. She felt him bending over her, and she opened her eyes. He murmured in Russian, 'Have you bought those shoes, Mama?'

'No. I haven't had time.'

'You must buy the shoes.'

'OK.'

'Junie can really do with the shoes.'

She grunted a yes.

'Don't get up,' he said. 'I'll get my own breakfast.'

It was weird. She had no intention of getting up. She had never got up to get him breakfast; on the contrary, he had often brought her breakfast in bed. She wondered if he were being sarcastic, though it didn't sound that way.

She wondered why he'd come on a Thursday evening. He usually waited till the weekend. But he hadn't seemed to mind that it meant he wouldn't see her this weekend, since you couldn't expect Ruth to put up with him so often. It was kind of her to put Marina up, and the two children, in return for Russian lessons. Ruth was nice, and her home was so clean; not like some of the dumps she'd had to live in with Lee since their arrival in Texas.

The separation seemed to be doing him good. He wasn't hitting her at the moment; seemed a little gentler. Maybe he was growing up at last. She would move back in with him – after Christmas. Families should stay together. She would give him one more chance. And he couldn't really look after himself. She was sure he starved, from the way he wolfed down Ruth's food. She couldn't see where he could get a steak and salad for a dollar twenty-five.

He hadn't wanted to make love last night. Their lovemaking was quite good. Well, OK. Lately he'd not ejaculated quite so quickly. She liked it when he sucked her nipples, especially when she was lactating. And he liked it; oh yes, he liked that a lot.

But he could be so cruel. Threatening to take her back to Russia. Stopping her from learning English.

She closed her eyes and went back to imagining she was in Leningrad. She heard the bathroom door open again and sensed, rather than saw, her husband enter and bend over Rachel's cot. Then he was in the next room, murmuring something to June.

Marina heard her little daughter say something, cheerfully, sleepily. She loved her daddy, that was for sure.

Marina's father, and the father of millions of others, had been Stalin. And, though her grandmother told her she shouldn't grieve for such a bad man, she had cried on hearing that he was dead. He still wasn't completely dead for a long time after. Not until they dynamited his statue in Minsk. Lee was lying beside her, his arms around her, when the muffled explosion came. He had joked about Russian secrecy, everything happening in the dead of night.

Next day, walking past it, she had averted her eyes. All the young men and women must have had similar memories to hers: the headmistress suddenly appearing in the classroom, tears streaming down her cheeks, her breasts heaving with emotion. The clapped hands for silence. 'Children! I have some terrible news! You are going to have to be very brave. Our beloved Father, Comrade Stalin, is dead.'

She listened for kitchen sounds, but there were none. Lee was probably munching a peanut-butter sandwich, and reading a book. She would wait for his workmate's car to honk, summoning him, then she would have to get up, dress June and give her breakfast, then feed and change Rachel. After that she would sit in front of the TV. The President and Mrs Kennedy were visiting Dallas. She wasn't interested in politics but she liked them both. Then in the afternoon she might go to the shoe store. Ruth would probably lend her some money.

The front door slammed. A few moments later a car drew away.

She got up, took a glance at the baby, sleeping peacefully, and padded to the bathroom. Lee had left hairs in the sink. It was such a beautiful, clean bathroom; she loved taking a long luxurious bath in the evenings, when iit was clean like this.

At least he'd flushed the toilet. That was an improvement. But what could you expect with a mother like that? Putting him into an orphanage. It was a wonder he wasn't cruel to the children; instead of which he was devoted to them, especially June. You had to give him that. Though he'd have liked a boy to take hunting and to grow up to be President. Such absurd dreams he had!

Ruth came to the bathroom door in her robe, rubbing her eyes, and they greeted each other in Russian, and Marina said she'd finished. She went into the kitchen, clucked at the mess Lee had left, and sat at the table sipping juice. She felt lazy. Well, there'd soon be more than enough to do when the baby started crying and June woke up.

She gazed at the watery pane. In the drizzly murk, you couldn't see very much, there was nothing to tell you it was Irving, Texas. The ships were out there in the harbour. Her grandmother was praying before the ikon.

Archangel.

3

He did envy those workmen a little. Not their lives, which were tough, but what they were. They were themselves, you could see it in their faces; they had not had their feelings knotted up by the Kennedy form of pre-season training, which started when you left the womb. Jackie, so cool and detached, had had a not dissimilar experience.

He saw often, in his mind's eye, that little tumbledown cottage in the West of Ireland, and it tugged at his heart. It stood for something lost within himself, he felt. Some capacity for emotion. Emotion was there still, but hidden; it gave hints, as when Caroline had brought the dead bird into the Oval Office. He'd shouted, 'Take that thing away!' surprising himself and everyone around. For a moment he'd felt the bird's death as if it were a child.

Well, there was no time for such brooding. Life was pretty good. If his parents hadn't taught him to love, particularly, they'd sure as hell taught him a good game of touch-football. Life – he towelled himself vigorously – had never been boring. His stubbly face, seen in the mirror, was pretty good still, though a little puffy because of the drugs he had to take. He enjoyed feeling the razor sharp against his chin, cleaving through the lather.

Aglow with health, he emerged from the bathroom. George, tactfully averting his gaze from the naked President, was laying out the morning's clothes: blue-grey suit, dark-blue tie, white shirt with narrow grey stripes from Cardin's in Paris. He picked up the shirt and handed it to the President.

Jack began to dress. 'Has anyone turned up in the parking-lot, George?' he asked.

'I don't know, sir.'

'I think I'll take a look.'

In his shirt and shorts, he opened the door into his wife's bedroom. She was waking, opening her eyes. 'Hi, Jack!'

'Hi, honey!' He crossed to the window. Below, in the fine swirling rain, he saw a drab parking-lot crowded with people. Mostly men: blue-collar workers. 'Holy shit, there's thousands of 'em! Terrific!'

'That's good,' she murmured sleepily. 'You're sure you don't want me to come.' It was a statement not a question. She pulled herself up on her elbow and reached for a pack of cigarettes.

'No, you rest. Stun them at the breakfast. They can make do with Nell Connally.'

'It's raining still.'

'Yes, but not so heavily. We could still be OK.'

Jack returned to his bedroom and finished dressing. A silent waiter had left a breakfast tray while he'd been in Jackie's room, and Jack drank coffee and munched a bun. O'Donnell came in bearing the overnight reports and a bundle of newspapers. Jack scanned the CIA pages as he ate. He paid particular attention to Vietnam. Since the assassination of Ngo, highly embarrassing to the White House, he hoped the tensions in Vietnam would calm down. There was no evidence of it in the reports so far.

'So what else has been happening, Ken?'

'Not a lot. The Bird-man of Alcatraz has died.'

'Ah! the birds will miss him.'

'The Legion in Abilene has taken down your picture. They think you're too controversial.'

Jack chuckled.

'We've got to tell our people in Dallas to put on the bubble-top.' O'Donnell glanced at the window.

'No way.'

O'Donnell looked startled. 'No way? It's pissing down. You've got to have it on.'

'Tell them I don't want it. The rain's clearing. Even if it's not, Jackie can get her hair wet for once, it won't kill her.'

'OK. You know best.'

'Let's see the Dallas *News*.'

Handed the paper, he saw 'STORM OF POLITICAL CONTROVERSY SWIRLS AROUND KENNEDY ON VISIT' and 'YARBOROUGH SNUBS LBJ'. He threw the newspaper aside. 'You tell Yarborough to ride with Johnson today.'

'He's refusing to.'

'In that case he's walking. You tell him that.'

The White House aide shrugged, nodded.

'I'd better get out there.'

Jack buttoned his jacket and O'Donnell followed him out. Agents crowded round him and ushered him into the elevator. In the lobby he paused in mid-stride, seeing over his shoulder an old lady in a wheelchair. He turned and strode up to her, holding out his hand. 'I'm Jack Kennedy.' The old lady looked to be on the verge of a faint. She held up her thin, liverspotted hand.

'I think you're doing a wonderful job,' her voice quavered.

She lived in this hotel. It was the most wonderful experience of her life to be sharing a roof with the President – and now to be talking to him. There were good people in Texas. I know that, I know that, he said. You look wonderful, I don't believe you're seventy-six, you're not old enough to be a grandmother, let alone have nine great-grandchildren.

Thrusting aside an offered raincoat, he slipped a hand in his pocket, thumb out, and strode along a corridor. The Bird-man. A lifetime penned in a cell. The inner life. Time for books, for poetry. And for birds. St Francis.

He met the rain. A loud cheer rose up. Grinning, he leapt on to a truck. He saw the near, worshipful faces. He warmed at once to them. Perhaps he knew how to love after all. He had loved that old lady in the wheelchair. But was it only vanity? He didn't think so.

'Thank you for showing the flag on such a morning!' he called. 'There are no faint hearts in Fort Worth!'

They cheered even louder. 'Where's Jackie?' a voice near him called. He pointed to her high window.

'Mrs Kennedy is still getting dressed! She takes longer than me, but the results are better!' He grinned his dazzling grin. They laughed, clapped.

The headscarfed office girls, telephonists, factory girls, stared up at him from the front rows, entranced. His wonderfully *open* face, thrown back, the sparkling eyes, the boyish grin, the sudden seriousness. Jack Kennedy, of Ireland the grandson, of the holy land of Ireland: saintly, human, prophetic, amusing, visionary. Singer of the word En–Masse, the word Democratic. Singer of a better future, of their children better off than the fathers, the mothers, lifting the hearts of mechanics, fitters, truckdrivers, cranedrivers, carpenters, plumbers.

They loved him. He loved them back. This was better than any woman's love. He knew how to charm them, sway them, seduce them, quieten them, then deliver the poignant thrust that brought them to rapture. He knew how to leave them wanting more. He had ten minutes in which to achieve it. Ten minutes was plenty, for a crowd or for a lover. They had already forgotten the rain. He felt the potency surge through him.

The TFX fighter plane. What a wonderful job they were doing. More grateful applause.

They were eating out of his hand.

The Bird-man.

4

On the outskirts of Dallas on this rainy, nondescript morning, one of Sister Agnes's sixth-grade pupils was upset. On the bus bringing her to school there'd been leaflets scattered around the seats, saying 'Wanted For Treason', with two pictures – full-face and in profile – of President Kennedy.

She decided she would ask Sister Agnes about it. The young nun was almost as fresh to the school as were Brenda and her classmates; she wasn't stuffy like some of the others and she didn't mind you interrupting her lessons with a question that was off the subject. So Brenda put up her hand when Sister Agnes asked for the reasons why the Pilgrim Fathers had left England. 'Sister, I found this on the bus this morning.' She held up the leaflet. 'It says the President was married before, and got divorced. Is it true?'

Some of the girls tittered; the young teacher's already pale face paled a further shade. 'Of course not! Let me see it, Brenda.' The girl rose and came to the front with the leaflet, then returned to her seat. Sister Agnes scanned the leaflet quickly. It was edged with a black border, like a funeral notice. Some other girls were calling out that they'd seen it too, it was all around Dallas.

Sister Agnes said, 'This is garbage. You can't expect anything sensible from someone who doesn't even know how to spell *marriage*.' She spelt out the leaflet's version to them. 'How should it be spelt, Janice?'

Janice spelt it correctly. 'Good. Whoever wrote this is

illiterate and just plain stupid. It's sick.' She scrunched up the thin, smudged paper and dropped it in a trash-can.

She thought it would be worth discussing treason with them for a while. The Pilgrim Fathers could wait, they weren't going anywhere. These kids weren't old enough to be able to grasp why a statement like 'turning the sovereignty of the US over to the Communist controlled United Nations' was itself a betrayal of logic and intellect, but they could be encouraged to think about the words traitor and treason. She invited them to name a traitor.

Judas.

That was an excellent example, she said. It occurred to the young nun fleetingly that the echo of Jew in Judas might have contributed to anti-Semitism. Into her mind flashed the memory of the Rosenbergs. She'd been unpopular, wearing a save the Rosenbergs badge at school, but her father had been proud of her. She'd cried herself to sleep the night they died in Sing Sing. Sister Agnes told her class about them: how they were convicted of having passed wartime atomic secrets to the Russians. If you did that, you were a traitor, weren't you? Yes! the girls chorused. Ah, but wait a moment! she said; what if they sincerely believed in the Russian system? And remember, the Russians were our allies in the war.

A few of the girls were furrowing their brows, she was making them think. Yet it was dangerous ground. She let them know, after they'd aired their thoughts, she believed the Rosenbergs were wrongdoers, though she wasn't sure they were traitors and she didn't think they deserved the electric chair.

'What if you're living under a dictatorship, or under an evil government? There were Germans who plotted to kill Hitler. Would you say they were traitors?'

No, they weren't traitors, the class decided confidently. You could say that Hitler or other dictators, such as Stalin, were traitors to their people. The girls agreed at last, with a lot of help from their teacher, that a traitor was someone who owed loyalty to a country or person *deserving* of loyalty, and who betrayed their trust.

By the time the discussion had finished it was a little late to return to the Pilgrim Fathers. Sister Agnes picked up her copy of President Kennedy's book *Profiles in Courage*, to read to them some of his fine, inspiring prose. The copy was a seventeenth-birthday present from her parents. Glimpsing the inscription her father had written on the flyleaf, she felt a familiar pang of guilt. She had betrayed them by going as far from their world as a girl of her background possibly could.

But she had done it for Him: she glanced up at the crucifix. Only for Him.

Her father's humour in adversity. 'I have been searching for piano sonatas composed for one and a half hands. There should be some. I'm rehearsing the kids to sing *I saw two ships a-sailing* for the Christmas service.' Grace under pressure.

She brought her attention back to the book and her students. 'He starts by quoting a definition of courage in a novel by Ernest Hemingway: "grace under pressure". Don't you think that's good?' They nodded, resting their elbows on their desks, arms folded across their grey-sweatered, still-hollow chests. Their eyes were on her. 'The President was a war hero in the Pacific,' she told them. 'I've told you about that. But I think it took even more courage, more grace under pressure, to write this book while he was lying on his back, in great pain from spinal operations.'

She began to read. As she spoke the measured, precise words, she thrilled to the thought that soon she would be seeing him. The President who had brought youth and excitement and glamour into politics, after the era of old men. He'd been a good officer, her father said; he felt he'd let him down in not going on to active service after the training Kennedy had given him; but *he* had courage too. It had taken courage, as a young teacher in Atlanta, to bring poor black kids in off the streets to teach them to read. He'd been attacked; but for the war being on he'd probably have been prosecuted under Georgia's racist laws. She only knew about her father's quiet courage thanks to an Atlanta newspaper cutting, sent anonymously to her after she'd organised a civil rights petition in college. The news story referred to a disciplinary hearing. She'd asked her father about it but he'd got embarrassed; she'd had to drag it out of him.

It was doubtless why, following his naval service, they had moved to Louisiana.

America! Sometimes she despaired of her country.

The young history teacher realised she was reading without concentrating, and she pulled herself together. But her class hadn't noticed; they were very quiet and attentive. They liked her voice; it was cool, even-toned, soothing, not like Sister Beatrice's, which was harsh, irritable. They reckoned Sister Beatrice had had no luck with men, because of the horrid birthmark on her face, so she had to be frustrated and angry. The older girls said she was quite nice usually, but this fall she didn't seem herself. Sister Agnes had an accent that was pleasantly not-quite-Texan. She also had beautiful grey eyes. She looked like Mary in so many pictures, holding the infant Jesus. Young and serene and lovely. The classroom lightened as the strengthening sun filtered through the windows; there was almost a halo of light around her head. The girls leaned forward on their elbows, scarcely hearing the words, concentrating on their teacher, worshipping her.

5

She appeared in the ballroom doorway, pink-suited, white-gloved. Aware that she felt and looked both vulnerable and resplendent, she was taken aback by the blaze of flashlights, the lights from the candelabras, and the impact of two thousand Texans clapping, roaring their approval, straining to see the belated vision of the First Lady. Hundreds towards the rear of the ballroom were standing on chairs. She stepped forward, almost stumbled, then saw her husband grinning his approval and she smiled back and he came forward to take her hand. The roaring and the clapping died down; waiters moved around; the guests, with a buzz of conversation from every table, fell to breakfast.

At the end of the meal the Mayor and Mayoress of Fort Worth presented Jackie with boots and Jack with a five-gallon hat. Chuckles, claps, as he tried his Texan hat on: he would never be a Texan, and knew it. He was a Yankee, he was Lincoln, he thought, in a Confederate gathering. He removed the hat quickly.

Then he was standing, to another storm of applause, and saying that two years ago he had introduced himself in Paris as the man who had accompanied Mrs Kennedy to Paris; that he was getting the same feeling in Texas; nobody gave a damn what he and Lyndon wore.

But beneath his good humour he was edgy. 'Today we're going into nut-country, Dave,' he said to Powers. The breakfast parties were milling around, unwilling to leave Camelot. His hand formed the shape of an imaginary pistol aimed at the wall. 'Those buildings we passed under yesterday – anyone could have taken a pot-shot at us.'

He was distracted over Powers' shoulder by Scarlett O'Hara. The young woman could easily have played her: petite; pale, almost English, complexion, in contrast to the healthy tans all around her; wide blue eyes; a cascade of curly russet hair. Her dress, though he wasn't interested in dresses, must have cost at least as much as Jackie's suit. She hovered, hoping for a word with him.

'It'll be fine, Dave,' he said, with a hand on his shoulder that dismissed him. He turned his grin on Scarlett. 'Good morning!'

'Good morning, Mr President.' She stepped forward, accepting his handshake. A gentle voice, not as drawled as most Texans', a distinct improvement on Lyndon and Lady Bird. 'I wanted to apologise to you on behalf of Texas.'

'For what?'

'For that ad in the Dallas *Morning News*.'

He didn't know of any ad. They hadn't told him about it. But he kept his smile, only narrowing his eyes slightly. He waited for her to tell him more.

'My husband – he's in Dallas for an oil convention – called me and read it out to me. He thinks it's great, but it upset me.'

'What upset you about it?'

'It's not Texan-style courtesy: that's what upset me. It would have been OK yesterday or tomorrow, but not today, when you're coming to their town.'

'Well, I accept your apology. Thank you.'

She edged closer. He could smell her perfume – or maybe it was shampoo. She must have taken as long as Jackie to get ready. He returned her upward gaze. Flames burned in the delicate cheeks as she said, 'But I have to tell you I agreed with the ad. If only it hadn't been today. I think you're a disastrous president. I'm sorry; there's nothing personal, just your policies.'

He chuckled. 'You put it much more charmingly than Dealey, when I entertained some newspaper editors in the White House.

And you're much more attractive. But I guess that makes it hurt more. That you feel this way. What policies don't you like, Mrs – what's your name?'

'Roberts. Elizabeth Austin Roberts.'

He turned away a moment as Stetsoned shadows loomed, thrust out brawny hands. 'Don't leave it so long before comin' back to Texas, Mr President!'

'I won't!'

He flashed them glittering smiles, then turned again to Mrs Roberts. 'What don't you like?' he repeated.

'Oh, everything. The way you're soft on Communism, as the ad says. Arranging for the CIA to assassinate good friends, like the President of South Vietnam, while buttering up to Khrushchev and Castro. Persecuting decent, patriotic American citizens, like Jimmy Hoffa – '

Hey, wait a minute, he said. America had had nothing to do with the assassinations in South Vietnam, and Hoffa was a Mafia gangster. He had fastened on to the Teamsters' Union and was draining its life-blood.

'That's just an opinion. Why are we selling wheat to the Reds? If they haven't got enough food that's their responsibility. I guess you're going to chicken out in Vietnam, leaving it for the Commies? That speech you gave in Washington about making the world safe for variety – '

'Diversity,' he corrected. 'How did you get a ticket for this Breakfast? I thought it was for Democrats!'

'Oh, I'm a Democrat! A good Democrat. I voted for Governor Connally. The snivelling liberals like Yarborough shouldn't be in our party. You couldn't fill an elevator with *your* kind of Democrat in Texas.'

He started to turn away, still smiling, but she touched his arm. 'I'm sorry! I got carried away! I've been as discourteous as the *News*.'

'Don't worry about it, honey.'

'Like I said, the ad was inexcusable. The only consolation is that it was signed by some Jew no one's ever heard of. At least it wasn't an American.'

He took a step back, staring at her. 'You're amazing. An amazing woman.'

Her eyes faltered. 'I'm just a patriotic citizen.'

Powers was tugging his arm. There was a hint of warning in his pressure. Jackie was leaving, a signal for all the reluctant guests to move off. He kept his eyes on Mrs Roberts. 'I'd love to talk about these things with you some other time.'

'Really?' She suddenly looked fragile, startled.

'I sure would. I should talk with my opponents. We're staying with the Vice President tonight: why don't you join us at his ranch?'

'Oh, I couldn't, it would be – '

'The Vice President won't mind. I'll get my people to lay on a helicopter for you.'

She dropped her head, thinking, confused. He wanted to kiss her splendid red hair; to draw her into an embrace. He pulled up her dress, yanked aside her panties, thrust her against a table and spread her legs, under the startled eyes of the Fort Worth Democrats. Her stockinged legs gripped him. It would have been fun. He was confident she felt the same.

'There's no need for that,' she said, looking up. 'I can come in ours.'

'Why, then, that's great!' He shook her hand. 'I'll see you tonight!'

Back in the suite, Jack changed into a light suit. He sensed it would be warm; the sky outside was still leaden but it had stopped raining. He urged Jackie to change too.

'She was very pretty,' she said; and he laughed.

'Believe it or not, we were talking politics. She's a Bircher. Probably a Kluxer. Her beauty is skin-deep.'

'I thought that was enough for you.'

He didn't hear; he called to her from the drawing-room, 'Come and see these paintings!'

The dull, anonymous hotel drawing-room had been transformed into a small art gallery. She recognised at once a Monet, a Picasso, a Van Gogh; the walls glowed, more colourful than the bouquets decorating the table and sideboard. 'It's amazing!' she said.

'Let's see who arranged it.' He picked up a catalogue. 'They've raided their galleries and private homes. What a wonderful gesture – it's for you, you know, Jackie.'

She was gazing at a glade of Monet trees. A hint of flowers leading into the shadows. I'd like to go into that glade, she thought; to breathe the scents and the quietness, to be alone. There I could commune with nature, and God, and my little dead son.

Jack placed a call to Mrs J. Lee Johnson III. She was too overcome to make sense. Then Jackie took over: 'We're both touched – thank you so much. We're so sorry your daughter's sick and you had to miss the Breakfast. I hope she's better very soon.'

Outside, the drawn-up cars and police outriders. There was an undignified scrimmage as somehow Jack's aides manoeuvred Senator Yarborough into Johnson's car. Jack was rapping orders: 'Push him in and lock the door! Threaten to blow his fucking head off if he doesn't ride with Johnson! The vultures are waiting to see where he sits.'

The western horizon was streaked with blue. 'We're going to be lucky, sweetheart!'

The procession moved off towards the airfield. It would have been easier and quicker to drive to Dallas, just thirty miles away, but nothing could beat a presidential landing. And the tall, shambling Vice President, sitting stony-faced by Yarborough, would be spirited ahead in advance to greet the Kennedys as they arrived. It was all an illusion, a brilliant masquerade. Tomorrow morning that cunt Dealey, the right-wing editor of the *News*, would be forced to print a picture of the President and First Lady stepping out of Air Force One, smiling, waving, at Love Field.

6

'I don't believe anything she says,' Emily observed, sitting with her history teacher under the pecans. It was a late June day of intense and airless heat; she was fanning herself with pages of notes.

'Why not?'

The girl shrugged. 'Just an impression I got. She was very nice, and gave me lemonade at the poolside as if she was JR's mother. But – she struck me as false. What's her background?'

'I know very little about her. I know she was involved in a messy divorce. From what I've heard about *Dallas* you're probably right to make the comparison. Her husband, Tom Rawlings, took over her previous husband's oil company and his wife in the same year. I'd say she's a go-getter.'

'Right!' said Emily, turning her large blue eyes on her teacher's and giving her cloud of hair, dazzling in the sun, a shake. 'I can't imagine President Kennedy making a pass at her.'

'Well, that was twenty-four years ago, remember. She'd have been attractive. But I agree, you couldn't trust her on it; it's the kind of thing she'd pretend in any case. But let's not bother about that, it's trivial, it's – '

'But I'd like to know what you think about his affairs,' the girl interrupted. 'They bother me.'

'Me too. Well, I think they've been greatly exaggerated. However, clearly he – he wasn't completely faithful. All I can say is – well, at least he preferred fusion to fission.'

Emily frowned. 'I don't get you . . . Oh – yes!' She threw her head back, smiling.

The smile faded quickly. 'This whole thing of sex bothers me,' she said more quietly. 'My boyfriend keeps wanting us to – do it. They get so angry if you don't go along. What do you think I should do?'

Sister Agnes looked away.

'I'm sorry, sister. I'm way out of line. Excuse me.'

'No, I'm glad you feel you can talk to me about it. I think you're too young.'

'That's what I think.'

'And these days, with – you know.'

'The plague! I know. It's very dangerous . . . Can I ask you something? Did you ever . . . I don't mean did you ever do that, but were you ever – tempted?'

The nun looked away again, towards the sun-drenched trees and, beyond, the unseen creek. Jake in his father's jalopy; begging her to let him touch her. And she thought. If only he did it without asking, it would probably be all right. But he didn't and she said no. And the next time, tense and beer-aggressive, he'd grabbed her hand and placed it over his groin. She'd pulled herself away, thrown open the rickety car door, and paused only to fling her ring back at him.

'I'm sorry,' Emily said, 'of course you weren't; you had a vocation.'

Sister Agnes placed her hand on Emily's shoulder, looked her straight in the eyes and said, 'Emily, do you really think I'm not human? I haven't always had a vocation. Of course I've been tempted!'

'Oh!'

'Even Christ was tempted.'

'Did he get erections?'

Sister Agnes blushed. 'I've no idea. I guess so. We should get on, don't you think?' She smiled.

Emily smiled too. 'I reckon we should!'

The nun took the sheaves of notes from the girl's lap, started to skim through them. Emily settled herself, her hands folded, looking over her teacher's shoulder. There was silence for a long time, save for the occasional chirr of a mocking-bird.

'You've got some good notes on their political discussions. You persevered longer with her than I did, and you got more out of her. And I think this information can be trusted more, don't you?'

It sounded like Kennedy's views, yes, from what Sister Agnes had told her.

And like Mrs Rawlings' views too, the nun said. And Oswald – what was she doing about him?

She'd got the address of Mr Truly; she was going to visit him at the weekend.

'I think it's going well,' Sister Agnes said; and the girl lowered her face, pleased. Then the frown-marks came again. 'It's maddening, though, isn't it?'

'How's that?'

'You can never *truly* know.' She smiled at her unconscious pun. 'You can never Mr Truly know.'

'That's true!'

'I mean,' said Emily, 'last lesson we were studying the eye with Sister Bridget. But I bet if you asked all twenty of us to set down the history of that lesson you'd get about twenty different versions. And that's just an hour ago.'

'All we have,' said her teacher, nodding, 'are some remnants of history that have casually escaped the shipwreck of time.'

'That's good! You're so clever!'

'Oh, it's not me! It's Francis Bacon.'

Emily scribbled in her notebook.

'He was writing about antiquities.'

Emily glanced aside, up. She saw decrepit old Sister Angelica passing them, hobbling down the drive, offering them a faint and gummy smile. They smiled back; then Emily glanced into Sister Agnes's mischievous, still-youthful eyes, and bit her lip.

7

Squatting on his haunches, he glanced through one of the high school history books. That knot of anger, rage even, he had felt in the pit of his stomach ever since he could remember formed again. It was all such pure crap. Who was it said history is made by the winning side? Had he read it in Marx? Nietzsche? The morons in the Book Depository would think Nietzsche was some baseball player. How many Americans could even spell his name? He would guess Kennedy couldn't spell Nietzsche. Lee had trouble with spelling, being dyslexic, which made some people think him stupid, but he could spell good enough in his head. It was 'N-y-e-t' which was the Russian for 'No', but you just had to memorise the rest, there was no way around it.

'That all men are created equal . . .' That was a laugh. You had only to look at Dallas; the old, bent Negro sweeping the gutter, and the fat cats in their limousines and Stetsons, spraying him with mud as they pulled up outside their plush offices. 'Pushing back the wilderness . . .' In other words, stealing the land of the Indians and Mexicans. How could anyone believe such shit? And now, they were set on blasting Cuba out of the water. First of all killing Castro. It had been a great shock when Ferrie told him that, in his Miami office. Kennedy had ordered his assassination. Lee had always liked Kennedy, thought his heart was in the right place. He still thought maybe Kennedy didn't know about it, that it was the CIA and the FBI who were secretly setting up the assassination attempts. He was prepared to give Kennedy the benefit of the doubt.

Lee had seen, right from the first, that Castro's Cuba was the bright hope for mankind. And meeting all those young Cubans in Minsk had confirmed it. Pedro and Rafael, their eyes shining, sipping juice while everybody else got drunk on vodka: 'You should go there, Lee! It's really government of the people, by the people, for the people! It's tough-going right now, thanks to America's hostility, but what little we have we share equally. And the sun shines on all, so we're happy!' As the cold, dank clouds of Minsk wrapped themselves around his apartment.

Well, tonight he would be there! He would be in a safe-house and Castro would come personally to shake his hand! He shivered; he could still scarcely believe it. In a few hours he would be famous; as the man who could easily have shot the President but had chosen to warn him off Cuba by killing Governor Connally instead. The way Ferrie had explained it, Castro had refused to agree to Kennedy's assassination, even though his own life was threatened. Now that was real nobility. It would be warning enough, Fidel thought, to put a bullet through the head of the most anti-Cuban politician in the motorcade. Connally was a typical fat cat. No, he wasn't typical because he'd been poor in his early days. He'd got rich and turned his back on his own kind. A traitor to his class.

Lee had no reservations about Connally. He was kind of sorry it would frighten Mrs Kennedy, who had been through a bad personal experience recently; and she'd probably get his blood and stuff on her clothes. But in the end it would strengthen her husband against the Fascists, and teach America it couldn't go on throwing its weight around, trying to bump off foreign leaders who were loved by their people.

He thought he would go down to the lunch-room and have a Coke. They must be in the building by now. It was so easy to hide, with such confusion, so many stacks of crates here, there and everywhere. They might even be hiding in a crate, with the rifles. Including his Mannlicher-Carcano and three or four bullets they'd fired from it. He had no idea who 'they' were, only that one of them looked like him, as it happened.

'*I* don't know who'll do the actual shooting, Lee,' Ferrie

had said. 'It's best we don't know. It's not a question of your courage, we know you'd shoot the fucker if we asked you to, but this really is going to take a crack-shot and you've had no practice.' Well, that was true, Lee had to admit it. He shouldn't have missed General Walker from so close. He could have become a crack-shot if he'd wanted to, but he'd never wanted to that much. His weapon was his brain. 'We just need you to be around when it happens. Keep out of sight from around twelve-fifteen till after you hear the shots; go to the john or whatever, just keep out of sight of anybody who could say he saw you.'

Because they needed an instant suspect, to give the real hit-men a chance to get clear. The night before, he should go visit his wife and kids, to say goodbye, but mainly to pretend to pick up the gun he normally kept in the garage there; and come to work next morning with a package that just might contain a gun. So Lee had found some curtain rods in Ruth's garage. His room at the lodging-house actually did need some curtain rods. The rods were now stuffed in a crate of biology books. It was his own idea to have this insurance: if anything did go wrong and he was arrested, he could tell them about the rods and they would find them. His small mouth curled into a smile as he imagined their surprise and consternation.

Not that anything was likely to go wrong. Everybody knew their role, Ferrie had assured him. The cop who would try to arrest him on Tenth and Patton was quite happy to get shot in the arm; he was being well paid for it, and would probably get a long-overdue promotion for having flushed out Connally's killer so soon. It was a clever idea, having him wound a cop. It would leave nobody in any doubt as to who'd shot Connally, once the identification had been made.

Tonight he would confess on Cuban television, explaining he had killed Connally as a protest against the plots to murder Castro. Ferrie had given him stuff that proved the plots. He'd be a hero – not only in Cuba but around the world. To decent people in America too. Fidel would deplore the assassination but say Lee Harvey Oswald had tried to do right in a confused way and in a corrupt society. He'd offer him political asylum. In time Marina and the kids would come over. They could get things together at last, have a good life in a just society.

Mr Truly, his boss, walked by as he sipped his Coke. He stopped for a word, friendly as always. 'How's that new baby of yours, Lee?'

'Fine.'

'That's good.' His eyes twinkled pleasantly. 'You going to take a look at the motorcade?'

'What motorcade?'

Mr Truly gasped. 'The President's! Jesus Christ, Lee, where've you been living! The President's in Dallas; he'll be along Elm in about half an hour!'

'Really? I didn't know.'

Mr Truly chuckled and shook his head. Oswald had his head in the clouds, or else buried in a book or magazine. 'Yes, they're comin' right by us, we'll have a grandstand view. The *News* has them going straight down Main, but apparently that's an out-of-date route; they're making a detour round the Plaza. Haven't you noticed the police activity outside?'

'No, sir, I've been real busy.'

Mr Truly nodded, patted Lee on the shoulder, and walked on.

Lee strolled to the end of the room. The grimy windows let in the increasingly warm sunlight, in which millions of dust-motes danced. He looked out and down. As the President's car turned right to move around Dealey Plaza there'd be a perfect direct shot. But Ferrie had suggested they might wait till it turned left into the last block of Elm, because it would have to slow almost to a stop.

Clusters of people had already gathered on both sides of the road. They would see more than they bargained for. A plane droned overhead in the clear sky. That could be the President. In a few hours Lee would be up there, in a tiny plane, heading east. Ferrie was a terrific pilot. A great guy all round. Those New Orleans years; Lee in the Air Patrol and Ferrie their instructor. That strange appearance: the brilliant red toupee and exaggerated false eyelashes, because he was totally bald. Red-hot anti-Communist, so Lee had thought as a callow teenager. 'I like killing Commies, and I also like training killers.' A bit scary, and not altogether comfortable, since Lee was already dipping into Marx, struggling to understand.

And that evening at Captain Ferrie's apartment, the boys who drank too much Lone Star and stripped naked with him and did things that Lee found staggering. He pictured it often; it bothered him that he'd got a hard-on, watching.

But Ferrie, though he might be a queer, wasn't a right-wing fanatic. It was all an act. Ferrie had revealed this only lately; that he was actually pro-Castro; and Lee had found this information even more staggering than the orgy had been. Because he knew he'd flown missions against Cuba. But of course, as Ferrie explained, that was all part of his cover, like his work for the CIA . . . Lee had done it himself . . . 'I'm prepared to learn Russian, sir. Act like a real Commie-lover. Have the guys call me Oswaldski. I know radar. I could maybe learn something over there . . .' To try it out, see whether the Soviet Union was as great as he imagined. Well, it wasn't, but he'd had a pretty good time, a real nice apartment, lots of roubles from the 'Red Cross'. He might still go back there one day; and after what he'd done for Fidel they wouldn't send him to some crummy town, he'd be right there in Moscow, yes sirree.

And Marina would be happy to be in Moscow, once she was there. She'd settle. She could get the books you couldn't find in Dallas – Turgenev, Chekhov, Tolstoy.

It reminded him he had Ferrie's New Orleans library card at his lodgings – left by accident among the assassination evidence for Castro. He must remember to pick it up and give it to him. Flying over the Keys, out over the dazzling ocean. 'By the way, David – here's your library card!'

A surprised sideways look and then Ferrie would laugh. God almighty, they'd laugh their fucking heads off!

Two young patrolmen in a Dallas–Fort Worth roadside restaurant watched a receding, jigging fanny in tight Levi's.

'Now that's a dessert I could go for, Davies,' said the plumper of the two men; 'and it wouldn't be fattening.'

Davies, wiping up egg with bread, nodded. He watched her out through the swing doors, then said, 'Do we report what she told us?'

The overweight patrolman, his shirt-front pouched like a woman's, glanced at his watch; shook his head. 'Anyone parking a van and carrying a gun-shaped parcel near the underpass must be security.' He stretched across with his fork and spiked a piece of pecan pie that the girl had left uneaten. 'They'd just think we was stupid.'

'Maybe. But I think we should have them check it out. The guy sounded pretty weird, the way she described him.'

'And you don't think Secret Service men look weird? . . . This pie's good. Try it.'

Davies shrugged, forked some pie and swallowed. A spotty, long-haired boy brushed past them heading for the silent juke-box. Nodding his head towards it, the plump cop said, 'I tellya what – if it's Chubby Checker, we'll go out to the car and call in. If it's Elvis, we won't, and I'll have a piece of that pie.'

'OK.'

But it was neither. The crowded, noisy restaurant filled with vigorous, raw English voices the patrolmen hadn't heard before. They waited to see if they liked it.

8

Patrolman J.D. Tippit was cruising quietly in Oak Cliff, a peaceful, gently decaying area of verandaed wooden bungalows several blocks from downtown. There was no activity at the moment to take his mind off his private problems. He had just one assignment today. It was clearly something covert, even slightly risky; from one o'clock he should be in the region of Tenth and Patton, on the lookout for a slim white man, twenty-five, about five feet ten. On seeing him he should pull up, get out and approach him in a friendly but very watchful way. The individual was somewhat unbalanced and it was possible he would pull a gun. Tippit had to be ready for that eventuality, and if it happened he should take no chances. Shoot to kill. 'Blow the fucker's head off.'

Otherwise he was to disarm him and bring him in for questioning. He was suspected of having been involved in the attempted shooting of General Walker. Walker had been a helluva good general, till Kennedy got him dismissed; he didn't believe in pussy-footing around with the Reds; so Tippit sure as hell wouldn't pussy-foot around with the guy who probably shot at him.

He felt happy that he'd been entrusted with this assignment. He'd always prided himself on being a good reliable cop.

But there was over an hour to go before he would have to watch out for the suspect. Too much time to think. He wondered how his wife was feeling. He didn't like hurting her. They had had good times. He remembered the honeymoon in

Havana – not so much the sex, though that had been good then, but the laughs they had shared. Though the sex had faded with the years, the laughs had gone on – really until this year, when Lynn had come bursting into his life. She never would have, if he hadn't taken the moonlighting security job at the Bar-B-Q, to earn a little more for his family.

It had been pretty crazy of him to tell Louise about the affair and that he wanted a divorce, one on top of the other, between the fruit juice and the scrambled eggs. He'd just wanted to get it over with, and give her a day to come to terms with it. She hadn't shouted at him, as he'd expected, but just cooed at the baby and taken her off to be changed. And shut the bedroom door. He'd thought it wise to get out.

He pictured her crying now. She wasn't particularly pretty or smart or much good at conversation and she would probably be hard-pressed to find another husband. She would be staring ahead into loneliness, with three kids to raise.

He pulled into a service-station, got a can of Coke from a machine, and sat in the car drinking. It was a warm day. He rolled the windows down. When he'd finished the Coke he sat on, as if paralysed. His problems suddenly seemed too great. The optimism and relief of early morning had passed.

Calling on Lynn on the spur of the moment to tell her the good news, and for the first time seeing her in her own apartment, hadn't given him the pleasure he'd anticipated. It had nothing to do with her appearance, though the bruises and the swollen mouth had been a shock; but seeing all the living that was a part of her and which he didn't share. Notably the swing in the garden. It was an awful responsibility, taking on a stepdaughter. Who would resent him like crazy. And wouldn't he resent her? Wouldn't he resent having to read her bedtime stories, knowing his own kids were fatherless?

It had been stupid of her to tell her husband she was pregnant – and not by him. She was damn lucky he hadn't done more than loosened some teeth. He was a violent man. It wasn't comfortable at all when they saw his white Buick shadowing them at night, when they drove to park somewhere.

Now that he had the time to think things through for an hour – instead of rushing from his police duties to the restaurant, seeing Lynn, going home for a few hours' sleep and then off on duty again – he began to wonder if he was making a big mistake. Even just financially, it would be fucking hard; he'd have to support two households. Lynn was already talking of giving up her waitressing for good, when she got near her time. Christ, he'd probably have to do even more hours at the Bar-B-Q. He would see even less of Lynn than he'd seen of Louise; he'd be too tired to screw. Hadn't that been the real problem with his wife?

'Will you still love me with dentures?' And of course he'd said yes. She thought the two teeth would have to come out.

Returning from the restaurant after midnight; wet diapers in the sink; greasy, unwashed dishes – there'd been a distinct whiff of slatternliness in her kitchen; the bathroom draped with two women's underwear and stockings; pop records blasting from Melanie's bedroom – for she would grow, she would grow, into a troublesome teenager. Lynn in bed, in cosy pyjamas, reading, offering him a gap-toothed smile; dentures in a glass.

He had to quell the rising panic. He shivered, despite the warmth. It wouldn't be like that; of course it wouldn't. Her hair in curlers, probably. Maybe another baby on the way. She liked babies, she said. She got pregnant easily. There'd only been that one time, when she'd been really hot for him and said, Don't use a rubber tonight, I want to feel you inside me, Jeff, it's safe, it's a safe time of the month.

Her mom, a whining, sickly widow living close by, forever dropping in. Wanting to move in with them in a few years.

He pulled out a crisp white handkerchief – Louise always kept his things so fresh – and mopped his brow. It was love that was the trap. It was sweet and fizzy as a Coke to start with; but then it was the empty can and cold metal cutting into your lips. He crunched the can and tossed it into other debris near a pile of re-tread tyres.

He saw in his mirror a white Buick, parked at a pump.

There were two men. Frank and his brother, who'd served time for robbery with violence. Was Frank keeping watch on Lynn's place? Was he following him, in broad daylight? There was no way of telling, and Tippit didn't fancy waiting round to find out. He switched on the ignition, released the handbrake, put it into first, and zoomed away, his tyres screaming.

After another ten minutes of aimless wandering he pulled up outside a record store. He dashed in and headed for the pay-phone. He pressed in the dime, dialled his home number. The phone, the familiar phone in the hall that he would never use again, rang and rang. Why the fuck didn't she answer? Had she overdosed, or was she simply at a neighbour's, pouring out her grief?

Distraught, he slammed the phone down and rushed out. Jumping into his car, he zoomed off again, and drove haphazardly, making turns at random, his eyes staring blankly, seeing nothing.

After a time he slowed down, feeling a shade calmer. She'd spoken of going to see the motorcade. That's where she would be, on Main, waiting for Kennedy. She thought he was good-looking. The plane would be landing in about twenty minutes. Yes, that's where she would be. Louise wasn't the sort to do anything rash; she loved their kids too much. He would carry out his assignment and then tell them he felt sick. He would drive home and she would be there, he would tell her it was all a big mistake, she was the one he loved, it wasn't too late to start over.

But what about the baby? Shit, there was a baby. But it wasn't real to him. Even though she'd made him press his hand to her stomach just before he left and said, Feel it, Jeff – it's ours! She'd been so fucking happy at his telling Louise he was going to move out.

Well, he would just have to tell her he couldn't leave his kids, and offer to pay for an abortion. He couldn't even be one hundred per cent sure it was his. There were those weeks when Frank moved back in. How could he be sure she hadn't got pregnant then? Still, he would do the decent thing and offer to pay. She would throw one helluva scene and he couldn't blame her. But then it would be all over. No dentures, no diapers. Louise had nice teeth and if he didn't have a rubber she would tell him to forget it.

9

They were breaking through the dispersing clouds and into dazzling blue. Jackie unclipped her seatbelt, removed her jacket and kicked off her shoes. She lay down flat on the bed and closed her eyes. It was good, so good, to withdraw. He, after unclipping the belt, stood and stretched, trying to shift the fierce pain in his back. It was still there when he sat again; it was always unshiftable. The only way of dealing with it was to pretend it wasn't there, try to separate your mind from your body. He gazed out of the small window.

Dallas was ahead and to the right. An island of skyscrapers rising from the plain. Its frightening beauty struck him first, then its loneliness. Islands in the wilderness. Homesteads. Ranches. Log-cabins. Cities. This America was so immense; Jack felt his mind expanding as he flew – almost blown apart by this immensity.

There was a timid knock; he called come in, and his secretary, Evelyn Lincoln, put her head around the door. Was there anything they wanted? Coffee? No thanks, Jack said, and nodded towards Jackie, whose eyes were closed, who was resting; who heard the brief conversation as at a great distance, the sound veiled by the trees and long grasses and flowers of Monet's glade. Mrs Lincoln put her hands over her chest in an apologetic gesture, almost as in prayer, and withdrew, closing the door gently.

Lincoln in the log-cabin. Feckless, illiterate father; mother-less by the age of eight; nine people crammed into that one

111

room. The perfect formula for creating a delinquent. The social workers would say, Look what he had to endure, your honour . . . Is it any wonder he turned into a thief, an addict, a murderer? But instead, he became the greatest president we've ever had. I don't know what the answer is, except to go on trying.

'With malice towards none; with charity for all; with firmness in the right, as God gives us to see the right, let us strive on to finish the work we are in, to bind up the nation's wounds . . .' Have I ever said anything so noble, even with my speech-writers? Your huddled masses. Life, liberty and the pursuit of happiness. They had an idealism that yielded memorable phrases.

Lincoln, with all his courage, had chickened out of visiting Baltimore before his first Inaugural. Even Lady Bird Johnson was scared of visiting Dallas. She and Lyndon had been spat on here in 1960. By ordinary housewives, with shopping bags and strollers. Good Baptists and Methodists. And Adlai had been assaulted just weeks ago. Nut country.

If I got hit, hope those Californian Polaroids don't flood the States. At least until after the funeral. Marilyn piling in on top of me. A special in *Life*. With an in-depth essay by Mailer. Wasn't it fun in the bath tonight? Poor Marilyn. She was quite a lady.

Kathleen, flying with her lover; in France too; flying into the storm, the clouds, the mountainside. Laughing and hugging, moments before oblivion. Or *in paradisum*. Or purgatory, her sins being scoured away. November 22, old Patrick Kennedy died on this date. Typhoid. Left not a picture, not a line. But brought us here. Out of the famine, but not to the paradise they hoped for. I'd like to have known the old guy. I guess some of him goes on through us.

'I am a part of all that I have met.' *Ulysses*. He'd read it first as a boy, lying ill at Hyannis. Spindly, weak, shortsighted. The bed piled with books. Gazing, weeks on end, out of the window, seeing the scudding clouds as knights in battle. Dreaming. He still felt that lonely boy inside him.

He glanced at Jackie drowsing. We don't talk any more. We speak in a kind of Esperanto. We're locked in, like the nuclear codes. I ought to have married an Irish girl. Who could sing the ballads and weave a spell of laughing words.

The roar of the engines seemed to stop for an instant, then resume. The long, slow descent. How far, yet how near, those souls who had sailed from Ireland a hundred years ago. To Boston instead of New York because the fare was nine dollars cheaper. How vast histories begin. With some businessman deciding to undercut another in the clipper-lines. And now – what was his father worth? Three hundred million? And then some. That worker was right this morning. But what could he have done about it? Just do his best for guys like that.

And for their kids. A safe world. The Test Ban Treaty was a start. A million lives saved in the next twenty years, Sakharov told Nikita. Ten thousand deaths per megaton.

He'd loved that little kid, fighting for breath. Patrick Bouvier. He'd give anything to know he was in God's arms, alive and kicking. Kick. She'll take care of him. Gazing down at his perfect little dead face, I cried. Powers was shocked, coming in on me. But it felt good, crying. Jackie, her face all pinched, her eyes red and wild. 'What would really break me up is if I ever lost you.' And like an idiot I said, 'I know.' God knows what I meant. Maybe I meant, at that moment, it would break me up to lose her. Which was crazy; but when you're griefstricken you say crazy things.

The cumulus piled and churned beneath them. In the distance a darker cloud cast down a shower and he saw the glimmer of a rainbow.

But this is a Godawful job. That first day, the red phone suddenly ringing, and I was too scared to answer it. Turned out it was a mechanical fault. And he said, What would you have done, Mr President, if it had been for real? And I said, General, made sure you were on the first plane. That was a damn good answer.

He stood up, stretching, shifting the ache to a different part of his back. He sat on the bed beside Jackie. Time to rouse her.

How strange that we're married. We're like North and South; I'm the practical Yankee and she's the Deep South. Black Jack, her father, as Gaylord. Swinging along with his fancy. And like North and South, we're only at one in a crisis or tragedy. Pearl Harbor. Patrick's death, holding her in the hospital. Other times we ignore each other. I guess she's resentful too, like the poor whites.

'Bobby, Jackie and I are all washed up. She's moving out and Monroe's going to move in with me. What's the constitutional situation – any problems?' His face like an ice floe. He's a little lacking in a sense of humour.

It would almost have been worth it, to see Mom's face, and Cushing's.

He stroked her sheer-stockinged legs, neatly together, then slid his hand gently up under her skirt. That was a good lay, last night. Never known anyone do that with a string of pearls before. Reminded me of Inga in Washington. The smell of her. Dad put paid to that; got me sent off to the Pacific. Fight rather than fuck; at least, fuck with Inga. Wanted her again himself, I guess. But Mom's won in the end. 'Shit' and 'no', the only words he can say, dribbling from the corners of his mouth. I'm glad I went back and kissed him a second time; I owe him everything.

He gazed down at her face. It was beautiful, delicate. He was too crude for her. Yet she seemed to like flirting with danger. Because of Black Jack. She was the only one who got on with his father, the old skirt-fumbler, she really loved him.

She stirred, feeling his caress. It was unthreatening, unserious, even affectionate. Yet from it came pregnancy and childbirth, and a baby struggling to breathe. Her eyes opened. He slid his hand out. She grasped it.

'What were you thinking about?' she asked. 'Politics or sex?'

'Oh, politics. History. The Irish potato famine. Lincoln's speech at the second Inaugural. What can I say next time, assuming I'm re-elected?'

She swung her legs off the bed and sat up, rubbing her

eyes. 'Men can forget so quickly.' Covering her eyes with her hands, she added, with a break in her voice, 'Oh Jack, I've been seeing him lying in that oxygen tent. Struggling, and puzzled, and hurt.'

'I think about him too.'

She removed her hand. 'You don't. You can't do. You never give him a thought.'

'We have to go on. It's John's birthday on Monday.'

'I know. We must make it a good day for him, we really must.'

'We will.'

The brown airfield came up to meet them, sunlight reflecting off car roofs, and then they nudged the tarmac and were taxiing. Leaning forward, Jack saw the familiar shapes of LBJ and Lady Bird, flanked by security guards.

'Lyndon's suits never seem to fit,' he said.

She looked out; smiled faintly. 'He sure is a giant . . . Your tie's crooked.'

Adjusting it, he said, 'It's hard to picture him and Lady Bird making love.'

'Maybe he just presses her elbow.'

'And she says, Oh, Lyndon, yow ain't lost your touch one bit. Yow make mah elbow go all goosepimply.'

Dave Powers knocked and entered. 'It'll be a few minutes, sir,' he said. 'The welcoming delegation are only just arriving. In a fleet of black limos. I should sit back and relax.'

'How many of them will actually feel like welcoming us, Dave?'

'One. Barefoot Sanders. Apart from him you have nine Republicans and two Dixiecrats.'

'Nobody from the Unions?'

Powers shook his head. 'There wasn't room.' He raised an eyebrow satirically.

When he had gone, Jackie picked up a book and opened it at random. Jack peered at the title. *A Dictionary of Symbols*.

'Jesus, Jackie, you sure go for some heavy stuff. I hope you're not going to be reading that during the motorcade?'

She grinned. She had once had Proust open on her lap during a motorcade.

'It's quite interesting,' she said in her whispery voice. 'A Jesuit priest sent it to me, after he'd seen me talking about the symbolism of various things in the White House. I thought it would be good on this trip since you can dip into it for the odd few minutes.' She was hoping it would help in the choice of emblems for cushions and curtains.

Gazing at the towering form of Johnson, Jack said, 'What's it got for prick?'

'I doubt it will have that.' She flicked the pages. 'It has *phallus*: "A symbol for the perpetuation of life, of active power and of the propagation of cosmic forces."'

'That's Lyndon.'

'Perfume,' she murmured, switching her eyes to the neighbouring page, 'is a symbol of memory, reminiscences. Which reminds me.' She searched in her purse and found a small bottle of scent. She dabbed some under her ears.

'Nice,' he said.

She lit up a Salem. He asked to see the book and she handed it over. He flicked through.

'This is too deep for me . . . There's nothing for ladybird, that's disappointing. – Oh, here's another one for Lyndon: *battering-ram*: "A symbol of penetration, that is, of an ambivalent force capable of either fertilising or destroying."'

She smiled, glancing out, exhaling smoke. 'Yes, he does look like a battering-ram.' The uncouth, hunched, gigantic figure.

He gave her back the book and she buried her eyes in it. He relaxed, if you could ever be said to relax with a back problem like his. Sunlight was sparkling off puddles on the wide brown field. He could see, in the distance, a cluster of spectators penned behind a cyclone fence.

'Why is it called Love Field?' she asked.

'I don't know.'

Well, he reflected, an airfield had something in common with love. Figures held at a distance. A sense of solitude, emptiness. Random departures and arrivals. Tension in the stomach before flying. Excitement. The search for novelty. A certain numbness. A poise between earth and heaven.

George entered, a clothes brush in the plump beringed hand. 'You want a brush-down, Mr President?'

'Thanks, George.'

He stood to allow his valet to tidy him up. 'The ramp's in place, sir.'

'Good. Get my clothes ready for Austin, will you? And something casual for the ranch.'

'Yessir, Mrs Kennedy, ma'am, you look terrific, if you don't mind me saying so.'

'Why, thank you!'

They stepped out, and stood waiting for the door to be opened. 'You know what, George?' Jack said to his valet. 'I wish we were going to the movies!'

George's teeth flashed. 'Oh, you'll have a good visit, Mr President!'

The door opened; light dazzled. Jack buttoned his coat; that familiar, hunched, round-shouldered look as he did so. It brought back to Jackie the slight, boyish figure of the wedding. Touching his arm she murmured, smiling, 'We don't make a bad couple, do we?'

'I should say not!'

He put his arm round her shoulder to move her ahead of him; she said, Just a moment, and made a last-minute check of her clothes.

He nudged her forward gently. 'OK, Mrs Kennedy, slay them!'

III

Love Field

1

On afternoons such as this, windless, almost cloudless, time
seemed to stand still at Love Field. The occasional plane landed;
another took off; the airfield parched and featureless. Only the
departure and arrival boards, recurrently flickering up and
cancelling, confirmed that time passed, despite appearances.

Kennedy would barely recognise it, Sister Agnes reflected.
The waiting area looked more like a seedy bus-station. It was
her first visit to Love Field for three years, since her father's
heart attack drove her to take the shuttle to New Orleans.

She sat over a book and a cup of coffee, waiting for her sister
to arrive. Jean had flown south from New York a week ago,
to visit their parents, and was coming on to spend some time
in Dallas. The New Orleans shuttle was delayed. From time
to time the middle-aged nun glanced up at the board to see if
the flight was announced. Anyone who cared to glance at her
would not have known she was a nun. She had changed much
more startlingly than the airport. Her order wore knee-length
grey skirts now and white blouses. The young girls – those few
who devoted themselves to the religious life – looked smart and
sexy. Sister Agnes wasn't sure it was good; it put temptation in
their way.

Finishing her book, she gazed out at the drab field. Always,
on her rare visits here, she saw Air Force One. It was always
that couple of hours when it waited for the motorcade to finish
and to take the President off to Austin. She visualised it so
intensely in its waiting that if she walked out she could touch

its warm fuselage. There was something infinitely sad about the empty plane's patience. She gave way to the pathetic fallacy; it would have known there was something not right, something terrible, when it was boarded again.

The book she was reading was the latest of so many about the assassination. Seeing its title, *Final Disclosure*, she had felt she just had to read it. Perhaps it really would have the answer, at long last. A detailed confession, perhaps, that would make sense of the whole maze. But the book was a great disappointment; written by one of the lawyers of the discredited Warren Commission, it simply insisted Oswald had acted alone, and Ruby had shot him without premeditation. Sister Agnes could see there was nothing new, nothing convincing, in the book. The author, who had gone on to become one of the lawyers for Nixon over Watergate, had mostly rehashed old stuff.

A rabbi, who had interviewed Ruby in his cell, was convinced he had indeed shot Oswald in order to save Jacqueline Kennedy from having to appear in a Dallas court. That was it; that was the final disclosure.

And yet . . . And yet . . . Sister Agnes wondered often if the Commission's simplistic findings might not, after all, be true. Any conspiracy would have had to be so complex and long-planned; yet Oswald got his job in the textbook warehouse apparently by chance, only a few weeks before. And Ruby: he was supposed to have dropped a bullet on the stretcher he believed to have been Connally's, in Parkland Hospital; yet how did he know, amid the chaos, that an extra bullet would need to be found? A magic bullet, which had passed through Kennedy and Connally . . . In any case, why didn't he leave a mangled bullet on the stretcher instead of a nearly perfect one?

Why did all the various bits of information or rumour not at least suggest some overall design? They weren't like jigsaw pieces, gradually building up a picture, but like elemental particles dashing madly around in space.

What would have happened if they had used the bubble-top?

For even if it wasn't bullet-proof it would surely have deflected the first shot and caused an instant speed-away . . . Months of preparation down the drain . . . Could one conceive of a vast conspiracy relying on chance events?

Of course, when you looked at all the evidence *for* a conspiracy, it became unimaginable that Oswald had acted alone.

It obsessed Sister Agnes. She found herself thinking of it during prayers, or while she talked to her class about John Paul Jones or the Alamo. Because she had perhaps been the very last person he had spoken to. Well, except for Sister Beatrice; but she despised him now, she had a different obsession. Besides, it was her – Sister Agnes – his smile had lingered on, driving away, when she'd pretended she was looking at Jackie. She sometimes felt he was appealing to her from heaven or purgatory to find the truth.

It was stuffy in the waiting area and she fanned herself with her book. A voice near her said, 'Would you like this paper? It'll be better.' She glanced aside, into the eyes of a woman who was smiling and offering her a newspaper.

'Thank you! It's so humid in here.'

'It sure is.'

The woman was middle aged, a few years younger than Sister Agnes; she was in green-and-yellow bermudas and a red blouse. Her long blonde hair had come out of a bottle. She clutched the arm of a man a good deal older than herself, who also smiled pleasantly at the informally dressed nun and joined in the small talk. They were waiting for their son – or rather *his* son – who worked in New Orleans real estate. Sister Agnes told them she was expecting her sister, whom she hadn't seen for ten years. She lived in New York but was coming by way of their parents' home, a small town north of New Orleans.

'I couldn't help noticing your book,' the woman said, touching it. 'I was in the Texas theatre when Lee Harvey Oswald was arrested. He was sitting right in front of me.'

The man leaned across her and said, 'I've heard her tell this story a thousand times!'

Sister Agnes scarcely heard him; the familiar excitement gripped her. She wanted to hear all about it.

Well, she'd been living in Lewisville at the time. She'd come in with her boyfriend for a day out in the city . . .

'It was the day they got engaged!' the man interrupted jocularly, winking.

'That's right, it was the day we got engaged. My first husband and me.' She touched her husband's hand lightly, affectionately. 'I guess it was about the nicest day we ever spent together: but that's another story. We didn't know the Kennedys were in town, nor even that they were in Texas . . .'

She continued with her story, leading up to the man who was Oswald sitting down directly in front of her. He'd leaned his arm back and actually touched her, accidentally, when she was reaching down to remove her shoes, which were hurting. They were new shoes, bought especially, and she and her boyfriend had walked a lot. So Lee Harvey Oswald had touched her. Then the lights had gone up . . .

Her husband leaned across again. 'Don't ask what they were up to!' He winked.

'We weren't up to anything! Young couples didn't get up to anything in those days! Specially if you were good Baptists from Lewisville, Texas.' No, they had simply been scared stiff by the police appearing and suddenly grabbing the man in front. He'd pulled a gun, but they'd wrestled it off him. They'd dragged him off protesting about police brutality, just like it said in all the books.

It was disappointing. Just like *Final Disclosure*. Sister Agnes was always disappointed when she came across some eyewitness, as she occasionally did, and his story backed up the official version.

People were beginning to stand up around them. They saw that the flight was announced, fifty minutes late. She and the friendly couple also stood up, and said it had been nice talking. The woman saw that Sister Agnes had stood up stiffly and had to lean a hand on a table for support. She touched her arm sympathetically. 'You OK, honey?'

Sister Agnes nodded. 'I've a touch of rheumatism in my hip.'

'You're young to have that.'

We all had to put up with *something* as we got older, the nun said, smiling. She joined the crowd waiting for the arriving travellers.

First one or two came, and then a stream. Galloping businessmen in Stetsons, for the most part, lifting briefcases to check their gold wristwatches.

She barely recognised her sister, grey-haired now and bespectacled, in a smart white pants suit, a bag slung over her shoulder, a suitcase on wheels dragging behind. Her face looked sad and drawn. But she broke into a smile as she saw her sister. They embraced.

'Sorry I'm so late; there was a bomb scare.'

'It doesn't matter; I'm just glad you're here.' They moved apart and started to follow the flow towards the exit. 'How are Mom and Dad?'

'Mom's fine. Full of energy.' Then she grimaced. 'Dad's not so good. He was in bed most of the time, he's so tired, you know. But his spirits are OK.'

'Well, that's good . . . And how about you? How are you feeling?'

'Terrible.'

'No sign of Mark coming to his senses?'

'No. But that's not the worst. I'll tell you later.'

2

Marina talked to Ruth for a while when her friend returned from her morning teaching job, then left her to prepare lunch while she herself got dressed at last. After she'd put on her slacks and sweater she reread Uncle Ilya's letter which had arrived that morning. He was as thrilled about the new baby as was Aunt Valya; he only wished they could see her. And Uncle Ilya led Marina, by a natural progression, to thoughts of her stepfather, Alexander. Just as good-looking as Uncle Ilya but so much less kind. To Marina, but more importantly to her poor dying mother. Downing the vodka when she needed decent food, for which there was no money left. And what was worse, when her mother was in the hospital wasting away with cancer, bringing a former girlfriend into the flat. Or at least, not raising any objections to his mother, that awful woman, inviting her along. The old girlfriend, plump and blooming with vitality! And her mother not yet dead.

'You ought to have married her, my son. This one's brought you nothing but problems.'

Marina took out her album of snapshots and gazed at her sweet mother. Her heart filled with guilt. Not that she hadn't tried to go to the hospital as often as possible; but it was on the Vyborg side of the Neva, which meant you had to make such a complicated journey; and it was winter. She was angry with her mother for being sick for so long.

'First to the hospital, Mama, and then to the cemetery!'

It was an unforgivable thing to say, and Marina screwed

up her eyes as she remembered it. She was referring to the abortion of the previous summer, but she didn't know why she had to be so brutal.

'I don't want to die, I don't want to die. Where's Marina?'

But Marina was at home that day, tired from her work at the pharmacist's. She could not forgive herself for not being with her mother at the end. And perhaps she would have told her, at last, who her father was.

'Don't put it in your mouth!' she said to June, shaking her head vigorously. June, sitting on the floor, took the lipstick out of her mouth, gazed at it then at her mama, and said, 'Nya!'

'*Nyet!*' Marina agreed, nodding.

The sound of Ruth percolating the coffee and rattling dishes mingled with the sounds of a quiz show on TV. Quiz shows were useless for her, she couldn't understand what they were saying. She'd watched the Kennedys arriving at Love Field – just as she and Lee had done. Jackie had on a beautiful light-coloured suit and hat; and Kennedy was – well, he certainly wasn't Khrushchev! But her thoughts were in Russia today. She felt homesick; but homesick for what lay beyond any passport or visa.

Standing between her grandmother and stepfather in the Nikolski Cathedral, her knees buckling, the tears streaming down her cheeks. The singing, so powerful; but mother would never hear singing again. Forgive me, Mama, forgive me!

She flicked the pages of the album. Lee. Crouched at the river, holding his fishing-rod. Surprised and thrilled when he actually hooked one, and they ate it that evening. Tchaikovsky's Fifth on the gramophone; he wanted to hear it twice. It was still playing when he took her off to bed, but he came in a flash.

'Don't worry about it, it was OK; I enjoyed it.'

'Have you ever been to bed with anyone else since we married?'

'Yes. Once. When you were in Moscow, Alik. But he couldn't make it. It was a disaster.'

Rising on his elbow, grinning. 'You're lying to me! You're just trying to make me jealous!'

'Why should I want to do that? It's true. I had a few drinks and I was tempted. If I wanted to make you jealous I'd have said it was wonderful. I'll never do it again.'

Still, he wouldn't believe her.

Slipping the album into a drawer she picked up a comb and ran it through her short dark hair. Lots of boys had loved that hair, stroking it. Tolya especially. Now, he could really kiss! Perhaps she should have married him, settled down in Minsk. Alik couldn't kiss, not passionately, hungrily. He could never have gone out with American girls who showed him what a kiss was. She suspected American women didn't know how to kiss. In Russia, where life was so bleak, you put your whole heart into passion. That Mrs Kennedy, she looked sort of cold in her pictures, though she was very beautiful. She wondered if the President got enough sex. Sometimes she dreamed she would show him how a Russian woman could kiss and make love. He was a handsome, sexy man; how sad if he'd never found out how to kiss and fuck.

The quiz show had been interrupted; she could hear the voice of the commentator who had reported the presidential arrival. He'd been excited then, though she couldn't understand what he was saying, but now he was almost going crazy. American commentators got so excited. Over the top. Perhaps because they didn't get any passion from their women, they had to put all that huge American energy somewhere.

Ruth appeared in the doorway, a saucepan in her hand; her eyes and mouth were wide open and her face had lost all its colour; she looked as if she'd seen a ghost.

3

In a corner of the trauma room, drenched in blood, Jackie hears nothing. She has become a deaf-mute. There are only inner voices and visions. He is at Love Field, following her out into bright, warm sunlight, and she is wondering if the woollen suit was a mistake. Red roses are being presented to her. Thank you. The first red roses in Texas. 'Shall I take this?' and Jackie doesn't hear her but nods and lets a nurse gently take the fragment of her husband she has been clenching.

A doctor leaned close to her and said, 'The President has sustained a fatal wound.'

She didn't hear him or understand what he was saying but tried to say, I know. She failed. Her lips moved.

Jack's own White House doctor grabbed her by the shoulders. His voice sounded strangled to others in the room, those who kept a toe-hold in reality. 'The President is dead.' Her head inclined, resting on his shoulder. He started to weep.

He ordered the room to be cleared.

Jackie sat by her husband and took his hand.

A priest entered. He was breathing hard; he had come as quickly as he could, through the impossible traffic. Gliding up to her, he murmured his condolences. He drew the sheet from the President's face and gazed at him. The question was, had the soul already left the body? The President had been strong; probably his soul still hadn't departed. But he would have to begin the absolution with 'If it is possible . . .'

His hands trembled and he dropped the vial of oil in its

cloth container. Stooping to pick it up, his eyes for a moment were level with the President's head. He saw the gaping wound, and grey substance within it. He straightened, took out the vial and unscrewed it, pressed his thumb to its neck and anointed the forehead: '*Per istam sanctam Unctionem, indulgeat tibi Dominus quid-quid deliquisti. Amen.*

He paused, his mind in a turmoil. His faith ebbed suddenly. It had only happened to him once or twice before, and with God's help he would recover. It had been the glimpse of the brain. Half of it had gone. Taking with it thoughts and memories and aspirations – everything that makes up a human being, a soul. This brain was perhaps where God had been born. Not Mary but the brain had been the mother of God.

He took a step back. The President's doctor rasped, 'Is that all?'

The priest looked startled. 'I – no, it's not all; it's only the beginning. I don't profess to understand God's ways, but – '

'I meant, can't you say some prayers, damn it!'

'Oh – yes, of course.' The priest bent his knees to kneel, but saw that the floor was covered in blood. He hesitated a fraction of a second; it was a choice. He chose to stand, closing his eyes, bowing his head, and murmuring, 'Hail Mary, full of grace, the Lord is with thee; blessed art thou among women, and blessed is the fruit of thy womb, Jesus.'

Jackie and the doctor responded, 'Holy Mary, Mother of God, pray for us sinners, now and in the hour of our death. Amen.'

'Eternal rest grant unto him, O Lord . . .'

The doctor could not speak, but Jackie whispered, 'And let perpetual light shine upon him.' She felt the world spin as she whispered the words; felt the icy stillness of space and the world turning under her feet.

She left the room. The priest came swiftly after her. He laid a hand on her shoulder. 'This has been a great personal shock to me. It's terrible, terrible!' He hesitated. 'I am convinced that the soul . . . you know . . .'

4

Over coffee in Sister Agnes's room, gazing out at the sun-dazzled, light-green foliage of the pecans, Jean poured out the full extent of her grief. Problems that were far worse than her husband's leaving her for a member of his church congregation. It involved her sons. John (named after the murdered President) was a heroin addict; Bernie, the elder, had revealed to her, in the one heart-breaking call from Los Angeles, that he was gay and HIV positive.

Of course it didn't mean he would necessarily get AIDS. Did it? She searched her sister's face anxiously – as if she would know. But she lied, pretending knowledge, saying there was a probability he would never develop AIDS.

Our children, Jean said: what have we done to them? Where have we gone wrong?

She cried softly, then wiped her eyes. It was too painful. She was tired, and for today she wanted to forget. Hearing girlish voices, she looked out of the open window. Pupils were leaving, heavy briefcases in hand. Two girls had paused under a marble statue of the Virgin, comparing notes. Dimly the sisters heard high-pitched laments: 'Could you answer number five?' 'No, I thought it was a shit-awful paper . . .' Sister Agnes blushed. 'They're talking about my history paper,' she said; 'they have exams all week.' That was how she'd been able to meet the plane; there were no classes and she'd had a break from invigilating. 'But I guess you pay for the break with hours of marking,' Jean said. 'That must be a bore.' She glanced at piles of work-books. 'They remind me of when we were kids.' Dad sitting out on the veranda, marking book after book, shushing the girls if they made too much noise. And that warm smell of baking from the kitchen, the radio on playing syrupy ballads for Mom.

The memory touched and saddened the nun. 'He just lived for teaching; he was a natural at it, as I'm not. It was criminal the way they made him retire early. Just for telling a class they mustn't take everything in the Bible literally.'

'Was that why it was? He told me it was because he read with his fifth-graders a story containing the word "shit".'

'He probably did both,' said Sister Agnes; 'he'd have been embarrassed to use a swear-word to me.'

'That's true! But he was foolish, he should have known you couldn't get away with such things in Louisiana, of all places.' Massive corruption, Huey Long and Carlos Marcello, were camels they could swallow, but they would strain at the word 'shit'. Maybe not so much now, but certainly in the seventies.

He was always courageous, the nun said; and chose the worst places to be liberal in. Look at Atlanta, the way he taught black children in his spare time.

Jean hadn't heard of that. 'Yes, he was teaching them to read. He got hauled over the coals. The school board accepted his resignation because he was enlisting; God knows what would have happened otherwise.'

'Jesus, Tessa! Doesn't it make you want to throw up?' She remembered her father placing his naval cap on her head, and it came down over her eyes.

But they thanked God for having had liberal parents. They'd been remarkably tolerant, Mom and Dad. They hadn't freaked out when Jean went joy-riding that time. Nor when Tessa started taking an interest in the Catholic Church. 'Well, Dad freaked out a little,' Sister Agnes recalled. It was understandable, and it had passed. He had stormed around the kitchen, growling about relics, the worship of old bones.

'Yes, I remember that evening!' Jean smiled faintly for the

first time since their meeting at Love Field. 'I've never seen him so angry. Mom was trying to calm him, assuring him it was just a whim.' The smile somehow twisted, became less pleasant. Actually she had a relic back home. Not in New York but at the house in Weston; the house that Mark, whose family was wealthy, had brought with him and would now take away, for the new woman. 'Guess what it is?'

'I can't imagine.'

'Well, it's from his accident – with the hedge-trimmer? I picked up his severed fingers. I didn't know what to do with them. I felt I could hardly throw them in the trash-can. I thought I'd burn them on the next bonfire, and meanwhile I put them in a cigar box he left behind.'

Sister Agnes's stomach turned over.

'But time went on; there was a lot of rain and we didn't have a bonfire; the cigar box got buried under other things in the woodshed. And I guess it's still there!'

She broke into a giggle, and her eyes, behind her glasses, flashed with amusement at her sister's horror. It was almost a flash of sadistic pleasure; and Sister Agnes remembered, from forty years ago, Jean's cruelty. How she'd enjoyed pulling her kid-sister's pigtails, twisting her arm! Yes, actually, there hadn't been much love between them. Once, in the marshy field, Jean had pushed her down into the mud; in revenge for something: nylons she'd borrowed and then laddered. Sugar cane, that old laughing Negro. She could only have been about twelve.

'I must burn them when I go back. I've got to sort all my things out.' Her smile vanished; pain returned. Abandoned by her husband at fifty-four. They used you and spat you out.

Tessa was wise never to have anything to do with men. 'And you look really well, honey – apart from that hip. You're getting to look like Mom. Isn't it strange how we grow to resemble our parents as we get older? I guess you wouldn't notice, not having seen too much of her in recent years. You're a bit too plump, like her – though she's fined down quite a lot, actually. And you really must get your hip done; I'll pay – or rather, Mark will pay. I'm going to fucking screw him. I'm sorry!'

'It's OK.'

After draining her coffee-cup, Jean said, 'They miss seeing you. They're old, you know, and Dad may not be with us much longer. You should try to get home more often.'

'I know. It's difficult.'

'Dad can't get to you any more.'

'I know that. I call them every week.'

They sat in silence. Really, Sister Agnes thought, we don't have much to talk about any more. Jean broke the awkwardness by standing up and saying she should get to her room and unpack. They walked through quiet corridors to the guest-room. It would be fine; the convent was blessedly cool compared with her parents' house; she'd left a cheque to help get the air-conditioning fixed. She liked it that this guest-room was rather bleak; she would have been disappointed otherwise. Space and time to think was all she needed – though it was nice to have TV, she hadn't expected it. She switched the set on and started to unpack. Sister Agnes helped her, but then felt weak and had to sit down. Jean's criticism, and her unnecessary reminder that their father might not live much longer, had distressed her. She saw him on their last visit, five years ago – in this very room. Saw his hand, with its missing index and middle fingers, clasping the panama hat; already looking frail. That business about the fingers had upset her too.

She loved him so much. It was cruel and unfair of Jean to suggest she didn't care enough. She felt so churned up that, while she replied to Jean's chatter, she withdrew into her obsession. The cowboy in the TV movie was holding a rifle. Both Oswald's workmate and his wife, who'd given him a lift that morning, swore he held his parcel under his armpit. Even disassembled, it couldn't have been a rifle, it wouldn't have been possible.

And yet, and yet, the long parcel was at least an odd coincidence, on that morning.

And Tippit. It was only a minor sub-plot, as Sister Beatrice would say, yet he might hold the key to the whole mystery. It seemed so incredible that, with all of Dallas to choose from, he'd recognised Oswald on the sidewalk from a vague description given by nobody knew who. And *could* Oswald have walked there from his lodging-house so quickly: a mile in about seven minutes? But then, there was no agreement about exactly when the policeman had been shot.

There were never any answers. But the brief meditation calmed her a little. And now that she felt more rational it suddenly occurred to her why Jean was being so bitchy, in her quiet way. She was put out because she, Tessa, knew something about her father's past life, the Atlanta resignation, that had never been confided to her. It was so simple! And so understandable. She ought to have explained to her why it had come out. He was excruciatingly modest; he'd asked her to mention it to no one, not even Jean; he didn't care to parade as a moral hero. He'd told Tessa so long ago she'd forgotten Jean didn't know about it.

Only Mom knew; and she'd been embarrassed when Tessa brought it up one day, saying something like, You must have been very proud of him, it was a very brave thing to do. Mom was weaker, a conformist; Sister Agnes could imagine how the scandal and the resignation probably hurt her a lot. Well, people had differing capacities for courage.

Feeling stronger and at ease, she talked to her sister with more animation. She was pleased, opening a package and finding a cassette of Chopin Nocturnes. Dad had suggested it, of course, and Jean had bought it at Slidell's only record store. Then the sisters sat watching the news together. Soviet tanks were putting on a show of strength in the capital of Lithuania.

It's starting all over again, Jean said. The Prague Spring. No, Sister Agnes said: long before that. Hitler has won. Germany is a superpower, with a huge market to the east. All perfectly respectable. And no Jews . . . Oh God, isn't that a terrible thing to say! Forget I said it, Jean. I didn't mean to say it!

Ich bin ein Berliner. The crowds roaring. History is a trance, she thought. We're all sleepwalkers.

5

The ambulance had left with the body of Patrolman Tippit. There was just a pool of blood on the ground. That was what your life was worth – unless you were a president, then everyone started wailing and gnashing their teeth. The policemen stood round the dead cop's car, hands on hips, or taking measurements. Another held a pencil and a notebook; around him clustered a group of residents and drivers.

'OK, let's go over this: which of you saw the shooting?'

Half a dozen people pushed forward, raising their hands. 'It was a man in a long coat,' a woman said. 'He ran to an old grey car, parked about twenty yards down.'

'That's not what I saw.'

'Nor me. He had a zip-up jacket. He was thin.'

'No, he was chunky. The cop chatted to him for a while, through the window, then got out and came round the car towards him. Then the guy shot him.'

'There was a chunky man and a thin one. After the chunky one shot him they just walked away in opposite directions.'

'When he was on the ground he stood over him and fired a last shot, right into his head. It looked to me like a Mafia-style execution.'

'I held his head in my arms and talked to him for about twenty minutes, till the ambulance came.'

'That's bullshit! He was dead before he hit the ground.'

'No, really, I talked to him, he was moaning.'

'OK, OK,' the cop said. 'One at a time. Let me take your names.'

An elderly man in a cardigan said, 'I need to go to the john. I'll be right back.'

'OK.'

He was gone some time. When he returned he stood next to the truck-driver who had seen the cop die before he hit the ground. He offered him a cigarette.

'Thanks, pal.'

'I took a look at the TV. They're showing the casket being taken out from Parkland. The guys carryin' him stumbled, they could hardly hold it. I can't believe what's happened. I saw them arrive at Love Field, I went to make myself a light lunch, and looked over the *Christian Science Monitor* as I ate it, and when I got back to the TV there was a casket bein' carried into Parkland! And they said it was for the President!'

'Yeah, it's unbelievable.'

'And now this. Right outside my own home. What's our country coming to?'

'It's a crazy friggin' world.'

The cardiganed man sighed. 'I'm almost glad my dear wife passed on. She was spared this. I liked Kennedy. Heck, I revered him. I'm about the only one on this street who did. I can't cry, though I want to. It just hasn't sunk in. It's like a part of my mind says it hasn't happened, it mustn't happen! You know what I mean?'

'I know what you mean.'

'It's the weirdest thing – Are these your shoes, lady?'

The woman who had talked to the dying cop for twenty minutes turned. He pointed to a pair of black high-heels on top of the dead patrolman's car.

'Oh yes! I took them off.' Her cigarette dropped through her fingers to the sidewalk. She looked close to hysteria. She squatted, in her tight black bloodstained skirt, to retrieve the cigarette. A bar-girl, she'd been running to catch her bus when the shots had rung out.

'Well, just don't forget them – Yeah, it's the weirdest thing.'

'I can't believe he's dead either,' said the trucker. 'But I can believe that cop is dead.' He nodded at the pool of blood.

'He's dead, he's a goner. But not Kennedy, that's impossible. No way.'

6

Lee walked quickly, away from the ambulance and the police-cars, the knot of onlookers. He didn't know where to go; everything was a mess, fucked up; what had seemed so simple a couple hours ago was now in a hopeless tangle, worse than when his mom tried to knit for the baby and threw the tangled wool away with a shriek.

The city appeared to be normal; the traffic rumbled past, people walked by him with closed faces that didn't look concerned. He tried to look unconcerned too, but it was hard. He couldn't quite control the way his brain was working, just like when he was trying to spell a letter. He was in Russia again, the first week in Moscow; he was spending almost all his time in his hotel room, but he did go out one afternoon to queue up outside Lenin's tomb. It's a bright October day, but Lee huddles in a coat, since it's cold after New Orleans. The Russians, mostly peasants from the provinces, stare at him curiously, suspiciously.

Lee, striding down a Dallas street, goes down into Lenin's Mausoleum, only it is President Kennedy he sees, waxen under the glass. No, he's only wounded; it'll be all right.

He walked into a seedy-looking store selling electrical goods. It was empty except for a hairy, muscular young man in a singlet who sat on a stool staring blankly at a TV screen. Lee saw a reporter standing amid chaotic scenes outside a hospital. There was the same or similar pictures from a dozen silent screens. The hairy young man, sweating profusely, slid off the stool. 'Can I helpya?'

'I was thinking about maybe buying a TV.'

The man's eyes came faintly alive. 'Sure. We got plenty.' He threw out an arm in demonstration. 'This one here's a nice one. It's a good picture, sharp. I can do you a good deal on it. I can give you ten per cent off the list.'

'What's the sound like? Can you turn it up?'

'Sure.' He moved forward and turned a knob. Lee heard the reporter say, indistinctly, that it was now twenty-five minutes since the President had been declared dead by the Parkland doctors.

'It's kind of muffled.'

'You think so? This one's real good. It's a little more pricey but I can knock maybe twenty off for a cash sale.' He tweaked a knob. 'You see, the sound's perfect.'

'The picture's fuzzy.'

It was showing a brand-new, light-coloured Cadillac hearse. The reporter was saying the casket had been taken in a few minutes ago. It was a large casket made of solid bronze.

'How about this one? You couldn't get a better picture. And the sound's great – listen.'

'It's expensive.'

'Sure it's expensive but it's the best. You want terms? I'll give you good terms. The manager's had to go out, but I can arrange everything, he's put me in charge. Pay over a year, eighteen months.'

Saying he'd think it over, Lee was out of the door and walking again. Dead. Dead. The hearse. Unbelievable. It couldn't be only an hour since everyone had been clapping the motorcade outside the Depository.

He came upon a shoe store.

I must buy shoes for June, he thought. He stood looking at the children's shoes in the window. He didn't know what size she took; he would have to guess.

He remembered his first sight of her, when Marina brought her home. She was already eight days old and they hadn't let him see her. Now he looked down at her and it was wonderful to think he had helped make her. He had cleaned the apartment and done all the washing and ironing. Marina had been astonished. He wanted to make love there and then.

He went off to celebrate the name-day of Marina's aunt and drink his daughter's health. He got very tipsy; but felt so happy staggering back to the apartment. While he had been away some friends had taught Marina how to swaddle her baby; and now she was tightly swathed and cosy in her crib. He'd insisted on dragging the crib over to the bed, on his side. He woke when Marina did and watched her give suck.

The little blue shoes in the window would look nice on her.

He walked in, but came to a halt just inside the door. He felt confused. What was he doing buying shoes? He probably would never see little Junie again. One of the men in the shop, perhaps the owner, was staring at him. Lee ran out. There was a small crowd of people standing around a hamburger stall where a radio was on. They were in front of a movie theatre. There was no cashier in the booth and Lee darted inside.

It felt good to be in the blackness. He fumbled around; most of the seats seemed to be empty. There was a crash of shell-fire from the screen. He saw a soldier throw back his arms and fall.

Three teenage boys followed Lee in. They went noisily down the aisle and sat almost at the front of the huge theatre. They left a seat between each of them so they could sprawl out. They couldn't believe their luck. Just as the first lesson of the afternoon was beginning, Miss Simpson, the vice-principal, had come in. She told them the President had been assassinated so as a mark of respect the school was closing for the day. The whole class had jumped up from their seats and cheered. Not just because of the unexpected holiday but because that Yankee, that Commie-lover and nigger-lover, was dead.

Miss Simpson had clapped her hands to stop them, but they could see the smile longing to break out on her serious face. The hint of a smile under the hint of a moustache. The solemn lips were desperate to break out into a big, joyful grin. She wasn't even trying to hide it. Not really.

In the blackness far behind them, Lee folded his arms and stared at the screen. At first he didn't really take anything in; but gradually the chaos became a hazy, violent story and he began to take a vague interest. Even to forget. It was comforting to be in a movie theatre; like being in the womb again. People were islands. To his left, across the aisle, a cigarette glowed; it fell like a shooting star as the man's invisible hand took it from his mouth. To Lee's right, over his shoulder, in the row behind but several seats away, a young couple were locked in a permanent kiss. She had a raincoat on her lap; the boy's hand was underneath the raincoat and it was moving. His hand in her pants. Young love. With Marina in Minsk. He turned back to watch the movie.

Suddenly the house-lights came on, dazzling him; he saw policemen moving up both aisles, looking from side to side. He brought his feet down from the seatback in front of him and tensed. But maybe it had nothing to do with him. A policeman came level with him and stared, then took a step in from the aisle. Lee jumped to his feet and pulled the gun from his belt. The policeman sprang and knocked the gun from his hand. A blow in the stomach took his breath away, and his arm was locked painfully behind his back. The other cop had grabbed him now too, and he found himself being frogmarched towards the exit. He shouted, 'I protest this police brutality!'

The young couple in the row behind him had frozen with fear when the lights had come on and they saw the police heading up the aisles. The boy had pulled his hand away and she'd clenched her legs shut. It looked as if one of the cops was heading straight for her, and her heart hammered in her chest. She'd got ready to say, We're from Lewisville, we didn't know it's not allowed here, we're really sorry.

When the man to their left had been leapt on, she breathed a sigh of relief. She watched with curiosity as he was hustled out. The theatre stilled; the movie resumed at the point where it had been broken off, the lights dimming and going out. Her face was being turned so he could kiss her again, and she felt a hand go up her thigh. But the mood was shattered; she pushed the hand away. She should never have let him go so far, much further than after the Barn Dance three weeks ago: swept away by the lovely day they were having, and by the diamond ring she could feel on her finger, bought that morning. What she'd let him do was utterly wrong before marriage. Her fear had been guilt speaking. She would hardly dare look the Minister in the eye on Sunday. She kissed him again, but with closed lips; they paused more often to watch the movie.

They had lost the track, however, and she didn't like war movies anyway. She'd only agreed to the movie because the streets had got crowded for some reason, perhaps a parade, and they'd wanted some privacy. 'Why don't we go?' she said now; and he nodded and they got up and left.

Emerging into the light, she looked at her engagement ring again. It sure was beautiful, she couldn't wait to show Mom and Dad and Sylvie.

The sunlight was strong, and they blinked. It had been raining when her uncle had driven them in from Lewisville in his pick-up truck. But it was as if God was smiling on their happy day. She grabbed his arm and swung on it, skipping. She wanted to do some Christmas shopping, but to their surprise they found some of the big stores closed. The crowds had thinned a lot. It was surprisingly quiet.

He bought hot-dogs and Cokes at a stall and they perched on a wall for a while. She lifted her hand, flashing the diamond in the sun. He was still on fire for her, nuzzling her under the ear, running his hand up her back under her new sweater, feeling for a garter-strap through her skirt and snapping it to her thigh, even with people passing, and she kept giggling and pushing him away. They dumped the wrappers and cans, and wandered on hand in hand. It was very warm; she stopped to remove her jacket. She wished she'd worn a blouse. They had passed outside a store selling electrical goods; in the window there were five or six television sets. The picture, repeated several times, caught her attention. It showed some men struggling to carry a large coffin up a ramp into a plane.

'What do you think that is?' she asked. 'Who's dead?'

He shook his head. 'It's just a movie.'

'On all channels?'

'Oh, yeah, I see what you mean. It must be for real. It could be the Bird-man of Alcatraz. He's died. I heard it on the radio this morning.'

'But this looks kind of official.'

'Well, he's become famous. Maybe they're shipping him off to his family, if he's still got any. I don't know.'

'You could be right. I really liked that movie.'

They strolled on. He put his arm round her shoulder, turned her sweet face to his. 'D'you love me?' he asked.

'Oh! So much!'

'How much is so much?'

'Completely! For ever!' They kissed and went on kissing, taking short clumsy steps, their heads spinning, all their nerves alive, tingling, and the blue sky wheeled above them.

'Let's forget the motorcade, Mr President; give Dallas a miss. It's too dangerous.' O'Donnell heard himself say these words as the massive casket dug into his shoulder and threatened at every moment to topple and burst open. Almost impossible to get it up the ramp. Sweat was blinding him. He could so easily have said those words; and it seemed to him he could still say them, was saying them now. And the President was saying, 'OK!' The alternative was madness, was this unreality. Servicemen standing around at attention in the utterly silent field; and not the President turning, with that familiar gesture, one hand in his pocket, to grin and wave, but in a coffin being lugged aboard. Delirium, insanity.

At last they got the bronze casket inside and laid it down near the door. The curtains drawn, the cabin was dark and stifling. The bearers, drenched in sweat, bent over their burden, gasping for breath. As their eyes adjusted they saw a lone figure, Jackie, sitting a few steps from them, watching intently.

O'Donnell moved to sit beside her; he placed his hand on hers; it felt deathly cold, despite the heat. He could see the bloodstains on her skirt. 'Why don't you go and change your clothes?' he said, still breathing heavily. 'You'll feel better.'

'No, I'm not going to change. Let them see the horror.'

He bowed his head. 'You're right.'

He knew her grief must be even greater than his, but he couldn't conceive how that could be. He was glad she hadn't witnessed the crazy, terrible scenes at the hospital: the Dallas coroner shouting that the body wasn't going anywhere, there had to be an autopsy right there; the Secret Service guys shouting that their President was going home. Scuffles and obscenities. Well, he was with the guys; fuck legal niceties at a time like this.

As if echoing his thoughts Jackie said, 'I want to get out of this place.'

'So do we all. I'll see to it.'

He rose, and started to walk up the plane. Pulling herself to her feet, Jackie walked to the casket and stood over it for a few moments, then turned away and opened the door of their bedroom. She recoiled: Johnson was there, lounging on her bed, dictating to a secretary. Seeing her, he hauled his bulk off the bed and shouldered past her clumsily, the secretary following. Jackie entered, closed the door, and stood lost. What was he doing on this plane? The President and the Vice President weren't supposed to fly on the same plane.

Someone had laid out her clothes for Austin: a white dress and jacket, and black shoes. She looked at her watch: two-twenty. Just two hours . . . It was still not time to fly off to Austin; she saw Jack pulling off his tie, stretching back on the bed, relaxing before the next motorcade; heard him crack some joke about Dallas. Her knees giving way, she sank on to the bed.

She heard loud and emotional voices: 'For Chrissake get this plane off the ground! D'you know what this is doing to Mrs Kennedy, hanging around in this fucking place?'

'We can't go yet. Johnson has to take the oath first.'

'What's that to do with us? He's on the back-up plane.'

'You go tell that to the tall guy with the big pointy nose and Texan drawl who's just pressed my elbow. We're not going to Andrews until the President has been sworn.'

'I have only one President, and he's lying back in that cabin.'

Her mind drifted away. It was all the same where she was.

Sometime later she heard a knock at the door. Lady Bird and Lyndon entered. Stooping, he put his arm round her and croaked, 'Honey.' Then Lady Bird, with tears in her eyes, embraced her and said, 'Oh Jackie, you know we never even wanted to be Vice President and now, dear God, it's come to this!'

Jackie rested her cheek against hers.

'And to think it's happened in my beloved Texas!'

'You should let the tears out, honey!' Johnson said. 'It'll do you good. I loved Jack; he was like a brother to me.'

'What if I hadn't been there!' Jackie said. 'I was so glad I was there.'

Lady Bird saw a bloodstained glove. 'Can I help you find some fresh things to put on?'

'Oh no. Perhaps later. Not now.'

'Honey,' said Lyndon, 'we have to think about the swearing-in. I know it's hard, but I'd like you to be there.'

'Oh – yes. The swearing-in. In Washington?'

'No, here at Love Field. I've sent for Judge Sarah Hughes; she should be here in an hour.'

'An hour?' She was gazing over his shoulder. 'That's a long time to have to wait here.'

'I called Bobby and he said I ought to be sworn-in as soon as possible. Now, why don't you stay here for a while, freshen up, change your clothes?' He hugged her again. 'It's a nightmare, the most terrible day of my life.'

They left quietly. Jackie took a cigarette, stared at the wall.

Johnson spoke to O'Donnell, seated straight-backed by the casket. 'Ken, I'd like a word with you in the state-room.'

O'Donnell came out of a daze, stood up. 'Sure, but there has to be someone with the President. I'll find one of the others.'

'Don't worry about that – everyone's in the staff-cabin holding a short service. I suggested it. It seemed right. These guys of mine can take over from you for a few minutes.'

Two Secret Service men were walking along the corridor towards them.

'Well, OK.'

Johnson led the way forward into the small state-room. Someone could be heard leading prayers beyond them in the staff-cabin. Johnson sat down by the President's desk and motioned O'Donnell to take the sofa. A white-coated steward appeared, bearing a tray of soup and iced water. 'Ah, that smells terrific!' Johnson exclaimed. The tray was laid before him: his hooked nose sniffed. 'It's a lifetime since I had breakfast. You like some, Ken?' O'Donnell shook his head. 'You should eat. Life must go on. You should keep up your strength.'

He began to wolf and slurp the vegetable soup and crackers. His hooded eyes concentrated on the food. O'Donnell watched, his head spinning.

Johnson finished the soup and pressed a buzzer. 'That was mighty good!'

'If you don't mind, sir, I'd like to go back to President Kennedy.'

Johnson waved his arm. 'I understand. It's difficult for you, seeing me here. But the country has to be run, I can't chicken out. It's the last thing I wanted, you must believe that.'

The steward appeared; Johnson, handing him the tray, said, 'Is there any more?'

'Yes, sir.'

Johnson nodded and the steward vanished.

Inadequate, quavery sounds of *Eternal Father, strong to save* filtered through. Johnson loudly broke wind. 'Ken, I wanted to say, I mourn for Jack as much as you do. Though not as much as that brave little lady back there. And I'd like you and your buddies to consider your future; see if you can face working for my administration. It's your choice. I want you. I need you more than Jack needed you.'

'Thank you, Mr President. I'll have to think about it. It's too soon to think about anything.'

'Of course.'

O'Donnell started to rise. 'No, sit!' said the President. 'Have some coffee with me.' He accepted the tray from the steward and started spooning the soup as hungrily as before. 'I need to talk about some things. The Presidency is very lonely; I'm just beginning to realise it. Especially when it happens like this. I understand how Andrew Johnson felt when he took over from Lincoln.'

O'Donnell settled, staring at the soup spoon, the cavernous mouth.

The President was still talking when a dark-suited woman, looking flushed and distressed, came in, followed by three photographers. Johnson lumbered to his feet and embraced her. 'Sarah!'

'Mr President.'

'I never thought, or hoped, we'd meet under these circumstances.'

O'Donnell left them; he returned to his President. The two Secret Service men stood at attention each side of the casket. At the Kennedy aide's appearance they melted like shadows.

The bedroom door opened and Jackie appeared. Still in her stained suit. 'They want me,' she murmured as if appealing to him to deny it.

'I'm afraid so.'

At that moment they saw Johnson's bulk heading for them. He stopped when he saw Jackie. 'Ah, there you are, honey! You've not changed your clothes. Well, never mind. We ain't got a bible; do you have one with you?'

'Jack always keeps one. Just a minute.'

She went back into the bedroom. Johnson adjusted the handkerchief in his breast-pocket, straightened his tie. Jackie came out clutching a black book to her breast.

When they had gone, O'Donnell stepped for a moment into the bedroom. It might be his last look. The pill-box hat was on the bed. He saw a speck of grey substance on it. Jack; his thoughts, memories, jokes, dreams, ideas. O'Donnell felt his knees buckle and he sat down hard on the bed. 'Jack!' he whispered. 'Jack!' But nobody replied.

8

Nine out of ten Americans, and countless numbers abroad, are experiencing deep grief.

Sister Agnes's great-great-aunt, Mabel Dixon, who lives at a rest home near Boston, is in a unique position: too young to feel deep grief for Lincoln, she is now too old and too confused to feel it for Kennedy.

Yet she is aware that something is amiss, just as she saw her father crying when Lincoln was shot. She caught something unusual in the grave, half-heard voice speaking over her radio; it is much more unmistakable in the demeanour of Amy, when she brings her afternoon milk. Amy is usually a cheerful, helpful girl, though very slow and clumsy like most niggers, but today she is crying. She is wiping the tears from her eyes and they are falling into the cup of warm milk she offers to her lips. She is clumsier than ever; most of the milk is spilled.

'What's wrong with you, girl?' she asks, as Amy wipes her lips.

'Oh Mrs Dixon, don't you know? I thought you'd have heard it on the radio. The President's dead! He's been shot!'

'Of course I knew that,' the old lady responds irritably. 'Who doesn't know that?'

'He was a wonderful President. It's wicked. I'm sorry, I've been crying ever since it happened, we all have.'

'My Daddy cried too.'

Amy ignored the remark. It was astonishing Mabel could

say anything even half sensible at her age. 'Poor Mr Johnson,' she said. 'He has to take over.'

'Huh! Johnson's hopeless,' the old lady croaked. 'He's a very weak man.'

'You think so? We must just hope and pray he's not. Peter – my son-in-law, who's real smart – has always said he's a good man. He'll need to be. Have you had enough milk, dear?'

She moved her mouth away irritably in response.

Amy wiped her mouth with a napkin, then lifted her in the bed so she could put the bedpan under her. She seemed to get lighter by the week: no more than a skeleton, really. Her head, with its wisps of white hair, lolled. Curbing a feeling of rage that this useless old woman was alive while Kennedy was dead, she fluffed the pillows to support her.

'They showed Mrs Kennedy getting on the plane to come home. She looked awful. I don't know how she can survive.'

She tucked her up again and smoothed the pillows.

'Mrs Kennedy? I don't think I know her,' said the whining old voice.

'The President's wife.'

'There's a Kennedy who worked for the President.'

'Bobby, yes. Poor man. But everyone's suffering with them. How could anyone want to shoot him? There's lots of evil people around, Mabel; lots of evil people.'

The old lady, peacefully lying, turned her thoughts to more important concerns. Her weak eyes flickered aside to her dresser. Someone, she thought it might have been the man with the grave, deep voice who had visited her, had mentioned Dallas. It had made her think of Tessa, her great-great-niece, who was a teacher there.

'Amy,' she says now, 'I want you to do something for me. You see that photo?' Her stick-like arm pointed. 'Not the one in the silver frame, the other one.'

Amy turned her raw, red eyes to the dresser. She stretched to pick up a plastic photo-frame. A handsome, moustached young man in First World War uniform. 'You mean this one?'

'Yes. Take it out of the frame.'

Amy did so.

'I want you to send that to Tessa. You've got my address book. He's my nephew, you know. A wonderful boy. My sister's son from Virginia. But I guess he moved to Texas; leastways the Army named an airfield after him in Texas. He died in training, his plane crashed. Lieutenant Moss Lee Love. There's a pen over there. Write on the back "Lieutenant M.L. Love. Texas".'

The woman picked up the pen and wrote with a trembling hand.

'Send it to Tessa for me. She keeps in touch, she's a good girl. Will you do that?'

'Yes, dear.'

'Send it instead of a Christmas card, I'm not made of money.'

Slipping the photo into her apron pocket, Amy stood staring out of the window at the falling darkness, her eyes brimming again. 'It's so unfair. He gave us hope. Now someone's just wiped it out.'

Mabel's brow furrowed. Then she remembered. The President. 'I feel sorry for Mrs Lincoln,' she piped.

'Mrs Lincoln?' Amy turned, startled; then she, too, remembered. The middle-aged lady shown in tears, like everyone else, outside the hospital. 'Yes, you're right, I guess. A secretary can feel almost as close to a man as his wife. She looked awful too. But you only have to go out on the streets here, everyone's in shock, everyone looks half crazy, just as if the world's come to an end.'

Picking up the bedpan and saying, See you tomorrow, honey, Amy withdrew and shut the door behind her. Mabel Dixon, as the silence fell around her, gazed up at the ceiling. Yes, there were evil people. Look at Esther Sumner, the way she stole that purse, even though Mama was so good to her and paid her for work when she was off ill that time. She was an ungrateful hussy.

The President had tossed her in the air and carried her on his shoulders. Her daddy had told her so. If anyone should be upset it was she; but you couldn't go on grieving for ever.

'Johnson!' she croaked half audibly, scornfully. He was a very weak President.

Roosevelt, now he'd been a fine President. Her husband had been happy to fight for him. Mr Roosevelt had stuck up for America, he hadn't let the Dagos push us around, no sirree. Was Dick still fighting in Cuba? She hadn't seen him for, oh, it had to be months. She was beginning to forget him, a little.

Today she will wear the blue dress, and she will do some sketching, sitting under the lime tree. She must be careful not to get the charcoal on her dress.

Judge Hughes hurries down the ramp, the President's bible under her arm, forgotten – she will hand it with apologies to a dark-suited man who steps forward and asks for it; the doors are locked and the plane starts to move. As it lifts off, placards welcoming President Kennedy are sent rolling about Love Field. A keen wind is also picking up and the sky has greyed.

'We're on our way,' Johnson says, and orders up bouillon. Jackie quietly excuses herself to go back to the other President. As she sees his friends, huddled around the casket, she begins to cry. It is the first time she has been able to cry. Now the tears come in a flood.

When there were no more tears to shed she whispered to them, half as a question, 'So – it's happened.'

'It's happened,' O'Donnell murmured.

The plane turned north-east, hurrying towards the darkness. Ahead, in its curving arc, lay Arkansas, Tennessee, Virginia. Yet, when Jackie closed her eyes for a moment, she could see him cat-napping on the flight to Austin while she dipped into her book. That was still more real than this.

O'Donnell sped a long, bullet-like pass, and Kennedy was in space, but he fluffed the catch. The students wearing Harvard scarves groaned, and O'Donnell hurled abuse. Motherfucker, prick. Jack grinned, sheepish.

The aide's head jerked erect. No one had noticed his drowse; their heads were drooping. The atmosphere was stifling; and of course shock made it imperative to escape, if only for a few seconds.

You can do with a drink, Jackie, he said, as her eyes flickered open in the gloom and stared blankly. He could use a stiff whisky; they all could. I've never drunk whisky, she said, but I guess this is a time to try.

He returned with a bottle and some glasses. She sipped, screwed up her face, then gulped. He filled their glasses again and they drank in silence. Later they talked of his love for Irish songs. 'The Rose of Tralee'. 'Macoushla'. 'When Irish Eyes Are Smiling'. 'Cathleen Mavourneen'.

It may be for years, and it may be for ever . . . His tuneless but enthusiastic voice.

O'Donnell's glasses were misty; he wiped them on a handkerchief, then his eyes gazed again at the casket. He leaned close to it, stared at it.

Excusing himself, he went forward to the state-room. Johnson, feet on the desk, was dictating to a secretary sitting before a clacking typewriter. He was describing for his diary how Youngblood, his Secret Service agent, had saved his life by pushing him down in the car and sitting on him. Lady Bird was scribbling in a notebook, absorbed. Johnson glanced up as O'Donnell appeared, and stopped the flow of words.

'Mr President, could I have a word with you in private?'

The typewriter halted. 'Sure. Though I don't know where's private.'

'The bedroom's free.'

'That's off-limits. Mrs Kennedy may want to change her clothes at any time. Besides, she kinda feels it's sacred territory. I don't blame her. We'd better go in the bathroom. I can do with a crap.'

Neither Lady Bird nor the secretary glanced up. Evidently they were used to Johnson's natural ways. He lumbered to his feet and O'Donnell followed him into the bathroom. Seeing the President remove his jacket and peel down his pants and shorts, O'Donnell closed the door and leaned against it. He glimpsed massive, swinging testicles before Johnson sat down.

'Well, what's so urgent?'

His neck muscles strained, his face reddened. O'Donnell heard a plop and smelt a rising odour. He tried to breathe through his mouth, but it was impossible to do that and speak at the same time.

'I've spent a long time just staring at that coffin. And something's odd about it. It's been opened, I swear it.'

A gurgle and splatter. Stench assailed the Bostonian and he fought nausea.

'How the hell can you tell that?'

'The angle of the screws; they're different. You wouldn't notice it if you hadn't been staring at it ever since we got on this plane. Well, that's not quite true; you know I had to leave the President for a while, and your Secret Service men took over. I find it unbelievable, but they must have opened the coffin.'

Johnson's neck strained again, and he grunted when there was another splatter. 'That soup sure goes through you. I believe you. They did it on my orders, Ken.'

'Your orders!'

The President tore off several sheets of tissue, separated them, then – rising – wiped himself. He glanced at each tissue before dropping it behind him. He pulled up his shorts and pants.

'My orders, though actually Mr Hoover suggested it. I talked with him on the phone. We had to check on something.' He pulled on his jacket. 'I'll be honest with you. I could spin you some cock-and-bull story but I won't. I trust you to keep it as secret as a Jewish jerk-off. We're not sure who's responsible for this tragedy. Hoover thinks it's just a lone Communist nut. As a matter of fact the Dallas police have arrested a guy by the name of Lee Harvey Oswald. They say he's well known for his Communist sympathies. Maybe he's the killer and he acted alone. But we can't be sure. A lot of people thought they heard shots from the knoll; and the Dallas doctors talked of an entry wound in the throat. It's just possible there was a conspiracy.'

'If there was a conspiracy, it's got to come out.'

Johnson stepped forward, grabbed him by the lapel. 'That's where you're wrong! How do you think America would react? Suppose we could show Castro was responsible? Or Khrushchev? This Oswald was a defector from the US Marines; he spent two years in the Soviet Union. Supposing they sent him back to assassinate Kennedy? Not Khrushchev, maybe, but some crazy generals in the KGB. And supposing it became known? The whole country would boil over; I couldn't stop the rage for revenge. We'd be at war, quicker than a kitten could piss.' His hand tightened on the lapel; his eyes glared straight into O'Donnell's, almost touching his spectacles.

'If on the other hand it was a right-wing conspiracy, it would tear the country apart: you know that. So what can we do? Just make sure it's Oswald. Well, it probably is. And probably he was the sole shooter. My men took a quick look and they don't see no entry wound in the throat. That would be good enough – to establish that no one else had a finger on a trigger. If there was some other country behind him – Russia or Cuba, or China, or South Vietnam – well, we ain't never likely to find that out, and it's best we don't.'

Nausea. From the still-unflushed toilet and the stench of a necessary cover-up. O'Donnell choked back a sob. The President loosened his hold on his lapel and squeezed his arm comfortingly. 'Besides, too many things would come out. Did you know about the assassination attempts against Castro? *I* didn't. Shit, they were even setting one up today. And they're using the Mafia! It's the CIA, of course, but it would damage Jack's reputation.'

O'Donnell's head was bowed, brushing Johnson's shoulder. The hand on his arm stroked him. 'There are other things that could harm Jack. The girls. Marilyn Monroe. Sam Giancana's mistress. A thousand others. Even in the White House. Even in this plane. Hoover's got a floor-full of files. He's a bastard, but I'll have to play along with him for Jack's sake. And for that brave little woman back there. I'm not gonna do a damn thing to jeopardise the love and respect people have for the President and Jackie.'

'God help us. God help us.'

'I say amen to that. Whatever we do we can't bring him back; I wish to God we could. From now on it's damage limitation.'

Johnson pulled a handkerchief from his breast-pocket and gave it to O'Donnell, who took off his glasses to wipe his eyes.

'The dream's got to hold, Ken. Camelot. For America's sake as well as Jack's memory. With that dream we can push through all the bills that have been held up; I'm damn sure we can. Civil rights, Medicare, the poverty program. I'm bound to be an offence to you Kennedy people, because I'm not Jack; but I know how to get bills through the House.'

Stepping back a little, he released O'Donnell. Turning, he pressed the flush.

'Now go back to your President.'

O'Donnell stumbled away; through the state-room with its two quiet women; to the dark areas where Jackie and the others crouched over the casket. He lowered himself to the floor, stared vacantly.

Jackie's cigarette glowed and faded. She was riding through Dealey Plaza.

10

The President wasn't smiling any more. Connally straightened in his seat and started to turn his head to the left, wondering if the shot had come from there. A bullet hammered into his back and he pitched sideways into Nelly's lap. The car had slowed, it was scarcely moving at all; Jackie felt the bump as the car behind touched them. Kellerman, next to the driver, said, 'Let's get the fuck out of here! Get to a hospital!' but Greer was slow to move.

People were screaming; some rooted to the spot, others running; a black umbrella kept pumping, under the 'Stemmons Freeway' sign. A young soldier standing on the grassy slope, home on furlough after basic training, felt a bullet flash by his ear and threw himself down, flattening against the grass. Connally heard the crump of this bullet smashing into bone behind him and screamed, 'No, no, no! They're going to kill us all!'

'You're going to be all right!' Nelly crooned, cradling him.

A child saw the president's head jerk violently back amidst a halo of grey and red. A police side-rider, behind and to the left of Jackie, felt the impact of flesh and brain and thought at first he'd been hit. Jackie felt herself drenched, saw bone fly back and she knew she had to get it, it was a part of Jack. She scrambled up on to the trunk of the car, hands outstretched. The Secret Service men in the following car were frozen; all but Clint Hill, Jackie's bodyguard, who she had insisted should come on this trip. He leapt on to the Lincoln trunk and Jackie's hands grabbed him.

A man who had unfurled a black umbrella to the cloudless sky furled it and sat down under the Freeway sign. The dark-skinned man who was with him sat too. They looked relaxed amid the screaming and the panic. Police with guns drawn ran up the grassy knoll, and dozens of onlookers did the same. There was a fume of white smoke, a smell of gunpowder.

But it was all outside of time. 'Mr President, you can't say Dallas doesn't love you!'

'I sure can't!'

The clutch at his throat, Jackie cradling him, Connally spinning, Jack's head jerking back in a halo of grey and red, Jackie crawling on to the trunk, grasping at the bodyguard's hands. The Lincoln springing away at last.

'They've killed my husband!' she sobbed.

Then, over and over, hysterically, 'I've got his brains in my hands! I've got his brains in my hands!'

IV

Historical Fictions

1

She was at Love Field, trying to board the President's plane, but her bad hip prevented her from getting up the ramp. Kennedy appeared in the doorway and said, Don't worry, I'll come down to you. She had on a black sweater, which was milk-stained. She said her sister would be very angry because of the stain, and because she was jealous and would think *she* ought to be with the President. He said, Don't worry, it's your turn. They strolled around the airfield; he clutched her arm as there were lots of pot-holes. He looked even younger than he was on the day of his death. She showed him her book, which was bound in black leather and had the title *Final Disclosure* printed on the cover in white. He examined it carefully and then said sadly, You know the trouble with this is, there's no plot.

The dream was clear in Sister Agnes's mind when she woke up, precisely twenty minutes – her body-clock was always precise – before the first prayers. Her room was dark. The familiar shapes appeared gradually as she lay there. She had lived in this room for almost thirty years; it had grown a little more comfortable in that time; but so imperceptibly that it still seemed to be the cell she had entered at twenty-one, straight from college. There was the same wooden crucifix on the wall facing her, taking shape in the darkness before dawn.

She had dreamed of Kennedy's death once before: a few nights after it had happened. Then, she had been driving through the triple underpass; in her lap had been, of all inappropriate things, a sanitary napkin, but it was imprinted with a man's face in blood. St Veronica. But when she had emerged from the tunnel she was old and she couldn't move. She'd looked down and she was a pillar of salt. Alongside her car were two others; in one of them the President, blood-covered, was lying in his wife's lap; in the other, they were driving through smiling and waving, perfectly normal.

That dream had only been a part of the general nightmare of those days. This dream, coming in isolation, had somehow a deeper, colder effect: in fact she had woken from it bathed in a cold sweat.

After dragging herself out of bed she washed, then put on sweater and jeans. Jeans were permitted in chapel only at Matins. She put on sandals and hobbled out to the chill, silent corridor. Slipping into the chapel, where about a dozen other teaching nuns were already kneeling, she eased herself painfully down and crossed herself.

Sister Beatrice was nearest to her, just in front and to her left. She was hunched over, totally absorbed. In spite of her secular interests, her love of literature and her feminism, when she came to worship she gave herself totally in a way that her friend could only wonder at, knowing that such saintly concentration would always be beyond her.

She didn't hear the prayers, which she repeated by rote. Her thoughts and emotions were concentrated on the dream. It wasn't difficult to interpret. The book was the one she was reading, had been reading at Love Field; but it was also the Bible. It was called *Final Disclosure* – yet it had no plot. There was no conspiracy.

But not only that, of course. All her life she had been looking for meaning and design in the universe. She thought at sixteen she had found it in Catholicism. Her certainty had been shaken by what had happened in Dealey Plaza, but a vulnerable faith had lingered on. If it hadn't been so, she could not have lived. She kept looking for evidence of design. She thought it was to be found in the night sky, the blaze of stars; in the yellow and red roses now luxuriant around the convent; in the smiles of her pupils when she told a joke.

She thought it was to be found too in history, her special love. You took the events of the past and you discovered a coherence in them. Even something dreadful, like Lincoln's assassination, seemed comprehensible, almost desirable, when one looked back over a century. The muffled drums seemed suitable for a great war hero and liberator. Far better than decline into a dull old age. Of course there were events you couldn't make sense of, such as the holocaust; but there were so many that did make sense, you could tell yourself the meaning even of the holocaust would be revealed in the fullness of time.

But with John Kennedy's assassination she had, in a way, entered history herself, and the shock had been enormous. History was what happened to you – to Sister Agnes, to quiet Tessa Mason, a hard-up teacher's daughter – and it made no sense. It began to make a glimmer of sense if you could see that death as the result of a conspiracy – a plot. Now she was beginning to get a similar feeling of chaos as she contemplated the end of the Cold War. It was something infinitely desirable, she had prayed for it endlessly; and yet the long struggle with Communism and atheism had been something not ignoble.

Yet now, it seemed, the fight was over; the enemy had laid down its arms. There was both a weird feeling of anticlimax and a sinister prickling at the nape. The Europe of between the wars appeared to have returned, essentially. It made no sense of the decades of struggle. Though she had wept for joy when the East Berliners first streamed through a gap in the Wall, now she hated the idea that they were selling the Wall off in little packages. Berlin, with the Wall, had a tragic dignity; without it, it was spiritually empty, the department store of Europe.

What if there was no universal 'plot'? If pure chance had called forth the Big Bang, in the same way as Oswald happened to be working in a warehouse overlooking the motorcade? As she knelt in prayer, it appeared to her that this must be so; and again she felt herself break into a cold sweat. It would explain the holocaust; and would explain on a humble personal level why her sister had been deserted by her husband in her fifties, and why her sons had a drug problem and HIV.

Yes, yes, it was so. The whole universe was nothing but a vast department store, created by chance and staffed by robots.

She stayed on the cold floor with her eyes closed, swaying, while the other nuns rose and quietly left. They assumed she was continuing to pray.

Her obsession had damaged others. Pupils she had encouraged to study the assassination. Jackie, in particular – the name a coincidence. Beautiful and intelligent. She had sat with her night after night looking at the video of the Zapruder film, helping her with her essay. And, whether or not the sight of the death was the sole cause, she had become deeply depressed and had to be hospitalised. Well, thank God she was all right now, taking history at Wesleyan.

Father had warned her against the obsession, told her to let go, even before it had really taken her over. Summer of '64. In Dealey Plaza, sitting on the grass verge with her. Self-consciously covering his left hand. Dear father. At that time she'd thought there was no need for such a warning. The obsession had really only taken hold when she started to learn how complex Kennedy was, how all too human.

Her thoughts grew hopelessly confused; she felt sick and hot, and thought she'd better struggle to her room. There, lying in her shirt and panties on the bed, shivering, she saw her mother, buxom and cheerful, standing near the wall under the print of a Tintoretto crucifixion, and she felt pleased to see her. They'd never really been close. She picked up her prayer-book but the words blurred and became unrecognisable.

Her sister called for her. It was a Saturday; they had planned to rent a car for an afternoon drive and go to a symphony concert in the evening.

'I'll be OK. Just give me an hour.'

But in fact in an hour she was flushed, covered in sweat, and alternately pushing all the bed-coverings off and demanding more. Nuns came and went, happy to leave it in the hands of Agnes's sister. But she herself didn't know whether to call the doctor. Maybe it was just flu.

Tessa began to talk, in a feverish, incomprehensible way.

'Love Field . . . I've left it too late . . .' Jean thought she imagined it was earlier in the week and she was late in going to meet her at the airport. But then, her eyes burning, she grasped Jean's arm and said, 'Sister Bridget . . . I need Sister Bridget.'

After that she closed her eyes and seemed to grow calmer. Her sister, on the point of going to ring a doctor, decided she would leave it a little longer. She felt her temple and she appeared to be cooling. And half an hour later the flush had gone and she was asleep. Alarm for her health gave way, in her sister, to a less immediate agitation. Had she, in her fever, revealed a deeply buried secret? Was she disclosing that she was a lesbian? She had perhaps misheard love as Love Field. Sister Bridget she had met briefly at supper last night: a vivacious biology teacher in her forties, Irish, attractive, freckled. Perhaps it explained why Bernie was gay; it was genetic. And it was why Tessa, who'd been neither unattractive nor stupid, had thrown her prospects away.

She sat looking down at her sleeping sister and was touched, for a moment, with a long-lost affection. She saw the wistful, large-eyed child of four or five years old, skipping along with her. And she heard her mother's voice, scolding or soothing; and then her father's, as he pointed to one or other of his girls and said, I want *you*, it's your turn to play for me. Or to practise their reading, or maths. And you were proud if you were the one chosen, yet also you felt nervous. It had been a problem having an elementary teacher as a father, because you could never really get away from school. And he could be stern. She rubbed her wrist reflectively, remembering how he used to grab it if she got something wrong. He didn't know his own strength. But they'd gained so much from him. He sure as hell had taught them to play. It was one consolation she still had. She still hadn't quite mastered that Brahms sonata.

She would fight Mark like crazy for the grand. It was enough to lose the house. Gall rose in her throat. That view from the drawing-room of the lush garden. It held only that one bad memory. Still it had the power to make her shudder as she relives it in every detail. Even though she's pregnant with John, she struggles up the ladder with the electric trimmer, since Mark won't do it. Says he has to prepare his first Thanksgiving sermon though it's weeks away. Her father sees her and says, Hey, you shouldn't be doing that! And grabs the trimmer-blade just as little Bernie, in the kitchen, being helpful, bends and switches on. And the lurch-back as her father grabs the blade makes her spring the on-button. She can still see the fingers sever and fly, as if in slow motion . . .

She shook her head to banish the image. It was a long time ago. He'd never once blamed her, though his inability to play the piano properly must have been painful for him.

She was able to leave Tessa to go and get something to eat in the refectory. It was mid-afternoon and several of the sisters were taking a coffee-break. She reassured them their sister was sleeping peacefully and her temperature had come down. They worried about her, they said; it was fine to have interests outside the convent, but the assassination magazine and the obsession generally seemed to consume her. A couple of the older nuns remembered her long illness in '64, and hoped she wasn't going to have a recurrence. Jean sympathised with their fears, and said she would have a long talk with her about it. When she returned to the sparsely furnished, whitewashed room, Tessa was sitting up in bed, reading glasses on, absorbed in a book. She smiled at Jean, said sorry she'd been such a bother; she didn't know what had struck her but she was feeling much better. They would still be able to go to the concert this evening.

'You worried me, darling,' Jean said, sitting on the bed and taking her hands. 'Do you remember anything you said? You were talking quite wildly. You can trust me.'

Sister Agnes frowned. 'I don't remember anything important. I wanted to put some money on a horse. I saw on the sports news on your TV last night a horse called Love Field was racing in Louisville today. The two o'clock. It was a rank outsider, but I made up my mind to place a small bet on it.'

'You bet on horse races!'

'Oh, a few of us have a bet occasionally. Bridget makes the

phone-calls for us; she knows about horse racing. Don't look so shocked! We've changed, you know. Sister Dolores even owns a vibrator. She showed it to me. Since she can't sleep with men she feels she's entitled to some solace.'

'I'm dumbfounded.'

Sister Agnes chuckled. 'There'll be an afternoon paper in the common-room; would you go and see how Love Field did, just out of interest?'

She left and came back in a few minutes. 'It came nowhere.'

'Oh, well, I saved my five dollars.'

Now that the brief worry about her sister was over, Jean collapsed back into her own problems. Sitting on Tessa's bed, she wept. There was nothing she could do for Bernie, except just be around, call him every day, visit when he wanted her to, be gentle with his boyfriend. Nothing either for John, who refused help. And nothing to save her marriage. It was finished, despite the briefly reconciling pain of their sons' tragedies. He was in love, and he looked at her, when they chanced to meet, as at some amiable, half-forgotten acquaintance; jigging his glasses quizzically like Woody Allen.

'It's not entirely his fault,' she said, drying her eyes. 'I was never a good wife to him, sexually. I've always been pretty cold.'

Sister Agnes stared at her in surprise. She had always seen her sister as hot-blooded. 'I thought,' she said, 'only Catholics had a problem with sex.'

'No. Lapsed Methodists can have it too. I guess it's because . . .' She paused, taking off her glasses to wipe them, thoughtful. 'Because Momma never told us anything, did she? Sex was always the no-go area.'

'You're right.'

Jean put her glasses back on and stood up. She would take a walk along the creek. Tessa should rest a while, if she really thought she'd be well enough to go to the concert.

'Yes, I'll be fine.'

Yet the Kennedys had had no problems with sex, she reflected, lying alone and staring at the crucifix. The men anyway. She stroked her stomach; you could hardly blame them, women's skin was so smooth.

She felt disturbed by what Jean had said. By thinking how much you could misjudge a person – even your own sister. She rested her hand guiltily on the cool, moist spot between her thighs. He had been obsessed with this.

Later, in the concert hall, Sister Agnes began to feel again that this beauty, this harmony, could not have sprung from blind chance. The harmonies of the *Eroica* had not been created from nothing by Beethoven, he had discovered them, drawn them out of the universal consonance.

But as soon as the applause thundered she thought: Why should God have the best tunes? Isn't chance capable of them? – and she felt sad, empty again. And rapture and sterility fought in her as she listened to the Elgar Cello Concerto. Though moved by the Chinese girl who played it, she could not help remembering a performance by Jacqueline du Pré in Dallas. Dazzling in a red dress, russet hair thrashing, she had played like a fury: the action like a frenzied masturbation, the effect like making love to life itself. Yet life was getting ready to screw her too.

After the concert they had drinks – in her case a soft one – with Jane Pulman Kendrick and her husband. Jane was a psychologist, and Sister Agnes could sense her subtle mind analysing the sisters' relationship; identifying tension; deciding it was envy of each other's freedom. Sister Agnes, tired, felt hot and a little unwell again; she was glad when Gary Kendrick's air-conditioned limo dropped them off at the Sacred Heart. She was even more glad when she had kissed cheeks with her sister and was alone in her room. How beautiful was silence.

Undressing, she turned away from Him.

She thought about the empty tomb.

2

Muffled against the chill night air, they stand behind the fence in their thousands: ordinary Americans, who have driven out to the Air Base simply to be there when the President arrives. They are in a trance of grief, with nothing of the undercurrent of excitement that everyone feels – so long as he or she is not personally involved – when something dramatic, tragic even, happens. There is only the shock, the agony, the disbelief.

They can hear a plane descending through the dark; they hear it land, but can see nothing because of the intense klieglights.

Suddenly the lights are dimmed, and they see a plane's shape loom up greyly out of the darkness. It ghosts towards them then turns, so that it is sideways-on to the crowd behind the fence and the reception party, standing at attention. A truck-lift rumbles up beside it. At the front of the plane a ramp moves into place and a door is opened. A figure leaps up the ramp before it has stopped moving.

There is the whir of a helicopter settling behind the plane.

'Jackie!' the widow hears softly behind her; and for a moment she is filled with joy, for it is his voice. She has been hearing that voice all afternoon, so it does not really surprise her. She turns and is in Bobby's arms.

Now she is standing in the doorway with him, and some watchers are surprised. They had not thought the President's brother had been with him in Dallas. She clasps her purse in one hand, his hand with the other. And the lights focus on her

171

pink suit, picking up the bloodstains on her skirt; her tousled shoulder-length hair and her tranced white face. Half the world is looking at her; no woman in the world's history has had so many eyes on her at one time. With supreme dignity she shows them the horror.

The widow and brother step back, and the bronze casket is brought out, glinting red. To those who bear it the four hundred pound casket feels somewhat lighter than in Dallas; but there they had to manoeuvre it up a ramp. Even so, it is heavy, and the truck-lift clumsy. Between the door and the lift there is a gap of five feet; the casket veers, trembles; and after it the men have to jump down and then turn to clasp Jackie and the other women round the hips to lift them down.

On the other, blind side of the plane, at the front, another door is open and a smaller, lighter, plainer coffin is being eased down a ramp. It is carried the short distance to the waiting helicopter. Its engines chug, ready for a swift take-off. The Naval pilot turns to the silent Secret Service man sitting beside him and says, 'Jeez, that's a coffin!'

'So?'

'I wasn't told to expect a coffin. Who's in it?'

'A Secret Service man was also shot. That's all I know. I don't know who he is or how he got shot. I just know it's classified. You get it?'

'Sure. Now where do we go?'

'Walter Reed Hospital.'

The helicopter rises, light as a dragon-fly, and darts away towards the white and amber glow of the city. The pilot reflects on the unfairness of life – and death. The President with his honour-guards and streets dense with mourners; while some poor guy has also got shot in Dallas and is being huddled off like this, as if his death were a matter of shame.

The grey ambulance bearing the bronze casket is crowded. Jackie, Bobby and four others sit crammed up, half-sitting on one another, their knees brushing the casket. General McHugh, the man who said he had only one President, talks quietly to Bobby Kennedy about the delay in Dallas. 'Johnson said he'd talked to you, and you said he had to be sworn in right there in Dallas.'

'I said nothing of the kind. The oath could be taken anywhere, any time. He was President the moment Jack died.'

'Of course. Well, he lied.'

'Does it matter?' Jackie murmurs. 'Oh, Bobby, I just can't believe Jack has gone.'

'No. No.'

'Have the children been told?'

He hesitated. 'I don't think so. They know something's wrong.'

There was silence for a time in the jolting ambulance, then she said, almost lightly, 'It was a wonderful motorcade. Well, it was terribly hot, I was wishing I hadn't worn this wool suit. But I looked nice. Jack said I looked nice. I wanted to look nice for him. I was given a bouquet of red roses at the airport. They called it Love Field. We wondered why they call it that, and we never did find out. Everywhere else we were given yellow roses. I wonder if the red roses were an omen. Do you think so?' Gripping his hand, she gazes frightened into his eyes, grey spots in the blackness.

'Who can say?'

He lays his free hand gently on the casket. It's impossible to believe his brother is in there. He searches for Jackie's hand and finds it. It is the nearest he can come to Jack. He feels grief like a sea of salt, buoying him up when he should be drowning.

Though the curtains are drawn he has a sense of the thousands outside, lining the streets. With his free hand he twitches the curtain and sees those silent, unearthly crowds, along Independence and into the Mall. He lets the curtain fall back.

'Everything was fine,' Jackie continues; 'until we turned into – '

She chokes on the words, and starts to shake all over. 'Don't go on,' he says gently.

If only, he thinks, there'd been something special about their last meeting, their goodbye. But no, just a handshake, a slap on the back. No sign that he'd had any premonition.

Lincoln; he thinks of Lincoln's last day. The friends he told about his disturbing dream. Moving through the White House, hearing sounds of lamentation but seeing no one. Then at last, approaching the East Room, he sees inside it a catafalque, an honour-guard. He asks an ensign, Who's dead? 'The President. He was shot.'

And a few hours later – to the theatre.

But Jack didn't go around telling people his dreams.

They ride in silence. Then someone says, 'Johnson! Johnson is President. It's too much to bear.'

The ranch, Jackie thinks. We weren't looking forward to it. Oh God, if we could only be at the ranch.

3

They gazed down on Lyndon and Lady Bird, bathed in the arc-lights. 'The last time, thank God!' Jack said.

When they alighted from the helicopter, Lyndon stepped forward, grasped Jackie's hands in his and said warmly, 'Light and set, honey! It's an old Texan greeting. Get down off your horse and come and make yourself at home! From now on you can just wriggle out of your girdle and relax!' Lady Bird stepped forward and hugged her. Lyndon led her towards the friendly lights of the house; Lady Bird and Jack followed, arm in arm.

The night was blustery; occasionally lightning flickered over the low hills.

Lyndon took Jack off for a quiet drink and chat in his office. They sipped cognac, and Jack lit up a Havana. He gazed around at Johnson memorabilia, even more dense than he remembered from his visit after the election. Portraits of Lyndon's homely-looking parents; a framed photo of Johnson City, looking still – in the thirties – like a miserably poor frontier town. Johnson welcoming General Clay in West Berlin, after the building of the Wall; and with various foreign dignitaries. Hunting trophies. A portrait of Johnson in oils. The enormous ego of the man came over powerfully, yet Jack found it easy to understand; he'd had to drag himself up out of the Hill Country dirt.

They discussed how the visit to Texas had gone. In many ways, they agreed, it had gone wonderfully. The crowds had been enormous and welcoming; Jackie had shown she would be a terrific campaign asset if she threw herself into it next year; the Democratic rift had been healed, at least to a degree. Yet they both felt downcast; one crazy old female Kluxer, at the Trade Mart, had spoiled it. Lyndon knew her husband well; he blocked everything progressive in Texas; he was to civil rights what women's slacks were to finger-fucking. Lyndon turned on a TV to get the news. The Trade Mart attack not only led, it took up almost all the time; there was little other news, so little they even announced the death in California of Aldous Huxley, the English author. Jack was sorry; he liked Huxley's books, he would send a letter of condolence to the widow. Of course he was an old man, but that didn't diminish the horror of death.

Lyndon switched the TV off and said, 'I'll make some calls later, see what I can get on that crazy crone.' He flung himself back into the armchair. 'What are you going to do about Vietnam, Mr President? Lodge will want answers when he meets you on Sunday. How do we deal with that little shit-ass country?'

Jack sighed. 'I wish to God I knew, Lyndon. Well, no, I think there's only one possible course, though a lot of people won't like it. We've got to pull out.'

'That'll be as popular as chicken-shit sandwiches around here, Mr President. They'll accuse you of getting even softer on Communism. You'll lose Texas.'

'We'll keep some advisers there this side of the election. But after that the Vietnamese will have to take care of themselves. I'll never forget what De Gaulle told me – that if we got involved there it would become a graveyard for us. And I believe that. We'd find ourselves having to throw more and more troops in.'

'I'm not sure you're right about that. And what price do you put on liberty?'

Jack said, smiling, one leg coiled high on the other, the ankle grasped, 'You're thinking we need to keep a strong Texan business presence there, Lyndon!'

'Hell, no! I'm only thinking of the domino effect. If you lose one country you lose them all.'

'We'll see . . .' He watched a moth burn itself against the ceiling-light and fall to the floor, wings whirling. He quickly averted his eyes. 'We'll see how things look a year from now. And that reminds me, Lyndon – I'm sure you saw Nixon's prediction this morning, that I'd be dropping you from the ticket. Forget it. You're doing a fine job. I'm telling you right now I want you to continue as my Vice President.'

Johnson's hooded eyes closed over, in thought, then he opened them again. 'I'm touched by your words, Mr President. I haven't decided if I want to go on with it after next year. I'll make up my mind before Christmas and let you know.'

'I hope you'll agree to stay on. And now – what about that walk?'

'OK.'

A Secret Service man was sent to bring overcoats, and they strolled out. There were few stars visible; the shapes of the surrounding hills were hidden. Johnson led the way, battling a wind; he brought Kennedy at last to a huddle of gravestones. 'This is where I'll end up,' he said; 'and where I'm happy to end up.'

'It's peaceful.'

Jack heard a hissing sound and turned his head to see Lyndon curving over a grave a windblown jet of urine. 'I like to piss in the open air,' he said. 'I used to like to go out of the house late at night and take a leak off the porch. But after I became Vice President that simple pleasure was denied me. I stepped out to shake hands with my wife's best friend and instantly there were flashlights shinin' on me. Security! They couldn't even let me take a quiet piss.'

It was too cold to stand around; they started back, the wind blowing them towards the friendly lights. Johnson said, 'And what about when your second term ends, Jack? I guess I can't hope to get your support for the nomination?'

Jack hesitated. 'I certainly wouldn't do anything to harm your chances. I think you'd make an excellent president. I would tell them that.'

'But if the Attorney General decided to go for it . . .'

'I don't think Bobby will be ready in '68. I've no idea if he even has that kind of ambition. But if he does go for it, I would have to stay well clear.'

Their footsteps raked through the long grass, a footnote to the gale and the distant rumble of thunder. Johnson said, 'Well, it's pie in the sky so far as I'm concerned. '68 will be too late. Before then I'll have another heart attack, and there won't be no third chance; my cattle will be munching me. My Poppa died at sixty and so did my grandfather.'

'Lyndon, you're the toughest guy I've ever known. You'll be in there fighting at eighty!'

'No – no. It's strange, I always had the feelin' I'd be President of the United States. Even when I was a boy, and we had no food to eat, I believed that. And I almost made it! Almost ain't no good, though. I just wanted one term, one term. I ain't greedy.'

Lightning played, more fiercely, along the invisible hills. There was a smell of rain in the wind that bowled them along. 'Winter's on the way,' Johnson said.

'Yep. I don't care for it.'

He had a sense of the seasons passing, year after year; of his energy declining. And finally death, which would leave nature totally unaffected. The lightning would still play over the hills, nights like this; the wind would still gust. Vanity of vanities.

4

The helicopter landed in the grounds of Walter Reed Army Hospital. In the darkness a ring of men stepped forward, and several of them assisted in unloading a coffin. They carried it to a small building, its windows lit. A door opened and the coffin was taken in.

It was carried through a short hall into a mortuary. Apart from the shuffling of feet there was complete silence. The coffin was opened by two men in short white coats; then two older men in long white coats stepped forward and looked in. They saw the President.

'Lift him out. Gently.'

He was laid on a theatre table. They examined him, asking for him to be turned over when necessary. They made an incision in his skull.

'It's impossible to do anything with this,' one of them said. 'The bullet tracks are clear. And they don't fit the picture.'

'I agree. The only thing to do is get rid of the brain.'

It was done with swift cutting movements. The sponge-like mass, incomplete, was dropped into a bucket.

'We haven't time to do much else. We could sew up the tracheotomy; that should make the entry-wound less visible. But it's going to be a mess.'

'It must be what they want. Break off more of the skull; open it out towards the front.'

'OK.'

They worked quickly and smoothly. Within ten minutes the coffin was on its way again in a black hearse. With the coffin were five or six of the men, black-overcoated, who'd received it from the helicopter, and in front were two more in white smocks. The hearse moved swiftly, and within a few minutes was turning off Jones Bridge Road into the back entrance of Bethesda Naval Hospital. A lot of top brass were there to greet it. There were no military honours; the coffin was taken out and carried, by the black-overcoated men and some naval ratings, to the mortuary.

Doctors were there waiting, and behind them were several big men in suits. The coffin – a simple metal coffin, such as had been used to transport soldiers home from Korea – was opened. Inside was a body-bag. The President was lifted out and the body-bag unzipped. All who were close to the naked body gasped as they saw the huge wound in the skull. And what was most sickening, most astonishing, there was no brain. Just a few tiny bits adhering to the skull. Otherwise nothing. A young orderly, whose job it should have been to section the brain, grew faint and dizzy; that such a thing could happen to his President. He was close to tears.

'There's been some head-surgery.'

'Uh-huh. There's a bullet-wound here in the back but I don't think it goes far. It wouldn't have caused much damage. Maybe a misfire.'

'The fatal wound must have been from the front. The right temple.'

One of the big men stepped forward and started an argument. The atmosphere grew tense, even hostile.

'OK, let's have some X-rays.'

While the technicians were setting up the X-rays, another of the burly civilians drew one of the doctors away into a corner. 'There has to be a brain,' he said. 'We can't say the President of the United States had all his brains blasted out. It would be indecent. Can't you get a brain? Any brain will do.'

'I don't like it.'

'I couldn't give a fuck. The President's going to have a fucking brain.'

'I'll get a message to pathology. Maybe they'll have one.'

Outside, moving slowly up Wisconsin Avenue towards the hospital, was the grey official ambulance leading a line of cars. Each section of the crowds lining the avenue gave a silent sigh as the ambulance passed. They all knew, in their minds, that the President lay casketed in that ambulance, yet in their hearts they could not believe it. He still smiled for them, still spoke in his flat Bostonian twang. The headlights turned in through the main gates and up to the entrance. The military honour-guard sprang to attention. The driver climbed out and opened the doors. He helped Mrs Kennedy to alight. She whispered, Thank you, and walked slowly towards the entrance, followed by Bobby and the others.

A technician was walking down the hall, with the President's X-rays for developing, when he saw Mrs Kennedy, wearing a bedraggled, bloodstained pink suit, come through the main entrance. He would never forget how tragic, how lost, she looked. He came to a halt. One of the Secret Service men surrounding her rushed up to him, with a worried look, and ordered him to get going. He rushed off towards the elevators. Doors were still slamming outside. An admiral saluted Mrs Kennedy and the Attorney General, then led them to an elevator which would take them to a VIP suite, high up in the hospital.

The technician waited in a lab for the X-rays to be developed. When he received them he couldn't resist taking a look. He saw the President's skull, and it resembled a black-and-white map of the world. The fragmented curve towards the back was shaped like the Americas; at the front it bore a vague resemblance to Africa and Europe. The huge black space in between was an Atlantic.

A tear splashed on the X-ray; he wiped it off with his sleeve.

On his way back to the autopsy, passing through the entrance-hall again, he saw an honour-guard shuffling in bearing a heavy bronze casket. He wondered why they were carrying an empty coffin.

He paused once more, and a litter, wheeled by two orderlies, almost knocked into him from behind. Turning, he saw a small wrapped bundle on the litter. 'What's that?' he asked.

One of them mumbled, 'Baby. Born dead.' And they rushed on towards the mortuary.

He felt sorry for the poor baby and its mother; sorry for the President and for Jackie. It was a helluva world.

It was ten-thirty before the autopsy started. Few of those who had been present for the earlier exploration, when the plain coffin had been opened, were still present. The bronze casket was carried in and opened. Everyone who was in the room at that time saw the President, clothed. Through the gaping hole in the skull a doctor removed the damaged brain and handed it to an orderly, telling him to infuse it with formaldehyde. The young man couldn't believe he was holding in his hands the brain of President Kennedy, everything that had made him human and great and a joy to look at on TV.

'There's been some head-surgery.'

'Uh-huh.'

'There's an entry wound in the right shoulder, here. It must have passed out through the throat, where the guys in Dallas did a trach. As for the head-wound, it must have been inflicted from the rear also.'

'I can agree with that.'

5

They heard the throb of a helicopter and, looking up, saw its lights. 'ROB OIL,' Jack read; 'are we expecting anyone?'

'Shit! I forgot to call that Roberts woman.'

'Jesus!'

'Don't worry, I'll deal with her. Unless you've changed your mind? She's mighty pretty.'

'No. I've had enough aggressive right-wing women for one day.'

'OK, you leave her to me. Her husband's company throw their weight around, they need a kick in the butt. They're not big time, you wouldn't fill a piss-pot with the oil they bring up each year. I'll see you later.'

Get her vote for me, Jack said with a grin, and Johnson said he sure would. They separated: Jack strolling towards the ranch house, past the lit-up outdoor pool, Lyndon devouring the ground with long strides towards the landing-area. He arrived just as shapely nyloned and high-heeled legs were alighting. She turned to face him, wrapping her fur coat tight around her neck, her vivid red hair flapping. 'OK, boys!' he said to the security men. 'The panic's over. Melt!'

They melted, sheathing their revolvers.

'Mrs Roberts!' Johnson exclaimed amiably. 'What the hell you doin' here?'

Her smile froze. 'I was invited by the President.'

'That so? OK, let's go inside.'

They walked in silence to a rear door, and he ushered her

along a corridor and into his office. 'Sit down,' he invited or commanded, and she did so, loosening her coat and crossing her elegant legs. Johnson stayed standing, pacing around her.

This was very awkward, he said. He didn't believe the President had invited her. The President would have been too polite to have invited someone to his, Johnson's, ranch without telling him first. The President had said nothing, and was already asleep; he'd had an exhausting day. Her story was unbelievable; he believed she had come, lured by the lies told about the President, hoping to fuck him.

Johnson's harsh, Hill-Country voice overrode the woman's denials. Her face was burning; she fiddled nervously with her purse.

'You're not the first groupie to come here tonight,' he continued, looming over her. 'I guess your husband doesn't know you're here, huh?'

'Well, no, but – '

'If I know Hal, he hates being pissed around. Your face is well known. Secret Service men gossip. There are a lot of press men here, looking for scandal. This could ruin Roboil.'

'The President will confirm that – '

'He ain't going to confirm nothin'.' Johnson, bending over her, stabbed a finger into her chest. 'The President's a busy man. He's met a helluva lot of people in Texas, and it just ain't possible for him to remember every stray remark he may have made. He won't back you up. And besides, you have a reputation to hide, Mrs Roberts. Half of Texas knows you fuck with Tom Rawlings, and there are editors busting a gut to have a chance to bring it all out.'

She turned pale.

Johnson rose to his full height, backed away slightly, turned and paced. He didn't want to cause her trouble. If they could find some plausible reason for her trip. Maybe a large contribution to the Campaign to Re-elect the President. Say a quarter million bucks . . .'

Her chequebook and pen were out of her purse. 'Who do I make it payable to?'

'You can make it out to me. The Re-election Campaign hasn't got an account set up yet. I'll see it gets passed on.'

She scribbled.

'Now, you go tell Hal what you've done. Tell him you were impressed by Kennedy, and that's why you flew in to give us this donation – which I'll make damn sure everybody gets to know about, and I'll praise old Hal to the sky – and he's got to get his fucking ass moving to work for us next time.'

'Yes, I'll do that.'

'That's swell. You needn't rush away. Have a drink.' Johnson sat down, sprawled his feet out; pushed the cognac bottle and Jack's emptied glass towards her. 'Let's talk about what you and your husband can do for the campaign. There's opportunities for Texan business comin' up in Nam. Play your cards right and Hal could get a piece of the action. You're a helluva nice-lookin' woman, y'know that? I'm even kind of envious of the President, you wantin' to screw him. Relax, take off your coat. I was with Tom the night after he bought you that sable. He was mighty proud of how you looked in it. And he was right – it's a mighty fine coat. And that's a swell dress too. They set off your legs real nice – you've got great legs. And the pearls – Hal buys you those? Hal's one helluva nice guy, but I guess he'll only ever get so far. Now the Rawlings Corporation – you just wait and see, in about ten years they'll really be going places. I know Tom is crazy about you, and I don't blame him. He'd split with Janice at the drop of a Stetson. Well, it's none of my business. Hal's a good short-term bet. But you'd make a terrific team, you and Tom. Specially if you had a friend who could ease the way, now and again. That's right, kick your shoes off. Light and set. You're one hell of a dame.'

The phone rang. 'Excuse me,' he said, 'have yourself another drink.' Pulling himself from the chair he turned his back on her and picked up the phone. He recognised the gravelly, unemotional voice of the FBI chief. 'There was a plot to kill the President in Dallas today.'

Johnson waited. The line crackled. Hoover continued. 'Four gunmen were picked up in the railroad parking-lot and the

Book Depository ten minutes before your motorcade was due through.'

'Who was behind it?' Johnson asked.

Again the long wait. 'Probably Castro. One of the suspects is Cuban.'

'You want me to tell the President?'

'No. The Attorney General doesn't think he should be bothered with this until he's out of Texas. There's a problem. A woman who was arrested this evening, on suspicion of aiding and abetting, claims she slept with him in Forth Worth.'

'And did she?'

There was an even longer, crackly silence. 'I thought you should know, Mr Vice President. Good-night.'

'Good-night, Edgar, and thanks.'

He put down the phone, stared at it for a moment, then turned to the woman.

'Gold garter-clips. Now that's real class. Hal buy you that belt?'

She shook her head. 'Tom.'

'I told you, he thinks big, he's got what it takes.'

'I know that,' she said. 'You've not said anything I didn't know already. Timing is everything in life – wouldn't you agree, Mr Vice President?'

'Call me Lyndon.'

6

He could hear the rumbles of thunder. That was fitting. It had been the stormiest day in American history.

It was late; Lee didn't know how late; they'd taken his East German watch. He stared from the bed at the cell bars. The day hadn't gone as he'd expected. He should have been lying on a soft feather-bed in a Cuban safe-house. Someone had fucked up, fucked up real bad.

Yet he was beginning to pull himself together. It could be worse, a helluva lot worse. Everybody knew who Lee Harvey Oswald was. Everybody in the world. And tomorrow they'd have to let him see a lawyer, and he'd tell him where the curtain rods were hidden in the Book Depository. That would wipe the smirks off their faces.

He didn't believe the screw-up was Ruby's fault. Ruby had been at the press conference. It had cheered him up, seeing the chunky, flashy figure. As if to say, Your friends don't forget you. He'd spoken up when some idiot had said Oswald was a member of an anti-Castro organisation. Fair Play for Cuba, Ruby had corrected him. Come to think of it, it had been a dumb thing to do, because someone might have asked him how he knew so much about this guy. But fortunately they were all pretty dumb, the reporters. And it was good because it showed Ruby's sympathies. He was OK, a rough diamond, even if he did knock his strip girls around a bit. Women could be cussed, they needed slapping down at times, even Marina.

At one point Ruby had kind of made a gesture of sympathy,

as if to step forward and defend him; but the reporters had got in his way. But he could see Lee wasn't saying anything to get him into trouble, and so he'd pull out all the stops to help him. He had very influential backers.

And Marina. Marina would say nothing. The FBI had her in some motel, protecting her. In other words, grilling her. But she knew how to keep her mouth shut. He just hoped June and Rachel were OK. Junie needed shoes; he must tell Marina tomorrow, when they'd promised she could visit him, she must get her new shoes.

He'd done real good at the press conference. Yes, sir, they could see there were no flies on Lee Harvey Oswald. He hadn't killed nobody.

He stretched out on the narrow, hard bed; gazed up at the naked light. He heard footsteps. Glanced at the bars. The portly, friendly cop. 'You OK, Oswald?'

'I need a book to read.'

'You got the Bible.'

'I need *Das Kapital*.'

'You can go fuck yourself.'

But the cop grinned, and Lee smiled faintly back. The cop turned away. Some of them weren't so bad. Some of them seemed to look on him as a kind of hero. He closed his eyes. He would sleep. He thought he would sleep quite peacefully. Last night, in Irving, he had lain awake most of the night. Marina had laid her leg over his after she'd got out to feed Rachel, and he'd kicked up angrily. He'd been so tense. But now it was over. He would sleep.

7

At midnight in the kitchenette of the VIP suite, Jackie perched on a stool, while the Secretary of Defence, McNamara, squatted on the floor, staring at her stained skirt and stockings. The autopsy was taking an age. The Defence Secretary let her talk. She wanted to talk about the murder. She was there. She was so glad she was there. But it was totally unreal. Half the day had been torn away like Jack's brain, and she felt she ought to be asleep in Lyndon's ranch. Part of her was there, she felt, although she couldn't explain it.

A telephone rang in the front room.

'We're almost through,' Mrs Connally had said, turning.

Robert Kennedy, shirt-sleeved, came into the kitchen. 'That was Hoover,' he said. He poured himself a glass of milk, then forgot it, wandering off to perch on a stool. 'Oswald's been charged with Tippit's murder. Those were Hoover's words in total. That's twice as many words as in his previous calls to me today. His first was, "The President's been hit," the second, "The President is dead." Was ever a death more tersely declared to a President's brother?'

'He's careful with the Bureau's budget,' McNamara murmured, his head almost touching his drawn-up knees.

'There are people who loved him too,' said Jackie.

The two men looked at her, startled. 'Hoover?' said Bobby incredulously.

'Tippit,' she said. 'That policeman. There are people who love him just as much as we love Jack.'

McNamara said, 'Do we know anything about him?'

Bobby shook his head. 'He's J.D. Tippit, a cop. I don't even know if he has a Christian name. He has a wife and kids. You're right, Jackie; they're suffering just as much. I'll call his wife tomorrow.'

And there were people dying in the hospital, McNamara said. As he came in the front entrance he had overheard an orderly, wheeling a trolley with a little wrapped-up bundle on it, telling someone it was a stillborn baby.

'Oh – really?' Jackie said, her eyes springing alive with anguish. 'Oh, that's terrible! Please, Bobby, find out who the mother is. I shall want to talk to her.'

He rose from the stool and left the kitchen.

'I know how she must be feeling,' she murmured. The ash gathered on her cigarette and fell to the floor.

Bobby came back. 'I called the registrar. No babies have been born dead here today.' He slumped on to the floor, beside McNamara. 'The only person to die here in the last few days was an eighty-year-old admiral's widow who spent the last thirty years in St Elizabeth's.'

He stared sightlessly at the wall. Jackie recalled the three catatonic old men on a garden seat at St Elizabeth's, that time she'd visited it. Our faces are just like theirs, she thought.

McNamara spoke in a racked voice: 'Bobby.'

The Attorney General glanced aside at him, focusing his gaze with difficulty.

'You know what your brother would be saying right now?'

'What?'

'That the fight must go on. And that you must pick up the torch.'

'Me! Why me?'

'You know why. You're a Kennedy. Joe was killed, so Jack picked up the torch. You're next.'

'We're not a royal line, for God's sake. I don't want it. Why put ourselves up for every nut in America to take pot-shots at us?'

'Well, I guess you're right. Forgive me.'

'You know what I think?' Bobby said bitterly. 'We created a myth; or we let the media create one. And my brother died because of it. We're just rich boys with an ambitious father and time on our hands. And a mother and sisters who are good at organising tea parties. Well – I pass.'

8

The Kennedy Myth

by Jane Pulman Kendrick, D.Psych.
Dept. of Psychology, Univ. of Texas

God knows that there were more horrific crimes before Dealey Plaza, and on an infinitely greater scale. The history of mankind is a chamber of horrors. Nevertheless, that weekend in '63 marked a shift of great psychological importance. Televisual death, observed from the comfort of an armchair, came into existence. Since then, anything has been possible, nothing unacceptable – as the Vietnam War itself amply revealed, with its scenes of napalmed children and its casual street-executions.

Death is the ultimate mystery of Dealey Plaza; and we are in love with it. Kennedy is the violent myth our time demanded. Myth in the true sense of the word, not in the sense of an illusion. In his balance of firmness and restraint, his good sense, his vibrant and uplifting personality, his ability to see the other side's point of view, and his preference for life over death (an excellent quality in a leader), he was in my opinion a potentially great president. Unfortunately he also had a serious moral flaw; to put it bluntly, he liked screwing women. Americans are intensely uncomfortable with him for that reason. They don't want to see him whole. It is a stain on our country that there has still not been a full and honest investigation of the assassination. It is because we want to forget him, want to forget all those women he humped, with the finesse of a stallion, while we thought he was hunched over his desk defending America.

It is noteworthy that there are only two kinds of Kennedy biography: Theodore Sorensen's hagiographic kind, in which JFK is the holy, ascetic statesman; and the what-stars-did-he-screw scandal-sheets. Mere profiles both, like the mugshots on the *Wanted For Treason* leaflets circulating in Dallas at the time of his visit. Before we can achieve a rounded portrayal of him we need a myth that can help us accept and celebrate sexuality. We have only been able to create a destructive myth, sex in death. The assassination was the *Liebestod*, the ultimate penetrative orgasm. He got really fucked. With all our violence and anger – Vietnam and other liberation movements, including the drug culture and feminism – it is quite obvious the myth for our time had to be a man's exploding head.

I think also of another potent Kennedy image, or rather blend of images: the body of Mary Jo Kopechne settling, Ophelia-like, in the muddy waters off Chappaquiddick; and, a few hours later, men in space suits nudging the ghostly lunar dust. Death to the feminine (I speak of values – they are not limited to women); victory to male technology and 'reason' (actually the most dangerous kind of madness, and not limited to men). In the last decade of the nineteenth century, Freud and others were beginning to explore the mind, and finding there imagination, fantasy, dreams, poetry, love and hate. Today these have vanished from serious study, but one may achieve a Nobel prize for keeping a primate's brain alive outside its body. Mankind has truly progressed.

So far, what can be dimly discerned in the Kennedy fate is some kind of religious myth. Life, created male and female, king and queen, arrives at Love Field, an earthly paradise. Roses bloom, and the queen wears that same tender colour. But tragically there is a violent son, who destroys the sacred marriage, the *hieros gamos*, through an act of terror. Creation's wholeness is broken up, intellect fatally separated from nature. The queen is robbed of her strength, which consists of intuition, imagination, tenderness. The brother next in line to the slain king attempts to restore the kingdom; he marries the widow (Bobby Kennedy would probably have liked to do that, but contented himself with befriending Jacqueline Kennedy). He too is destroyed. A third, much weaker brother steps into the breach, but instead, through misjudgement, completes the queen's destruction; she (in a different persona) is drowned. The violent son is all-powerful.

All theories of what happened in Dealey Plaza seem unbelievable, whether they posit a single assassin or a conspiracy. This backs up my suggestion that the event was mythic – essentially mental. All myths are unbelievable yet intensely real. Children no longer have an Oedipus Complex – many do not even have a father. They have a Kennedy Complex. They grow up believing that the mind, the psyche, is just expendable and explodable grey matter. Less efficient in many ways than computers. The spaceflights marked a profound change; how could you believe in the soul when you could see the whole earth no bigger than a tennis ball in space? Yet the damage had been done six years earlier, when a brilliant mind was blown into the bracing Dallas air, then settled on a pink hat, a patrolman's tunic. The soul has been blown apart; we have quite literally lost our mind.

As with the Oedipal myth, there are also innumerable personal outgrowths, depending on the psychological make-up and background of each individual. Procreation is crossfire; domestic life is a conspiracy. I have no doubt that I have been affected by the profound grief both my parents felt for Kennedy. My father ought to have been sitting next to Kennedy at the Trade Mart lunch; my mother was a patient at Parkland Hospital, recovering from a mastectomy following cancer. She heard the commotion as the dying President was brought there. My father plunged into deep depression, and was unable to give my mother the emotional support she needed. I am convinced that my observation of their deepening spiral of unhappiness led unconsciously to my choice of psychology as a career.

For my mother, Kennedy represented a lover: hence guilt. She confessed to me, a few months before her death in '88, that she had slept with Kennedy during the Democratic Convention of '60. She loved him; she believed, very foolishly, on the basis of ten minutes in a senator's bedroom, he reciprocated her love. For my father, he was probably the beloved younger brother who was reported missing presumed killed flying over Germany in the Second World War. For a former elderly patient of mine, now dead, Kennedy was a son: the son whom she had driven out of her home through her alcoholism, and who was killed in Korea. My patient's remorse was due to take the form of an attack on Kennedy at the Trade Mart lunch. For a British author who interviewed me during his writing of a book about Kennedy, the President stood for his father, who had been very pro-American and democratic. He had died three years before Kennedy of a sudden brain haemorrhage, when apparently in full health. The author only discovered this association, hidden in his unconscious for twenty-five years, after his meeting with me, and through a dream. In his dream he had consoled his father by saying that he had not died alone, but surrounded by people he loved and who loved him. Waking, he realised that there was an echo of something I had told him about Kennedy, that he sometimes slept with women in Jackie's absence because he hated to fall asleep alone. The author now knew why he had never been able to accept that Kennedy was dead.

For all of these people – and they could be multiplied – the assassination occupies a kind of dreamtime. Kennedy is dead, he is not dead. He is being taken back for burial at Arlington; he is flying on to Austin. A physicist said to me that those few seconds carried too great a burden of event, of shock, and it was as if that weight caused time to cave in, creating a vortex, a whirlwind, in which past, present and future, and reality and illusion, became confused. In the same way the mythic Arthur, who also carried the burden of a people's hope, has not died, but lives on in Avalon. And there are some who would add Jesus.

JFK was the ideal persona for the myth of our violent age to home in on. Not only because he was the most powerful man in the world; not only because he had launched the space programme. He was emotionally split already as a result of his background: the sexually rapacious, energetic and capitalistic father; the undemonstrative, puritanical, intensely religious mother. He had no proper home; woman was his only home, or rather it was her womb and her vagina where, for the last time, his mother had truly hugged him. So he kept wanting to find it again, and the women were all too eager. Home is where, as Frost said, if you have to go there, they have to take you in.

The mother, Rose, is the central person in his life; the woman he always sought in vain: most determinedly through his marriage to the similarly cool Jacqueline. He was reputedly a bad lover because there was an element of punishing his mother in every act of 'love'.

Yet he kept trying. I have mentioned that, according to at least one of his sexual partners, he was afraid of falling asleep alone. If this is true, nothing could more clearly evoke the importance of Rose; for by sleep he implied death. We share birth with our mother; he longed to rediscover the sharing in death, that most solitary of experiences. He thought he was after votes, after power; I would guess that his real quest, so painful and exhausting that it made him sickly from childhood, and later all but broke his back, was for Love Field.

9

In the summer of that year, a few weeks after Jean's visit, a November 22 Museum was established in a Main Street building, overlooking the motorcade route. Its creator was a wealthy member of the assassination class Sister Agnes attended; he'd been gathering material over many years. Now at last it was ready, and the class members were invited to a preview.

Time was in the nun's mind on the bus ride into the city. The bus passed through Oak Cliff, where now the people sitting out in front of their faded houses were mostly black. Oak Cliff was being ghettoised; here lived the housekeepers of the rich whites. Time was a very subtle assassin. Though the walking stick which she increasingly had to use was not so subtle.

An elevator took her up past the Ford-Markham Acquisition Company, Duttington Finances, attorneys' offices, and Hartford Assurance, to Assassinations. Stepping out, she saw a familiar group of *aficionados* in a reception area. Timidly, her heart sinking a little, she joined them; and Jane Pulman Kendrick, with a welcoming smile, detached herself and joined her. Sister Agnes took an orange juice.

The tall, rather austere psychologist, her short, sandy hair on the turn to grey, asked after her sister. Oh, she was much better, the nun said, screwing up her mouth. On the flight back to New York she had sat next to a handsome wealthy widower, and they had been inseparable since. A lawyer, he was even going to do battle with Mark on her behalf, and she had good hopes of keeping the Weston house and the concert grand.

Well, that's great! Jane said. I liked her a lot, remember me to her. And that reminded her: her daughter Marilyn had asked her to pass on her good wishes. Marilyn was a glamour model in Miami.

Your essay is wonderful, Sister Agnes said; it'll be in the fall issue. Though she would have to cut the explicit words. Jane flushed, and said she had felt it necessary to use the brutal terms, to convey what she meant. Still, she understood; she'd expected it, it was OK. And did she feel it was also OK, the editor of *November 22* asked, to reveal her mother's involvement with Kennedy?

Yes. She'd thought a lot about it. No one would blame her mother.

Well, Sister Agnes was really pleased. She was proud of her old pupil; and Jane flushed again. She turned aside, her arm touched by one of her male colleagues, a distinguished-looking black social worker, and the nun moved away. She gazed up at a blown-up picture of Marina. She felt in tune with her; her alienation, foreignness. She felt closer to her than to Jean. All that sympathy she'd wasted on her.

And now, according to magazine articles, she was Marina Porter, spoke good English and loved greenhouses. She had three children, and no doubt the older ones had often said to dates, 'My father was Lee Harvey Oswald,' and sometimes the response would be a puzzled, 'Who?' She preferred that earlier, Russian, enigmatic Marina, with Lee on the train at Minsk, leaning her head out to say goodbye, clutching a thin bunch of flowers, headed for the States.

How could you go through all that, and become a poised, attractive American, as American as apple pie?

Around the corner of the L-shaped reception area the walls held blow-up portraits of world leaders in '63. Fidel, in his guerrilla cap, scowled down at her. So much hysteria at that time, she reflected. Everyone scared Communism would take over the world. And now Castro was an aged, frightened conservative, his country's economy collapsing. All but alone in the abandoned house of Marxism, like the old retainer in *Cherry Orchard*, mumbling, 'Everyone's forgotten me.' It was almost sad; like so many young idealists she had stirred to his vision. Che Guevara – she'd had a poster of him on her wall.

She avoided people's glances, so as not to be drawn into a circle of conversation; she wanted to be alone, sipping her juice. She reflected on Jane's essay. Kennedy wasn't a myth; people grieved for him because there had been a single lantern in a dark, stormy field, and someone had come along and kicked out its frail light.

A hand waved in front of her abstracted eyes; she blinked; was uncertain; then smiled with genuine pleasure as she saw another former pupil. 'Emily!' Emily was flashing her perfect, dazzling teeth, between lips that were unfamiliarly glossed. Sister Agnes had a moment of guilt that she hadn't immediately recognised this sophisticated young woman, her hair no longer flying wild, but drawn back: one of her best pupils, with whom she had spent many untimetabled hours. They had helped Emily to achieve the highest grade of her year, in a study of Kennedy's last morning. *Morning Glory to Red Roses* – the cover ornamented with Emily's design of intertwined flowers.

The girl embraced her old teacher warmly, a little shyly. It was always difficult to make that transition from tutelage to friendship. She was thanking Sister Agnes for sending her the invitation; she'd been looking forward to it so much – not the museum particularly, but to see her again. It had been too long. Her brilliant blue eyes were shining; and left Sister Agnes's reluctantly, to accept a cocktail from a waiter.

They chatted, and the room filled, grew noisy. She had a summer job at a gas-station; she was enjoying university life, getting good grades; but she missed that personal contact she'd had with Sister Agnes, those hours under the tree or alone in a classroom. She'd given her so much. Come to tea some time, Emily, the nun said. Make it soon. 'I'd love that – thank you!' The room was thinning out again as people started to inspect the museum; and suddenly Emily was saying she must go, she would see the museum when it opened to the public, she had a date. She kissed Sister Agnes on the cheek, pressed her arm lightly; and was gone, heading for the door, her full yellow skirt swirling as she walked. Sister Agnes felt abandoned. Felt as she did at the end of a semester, when all the cheerful voices had vanished. Leaving, here a hair-slide; there, a school photograph they didn't want.

She put down her empty glass and started to drift around the museum in a daze. The most dramatic exhibit, supposedly bought from a former orderly at the Walter Reed Army Hospital in Washington, made her want to throw up. She had to lean for a long time over a display case holding a variety of more modest, and probably more authentic, items: drafts of the speeches Kennedy had been due to give at the Trade Mart lunch and the Austin banquet; a baseball cap he should have been given at Bergstrom Air Base; a list of the phone-calls Jack Ruby had made to Mafia bosses in October and November; a slim typewritten anthology of German writings, prepared and donated by Ted Sorensen, which the President had been reading during his trip.

When her stomach had settled she moved on. There was a display devoted to Robert Kennedy. The open pages of his copy of Aeschylus, in English translation, moved her more than anything in the museum. Robert Kennedy had pencil stroked three lines: 'God, whose law it is that he who learns must suffer / And even in our sleep pain that cannot forget / Falls drop by drop around the heart.' Tears gathered behind her eyes and in her throat. She knew how Jack's death had torn him apart, driven him into study, into philosophy and poetry, into intense moral concern, as he too sought the final disclosure. Until he too . . . The pain suffered by the Kennedy family, heroic whatever their faults, seemed to her too great for anyone to have to bear.

Totally drained, ignoring the figures that shuffled past and sometimes greeted her, she slumped on a black leather sofa in front of a full-scale blue Lincoln limousine with wax figures fixed eternally in the gestures of the fatal moment. She closed her eyes; her mind drifted.

'Sister Agnes?'

Her eyes opened, her head jerking forward. She saw standing over her a burly, grey-haired man, his grubby white shirt straining over a beer-gut.

'Oh, hello! I was miles away.' She pulled herself up straight. The blue Lincoln confronted her. The flung-back head, the pink suit. 'What do you think of the museum, Wayne?' she asked.

'They got some good stuff.'

She nodded.

'But I don't hold with showing the brain,' he said.

'No, that's terrible.'

'You think it's Kennedy's?'

'I don't want to think so.'

'Yeah, I know what you mean.' He sat down heavily beside her on the leather sofa, easing his shirt-collar from his neck. 'It sure is hot. They want to do somethin' about the air-conditioning. We're on our own. The others have gone to some bar.'

She glanced around. Yes, the spacious rooms were empty and silent; the familiar faces had vanished. 'You didn't want to go with them?'

He shook his head. 'I can't talk to 'em. I ain't educated.'

She felt a pang of sympathy. He'd been an oddity in the assassination class, among the neat suits and designer jeans. She'd tried to talk to him, to make him feel at ease, but he had stopped coming after a couple of times. She had been surprised to see him turn up this evening.

'Besides,' he said, 'I put back a few beers before I came.'

She knew that was true from his breath. He had put back a lot of beers in his life, she thought. There was a yellow tint to his haggard face. She'd never taken to him, which made her feel guilty.

'Are we goin' to whup Iraq?' he asked. There were rumours of war, as in so many Augusts. Without waiting for a response he said the US should make an immediate air-strike. Some general had said there'd only be about thirty American casualties if there was a strike.

'I think the general should lead a commando raid to take out Saddam,' Sister Agnes said – hearing, like an echo-effect, Kennedy's ironic East-Coast tones.

'Well, whatever it takes, they can't get away with this. But that ain't what I wanted to talk to you about. I got somethin' on my mind, sister. I ain't nothin' religious, but I got respect for nuns, and you bin nice to me.'

'I'll help if I can,' she said, turning to face him. Their knees brushed and she moved away slightly. She waited. He lowered his head and covered his eyes with his large, rough hands.

At last he raised his face to her, though his eyes stared over her shoulder. 'I got things on my conscience. Bad things. I've been in prison a lot of my life. Also the nut-house. I've tried to kill myself twice. The last time, about a month ago. I stole and I killed, when I was young. Most of the guys I killed were gangsters, I don't feel nothin' about them. But one of 'em wasn't like that; one of 'em was that guy.' He nodded towards the Lincoln.

Sunken, bloodshot eyes stared into hers. Her head started to spin. It was a long time before she could gather her senses enough to whisper, 'Is this true?'

He nodded. 'You see, nobody'll believe me. It's drivin' me crazy. I'm in bad shape, my liver's shot to hell, and I want to clear my conscience. I told my story to the cops and the FBI, but they don't want to know. That's why I went to the evening class, I figured I'd tell the guy who ran it, but he don't believe me either. He just thinks I'm a harmless nut.'

The room seemed to be moving around her like a fairground waltzer. 'Tell me what happened,' she whispered.

He'd been taught to shoot by David Ferrie; had become a real crack-shot. Ferrie had come to him just a couple of weeks before Kennedy's visit, and told him what he wanted. But he didn't think he'd set the whole thing up. It was too big, there were too many guys around pretending to be Secret Service men. He'd fired from behind the fence of the grassy knoll, and saw Kennedy's head explode. Then he'd run along the fence and tossed his rifle to somebody else. After that, he'd walked casually away in the confusion.

'I went straight off to work – I was workin' afternoons in an appliance store. I was on my own that afternoon – the guy who ran it pissed off to see the excitement. I was feelin' pretty cocky on account of I was in charge of somethin'; though not many people came in because of what happened. It was all on TV but I didn't even bother to watch or turn the sound up. For me it had just been a job; I didn't give a shit about Kennedy. This thin, scrawny guy comes in, says he's lookin' to buy a TV, then walks out. I didn't know him from Adam, till I saw him on TV later – Lee Harvey Oswald. I guess he was hidin' from the cops.

'I saw Ferrie that evening and pocketed a lot of dough – two grand. And you know what? Somehow he'd got hold of Kennedy's bible. He showed it to me; he was laughin' about it. Well, we know what happened to Ferrie, the night before he was due to give testimony. Had a heart attack, but left two suicide notes! Typewritten notes! Jesus, do they think we're idiots? They killed him, just like they killed Ruby with injected cancer cells, and a whole lot of others. But I'll probably be dead in a year anyway, so what the hell does it matter?'

He had bad nightmares. The weight of guilt was like a ball and chain he kept dragging around. What should he do? What should he do? He stared pleadingly into her eyes.

He was the second person to ask that of her this summer; but Jean's problems were nothing like this. If he could be believed. There were many screwballs who had confessed. She was horrified and sickened, yet she wanted to believe him.

'You're not religious,' she said, 'and you felt nothing for Kennedy. Then why do you have nightmares?'

'Lady, I wish to God I knew.'

He put his head in his hands again and started to cry – to sob. She had never heard such sobbing from a man and, whatever he had done, she felt compassion. She touched his knee; he clutched at her hand. The next moment he had buried his head in her breast, just like the waxen President with Jackie in the

Lincoln. As he went on sobbing, she began stroking the back of his head. She kissed his brow, and whispered, 'Hush – hush!' She breathed in liquor and sweat. His sobbing eased gradually, and his stubble rasped against her cheek. She felt nausea, horror, repulsion, and gratitude that he had chosen her.

'And do you forgive me?'

'Only God can forgive you,' she gasped.

'No – you've got to. You can forgive people, surely? You're a fucking nun, aren't you?' She removed her hand from his, taken aback by the crudity; but he grasped her wrist, and for a moment she thought he was going to scream at her, telling her she was a failure, and she felt a wave of panic. Instead, with a deep, wrenching sob, he said, 'Forgive me, please!'

Her eyes misted. He was in despair, a soul in torment. She whispered, 'I forgive you! You're not the same person now. I forgive you.'

It astonished her that she could say the words, and mean them – just as if he were a schoolgirl crying over having copied from someone else's essay. A weight lifted from her; she'd been right all along. There *was* a conspiracy! The relief was so huge it became a sense of rapturous flight, and she almost loved this loathsome man who had brought her such happiness. She squeezed his hand.

10

'Mr President, this is Beth – Beth Pulman. I hope I'm not disturbing you, calling so late. They told me you'd only just gone to your room.'

'That's right.' He loosened his tie with one hand, undid his collar. 'Lyndon and Bird have been very hospitable, we've sat up talking. How are you?'

'I feel wonderful!' She gave a slight giggle. 'Henry's only just left – we've been drinking champagne to celebrate your visit! You gave me a terrific lift, Mr President, you really did! I just wanted to thank you.'

'Well, it sure gave me a lift too.'

After a hesitation she said, 'I think what we talked about is going to happen. I have a feeling. A gut feeling, if you know what I mean. I'm always right about my gut feelings – leastways I have been to date – all four times.'

It took him a few seconds to decipher her words. 'Well, if that happens, that's OK by me. How about you?'

'Oh, I'd be real pleased. It would help take my mind off – you know what.'

'I know. But that problem's not going to recur.'

'I hope not. I know Henry would be pleased too: you saw how he reacted. He's wanted another for years.' A longer pause, then, 'I'd have to tell him, though, I think. That your visit to me might have something to do with it.'

'Hey! wait a minute!' he said, alarmed.

'Don't worry, Mr President. Oh, sure, he'd be mad as hell,

for a coupla days, but he'd come to terms with it. I know Henry. He throws his weight around like a wild bull, but he's soft underneath and it soon passes.'

'We should talk about this.'

'Sure. But I'd have to tell him. I couldn't stand having it on my conscience.'

'If it happens, get in touch with me before you do anything.'

'Of course.'

'Well, good-night. You keep well.'

'I will. And thanks for everything, Mr President.'

He replaced the phone, and felt the soft, quick thud of his heart in the stillness. This could screw everything up.

Yet he had survived worse scares. This was no match for Marilyn. It was foolish of Beth to think she could tell if she was pregnant. It was hysterical thinking, natural after her operation. But even if it happened, and she still threatened to tell Henry, he could send Bobby or someone down to talk to him, make him see it was in no one's interest to make this public.

He was walking on a tightrope, though. Just let one of those Polaroids emerge that Lawford had taken and he'd be dead meat. The great American public would have his balls. Americans approved of serial adultery in the form of several marriages, but they wouldn't forgive him even a hint of infidelity. It would be absolutely no use pointing out how the Test Ban Treaty had saved millions of lives. Maybe even their own kids, now or in the future. They'd say, Screw that, you fucked around. You liked pussy too much. If you want a fresh piece of ass you gotta get a divorce and remarry, like the rest of us do. Get yourself a weekend retreat in Reno. We always knew you couldn't trust a Catholic. Move over, and we'll have us that nice Mr Johnson instead. He doesn't love pussy, he loves Bird. Or nice Mr Nixon.

He should call a halt.

And yet, that whiff of danger – it made the juices flow, made you feel alive. He couldn't do without it. He stood up from the bed, flexing his back, and took a few steps around the bedroom. He didn't feel like sleeping yet. He might have talked with Jackie, but the light was out under her door; she'd left the fireside an hour ago, saying she was exhausted. Well, it had been a heavy day for her; she'd been terrific.

He took out of his briefcase a slim document, a collection of German writings which Ted Sorensen had put together for him. The intention was to provide a source-book for some apt and elegant quotations that he could use for the visit of Chancellor Erhardt next week. He sat at a desk and started browsing. The earliest passage was from the medieval Gottfried von Strassburg. Jack smiled; Sorensen had the kind of wide-ranging taste he liked to see in an aide.

His attention was caught by a short poem by someone called Rainer Maria Rilke. He read it through several times, memorising it. It was called 'Time and Again' . . .

Time and again, however well we know the landscape of
    love,
and the little churchyard with lamenting names,
and the frightfully silent ravine wherein all the others
end: time and again we go out two together,
under the old trees, lie down again and again
between the flowers, face to face with the sky.

He thought it was a touching poem. He couldn't imagine it would be of any use in the meeting with the German Chancellor; indeed, its third line might even be interpreted as hinting at the holocaust; but Sorensen had put it in simply because he thought the President would like it. Ted knew his mind well; he could write a speech that would convince Jack he had written it himself.

He thought of Love Field, and Lyndon's little churchyard. He thought of Jackie asleep.

He undressed and knelt beside the bed. He did it every night for his mother's sake. He wasn't certain there was anyone there to hear his prayers, but that was no reason not to try. He persevered, as he persevered in the personal correspondence with Khrushchev. With God, as with the Russians, you had to keep talking.

He lay down on the hard bed. Very quickly he had an erection. He regretted having passed up Mrs Roberts. Shit, she was beautiful; that red hair, so delicately scented; the cleavage down which he had stared. The chance had been lost probably for ever. No, he would find an excuse to bring her to Washington. Get her to pair up with a cheap hooker – it shouldn't be hard. He would fuck them both and then watch. But his imagination didn't catch fire.

And again – it was risky. She hated his policies too much. What he should have done was invite Sister Agnes here. Telling her he wanted her views on moral questions. A young Catholic's views. Then there'd have been the excitement of being within reach of temptation, but having to resist it. He could hardly thrust his hand up her habit, during a discussion of divorce or contraception; though it was an amusing fantasy and he grinned, picturing her surprise. He loved the games of love, the pranks. The great thing about sex was that you could be a child again – or even for the first time.

Girls' breaths. Sails billowing. Salt spray off Nantucket.

Watching Kathleen, at ten, rescue a beetle from the swimming-pool. Dear, soft-hearted Kick. Grass-scent and blossom.

'A child said *What is the grass*? fetching it to me with full hands.

How could I answer the child? I do not know what it is any more than he . . .'

All flesh is grass. I like holding it.

11

In the real world, the world that could not adjust to his death, people were beginning to dream of the assassination. By 1990, Jane Pulman Kendrick had collected over ten thousand assassination dreams: mostly from the States, but spanning the globe. They could only constitute a minute percentage of all the dreams dreamed; she guessed there were probably ten thousand a night, the number only now starting to fall off.

Every one of the dreams was about Kennedy's death, but also about the people themselves, of course.

She believed her mother might have been the very first dreamer of an assassination dream. Jane had 'collected' it from her on her deathbed.

Beth Pulman, lying in Parkland, had been very conscious of Kennedy's visit. She should have been meeting him at the lunch, with Henry; but the cancer had struck. The cancer was perhaps punishment for her past adultery and present longings. There'd have been no time for a private meeting – yet the President was always capable of creating a miracle.

She heard, just after twelve-thirty, a screaming of many vehicles far below her fourth-floor room; shouts, cries, doors slamming. A few moments later a nurse came in, tears pouring down her face, saying the President had been shot. Beth Pulman had fainted.

She came round a few minutes later, a young intern, red-headed, lantern-jawed, bending over her. 'Will he live?' she asked.

The intern smiled. 'They're working on him, they'll do their best.'

She asked him where he'd been hit, and he placed his index finger hard against his forehead. 'He's got about half a brain left,' he said briskly; then smiled again. 'I shouldn't think we'd notice!'

She was sedated; but remained on a hysterical high. Henry came, and they sobbed together. Nurses talked about what they'd seen: Mrs Kennedy, in a tranced state, still clutching a piece of bone in her stained white gloves; one of the nurses had had to prise it gently from her. The chaos; and, above all, the blood everywhere, like a Civil War field hospital. The nurses still had blood on them.

One of them had heard the priest say to Mrs Kennedy, after, that he believed his soul had still been in his body when he'd given conditional absolution. Because the President had been young and strong.

And there were stories of crazy callers on the hospital phones. A boy laughing and saying three times he wanted to speak to his father, the President; a woman saying it was God's vengeance on account of them being Catholics; another, that it served the nigger-lover right.

Jane's mother eventually fell asleep at around nine in the evening. And dreamed she was in the Trade Mart with Henry. The President arrived, and kissed her on the cheek. Beth accepted a steak, even though it was a Friday and Henry looked at her angrily. She explained she had to have steak because their daughter Jane had grilled it. (Jane was supposed, that evening, to cook her first meal for the family left at home.) The steak seemed well done, but when Beth pressed her knife into it blood oozed out and went on oozing. Soon it was covering her and everyone near her, including Kennedy. Kennedy most of all; he was all blood, from head to foot.

She tried to exonerate Jane by whispering to the President that it was her period. He smiled; he recalled she had been bleeding when they'd made love in San Francisco. The smile froze into rigor mortis. There was confusion as he was laid out on the table and the diners and waiters, wearing surgical gowns, set to work with the table-knives, trying to save him. Someone said it was fortunate the Trade Mart was so close to Parkland – the real surgeons would be here any moment. And the red-haired intern arrived, breathlessly.

Henry was crying and telling everyone *he* should be the one to die, to sacrifice himself; and Beth found herself agreeing. Kennedy was helped up, and Henry's corpse was laid out in his place. Everything calmed down a little, and people got on with their lunches. A priest came carrying a great salver of sole, which he proceeded to slice up. Beth took a slice; the priest left and returned with a tiny jug of lemon juice, and he poured some on her sole, saying, this sole is good, I promise; it's fresh; and as he poured on the lemon juice he pronounced the blessing: *Si capax, ego te absolvo* . . .

Jane had not discussed her mother's dream with her. She just leant over the pillow and kissed the tear trickling down the dry, yellowish cheek and said, 'Thank you, mother.'

Another dream on that first night of his death was dreamt in the White House, several hours after the silent procession of cars had followed the slain chief from Bethesda. This dream was not one of Jane Kendrick's collection.

An honour-guard had been established in the East Room. Finally Jackie was able to take off her suit, on which the stains had turned stiff and dark. After bathing, she lay down on the double bed, the softly sprung side of it, and allowed a doctor to inject her with Amytal, since neither whisky nor an earlier, milder injection had had any effect on her.

'Why are you all facing away from him?' Jackie asked the Marine Corps officer, stiffly at attention. 'Surely you should be facing your President?'

The young officer's face turned red; his lips moved but at first could say nothing. Then she thought he whispered, 'Because we're embarrassed. It doesn't seem right.'

'There's no need to feel embarrassed,' she said, turning her head towards the catafalque. What she saw made her cry out softly, 'Oh no! . . . Yes, I see what you mean!'

The bronze casket had gone. There was an ordinary bed and two naked figures were making love on it. Jack and a blonde-haired young woman. Jackie walked closer. The woman's face, eyes closed in the ecstasy of the embrace, turned towards her and it was Marilyn Monroe. Jackie swerved abruptly to avoid the sight. The swerve brought her level with another of the Marines. The young man relaxed from his stiff pose to light her a Salem. 'I'm sorry,' he said.

'It's OK. It's not your fault. But I should have been told. They told me he was dead.' She felt in herself a mixture of huge relief that Jack was alive and a horrible embarrassment and resentment. Did he have to do it so openly? His parents would be coming, and the children. Dear God, the children!

She walked to the exit, hearing her high-heels echoing. Coming towards her was the tall, bleak, camel-like form of General De Gaulle in uniform. Stopping in front of her, he stooped and kissed her hand. *'Dommage!'*

'Ah, oui! Merci.' You mustn't see him, she said; he's too defamed.

'N'importe. Je dois le voir. J'insiste.'

He had gone, stalking past her; and now she was with Bobby. You have to do something! she said. Look at all the people waiting to see him!

And there were thousands, broad rank after rank, stretching away from the White House doors and all around Lafayette Park.

Bobby was crying. How could he do this to me? I loved her. Jack didn't love her.

I know, she said; he loved me.

She started to cry too.

She begged him to persuade Jack to let him take his place. Since he loved Marilyn it would be OK, the people would be sympathetic; and they also knew he was devoted to Ethel and the children. Maybe he wouldn't even have to resign. And even if that wasn't possible, it was better he should resign than for the President to be impeached. That would be a terrible shame on the whole family.

Think of your father!

I can't do it, he said. Not even for Jack. It wouldn't help him, either. There would still be the family disgrace. *You* must get rid of Marilyn and sleep there with him.

She couldn't. She'd just lost a baby. It was too soon.

Then it must be a family member.

They were with Rosemary in a convent. Black-robed nuns flitted around. Rosemary had put on a lot of weight. You must sleep with Jack, Bobby said; it's the only answer. A sister, a family member, would be OK. Rosemary nodded and smiled and Jackie felt relieved.

But Bobby was not happy; he felt guilty about Marilyn; the poor woman had suffered enough from the Kennedys. Perhaps if they gave her a lot of money she would feel better about being tossed out yet again. They'd have to have a family conference.

Her father-in-law in his wheelchair at the head of the table in Hyannis was animated; she hadn't seen him so lively for years. He punched the air, insisting that everything must be done to save Jack. Even if they had to sell all their stocks.

But Rosemary doesn't know how to, one of the girls said. And harshly he replied, Then she'll have to learn quick!

His wife was pouring water from a jug into all the glasses, but by the time she reached Jackie the jug was empty. Jackie felt resentful, and she was consumed with thirst.

The thirst half-woke her; she opened her eyes and saw Provi, her maid, sitting by the bed, neither awake nor asleep, in the faint nightlight. 'Can I have some juice, please?' Jackie murmured thickly; and Provi got up to pour orange juice into a glass and hand it to her. Jackie rose on her elbow to drink it. Handing the empty glass back she collapsed on to the bed again, her eyes closing.

She returned to Jack's hospital room, where he was making love with Marilyn. A priest covered in his blood was giving him the last rites. The naked woman, who had been sitting on Jack, clambered off him, turning sadly to face Jackie. She saw it wasn't Monroe but Princess Grace – so much more refined, how could she have mistaken her for Monroe? Well, she'd jumped to conclusions because of the poster of Monroe, upside-down, legs apart, above the bed. She herself had put it there to try to boost Jack's morale after the terrible back operation. 'I'm sorry,' she said to Grace, embracing her.

It was hopeless, the princess said, tearful, looking down at the clothed President in his casket, the priest babbling over him. – I thought maybe I could revive him. I must be losing my touch.

'Thank you for trying.'

Dressed in black, numbed with grief, she was in a Greek museum with her sister Lee and Aristotle Onassis. Passing a display case holding a number of famous black bronze heads, Jackie caught sight of one of the heads, that of Socrates, trying to address another, Plato. She saw Socrates' black lips move silently. She caught hold of Ari's sleeve, and he turned. When she'd described what had happened the fabulously rich shipowner said, It's possible; the dead can come alive in Greece. Our myths prove it. Euridice. Alcestis.

His broad lips curled; she couldn't see his magnetic eyes behind the dark glasses. Could *he* help her, she asked? To bring the dead to life? He shrugged. But who? Jackie hesitated, seeing Lee's eyes upon her. It had to be their father. That would be wonderful, it would console her for Jack's loss. My father, she said.

OK, yes. He shrugged again. It should be possible. We must go to Crete.

They stood at the entrance to a labyrinth, the brilliant blue sky burning their faces, their bare legs. Onassis stopped Lee from entering; he was sorry, it would be dangerous for more than two to enter. Jackie, who had lost father, husband and son, should have first claim.

Jackie saw jealousy flash into her sister's face; though she nodded and turned away.

Far underground. they were threading their way through a

maze, moving ever closer to the secret at the heart of it. She was stiflingly hot and her heart thudded. She asked would they find the Minotaur?

Not the Minotaur – your father. His voice echoed many times.

They turned one final corner and there, in a central room, stood a magnificent, black, shining horse.

I told you, Onassis said. Shall I leave you with him?

But this isn't my father.

He looked taken aback. 'But his name is Black Jack. This is Black Jack.'

Blinking back stinging tears of disappointment, she explained that Black Jack had only been his nickname. 'Oh – I'm sorry!' He was an ignorant Greek; he'd tried. And then he brightened. 'The riderless black horse can lead you to its master in the underworld. Mount it, and it will guide you to your husband.'

Full of hope again, she sprang on to Black Jack's back, tugged its mane, and it was bounding off. They flew through the Cretan landscape of stony mountains. She saw a brown deer leap away anxiously, and she suddenly thought: There are no deer in Greece! This landscape is familiar; I was here with Jack before the Inauguration. It's Johnson Hill Country! The wind taking her hair, she threw her head back and laughed in sheer relief. It was nothing but a dream, a trance. She and Jack were in the Hotel Texas. She had dreamed of his death because Dallas was worrying, they weren't looking forward to it. And the wound in his head was a memory of the weeping wound in his back, when he'd had the operations and nearly died.

When she opened her eyes she would see the pink suit hung up ready.

God, what joy it was! But perhaps the bad dream was a premonition. She should tell him about it, they must give Dallas a miss; those shots, his recoil, her scrambling up on to the trunk, had seemed all too real.

12

It's five in the morning in Washington. A white-coated technician, thinking herself alone in the FBI laboratory, jumps as a hand grasps her shoulder.

'Oh, it's you, Rick! You scared me!'

'I'm sorry, sweetheart. I couldn't get here any quicker. It's been quite a night – and I got stuck for a half-hour behind the funeral procession. You shoulda seen it! There were cars, three or four abreast, miles of 'em, just driving slowly towards the White House, following the hearse from Bethesda. It was spooky. There wasn't a sound. Anyway, how's it going?' He nods at the blank screen in front of her.

'It's awful. I'll have nightmares over it for the rest of my life.'

'Show me.' He straddles a chair, lights a cigarette. She switches the projector on. He sees the Lincoln in the middle distance, being driven slowly towards a seven-storey corner building; police outriders; spectators – a man with an arm resting on a woman's shoulder, a boy sitting astride a wall; the motor cycles and car turning the corner. For a moment a big sign obscures the car. Then the camera, held by an onlooker called Zapruder, concentrates on the Lincoln as it draws level.

'Holy shit!' the agent exclaims, the cigarette dangling from his lip.

'I know,' the technician whispers.

'What the hell is Mrs Kennedy doing? Is she trying to escape?'

'No, I don't think so. She picks something up off the trunk. A bullet? You can see it in slow motion.'

'OK, take it through again, frame by frame.'

He adds that she shouldn't speak about it; and she should forget what he's said about the shots. I wasn't listening, she says.

He waits for her to clear up, and turn out the lights. Then they walk out of the building together, past a tired security guard to whom they say good-night. Her high-heels clattering beside him, they head for their cars. Office windows are lit up, but there is no one about on the sidewalks, and few headlights pass them. The initial panic, in which many families drove out of the city in fear of a nuclear war, has faded. The city will soon be waking to its grief; hands will fumble for the knobs of televisions before switching on the percolators. The sets will stay on all weekend. JFK will smile at them in a thousand images, and still they won't believe he's dead. He's more alive to them on November 23, 1963 than he's ever been.

V

Black Jack

1

The phone by his bed roused Jack early. After talking to Bobby for about ten minutes he rang the kitchens to ask for coffee. It was brought by a stout, overawed Negress. He chatted with her for a while, setting her at ease. She'd worked for the Vice President here at the ranch for ten years. 'I don't remember seeing you on our last visit,' he said.

No, she'd missed that; she'd been in labour. In answer to his question she said it had been a boy. Lyndon. Her employer was a wonderful man. Jack promised her they'd have a photograph taken together.

When she'd gone, and he'd drunk the coffee, he opened the door leading into Jackie's bedroom.

Light glimmered between the curtains. He bent over her. Her eyes opened.

'Hi, sweetheart!' he murmured. 'Sleep well?'

She stretched, slid her hand out and stroked his silk-robed arm. 'I guess so.' Lifting herself on her elbow and switching on the bedside lamp, she smiled as she saw he was wearing the orange-and-white Longhorns cap given to him at Bergstrom Air Base. Idiot! she said, and he grinned and took it off.

She reached for her cigarettes and he lit one for her. Austin had been nice, she said. OK, the crowds hadn't roared like in Dallas, but they struck her as more sincere, more relaxed and human. She liked the little country-and-western bars and honky-tonks they'd glimpsed. She wouldn't have minded spending all the time in Austin.

221

He agreed it was her sort of town: artistic, full of character. He took her hand. He was grateful she'd come. Oh, I wouldn't have missed it, she said.

'Bobby called. He's very downhearted.'

'Oh why's that?'

'Well, mostly because of what happened at the Trade Mart. There's a big picture of me with my eyes closed and my hand to my cheek on the front page of the *Post*. I told him apart from that we've had a successful trip. But he's also depressed because Marcello, one of the top Mobsters, got acquitted yesterday. Bobby works his butt off trying to put the Mafia behind bars, and he gets them to trial, which is a miracle; but then jurors are bribed or threatened and find them not guilty. Bobby's really pissed off about it; I've rarely known him sound so down.'

'Uh-huh,' she murmured distantly, her eyes closed. It wasn't, he told himself, that she didn't feel for Bobby, she just couldn't raise an interest in political issues. He cast about for something else.

He had discovered a poem she would like. She stirred; opened her eyes. He recited 'Time and Again'. Yes, she murmured, that's beautiful. It was by Rainer Maria Rilke; did she know any other poems by her?

Her? Jackie laughed. 'Rilke was a man!'

'Oh! Then why the fuck did his mother call him Maria!' He grinned. 'He must have had real problems. Thank God I found out before Erhardt gets here!'

'I'm useful to you occasionally,' she said rather wistfully.

'No: time and again.' He squeezed her hand. Then, slipping off his dressing-gown, he pulled back the cover and climbed in; they nestled together. He lay with open eyes. The heavy curtains shone in the half-dark.

'I was reading Frost,' she said, reaching out her arm to touch a book on the bedside cabinet. 'A poem called "Home Burial". Do you know it?'

Jack shook his head, and she said it was very moving. About a woman who, from a window of her farm, can look out at the family graveyard where a recent baby is buried.

'I'll have to read it,' he said; though it was clear he wouldn't. The woman's husband doesn't even know why she stands at the window. Men are blind.

Birds had been singing for some time, but Jackie only grew aware of them now that she thought about the New England poet, who had died in the spring. At the moment there was a solo bird. 'That's a mocking-bird,' she said. 'It's honouring Frost.'

The white-haired, craggy old man at the Inauguration. Stumbling as the wind caught his paper. Then throwing it aside, and reciting a poem from memory. 'The land was ours before we were the land's . . . The land vaguely realising westward . . .' Vaguely realising, that's a helluva phrase. Then what a night I had! Two girls separate and then two together. Jesus Christ!

His arm around her, he stroked her soft, full hair. He felt no guilt about having just called a girlfriend in Washington, saying all sorts of crazy things like, I'm crazy about you, I'm dying to fuck you. It was meaningless; well, not meaningless, but it had nothing to do with his marriage to Jackie. He felt not tenderness exactly, as he stroked her hair, but a reaching out for tenderness. That emotion had surprised him a lot lately. He guessed that in the end of things he and Jackie would lie down together; though probably not in a little churchyard.

Why is he incapable, she thought, of saying, I love you? Is it because he doesn't feel it? Cannot feel it?

Gently disengaging from his arm, she got out of bed and walked to the bathroom. On her return she stood, in her white nightdress, with her back to him, gazing out through the chink in the curtains. She saw, and remembered from their previous visit, the grey-green hills, strewn with shrub-oaks and cedars. Dry, harsh, beautiful. 'It reminds me a little of a Greek Island,' she said. She had spent a few weeks in the summer on a Greek shipping-magnate's yacht.

She saw, close at hand, a big black bird on a branch, and then they heard its call: a long whistle followed by a chirr like a wind-up child's toy. The familiar bird-sound reminded her of John and Caroline, and the coming birthday party. She must not let it be tainted by sadness. She lay back down on the bed, outside the sheet.

She'd better get dressed, she said. She and Bird were going riding.

'Did you sleep with Onassis?' he asked.

'Of course not! What a stupid question!'

'You could have done, if you'd wanted to. We don't own each other. Nobody owns anyone else.'

'Well, I didn't want to. We've sworn to be faithful, do you remember?'

'I'm always faithful to you.'

She was out of breath, having run, kirtling her robes, to the Mother Superior's office, where the phone lay off the hook. She picked it up.

'This is Sister Agnes.'

'Hi! How are you? It's the President here. Hope I haven't dragged you away from something important?'

She still felt breathless, wondering why he was calling her again. 'No, it's a conversational period; Sister Beatrice and I were discussing some school work, that's all.'

'That's important. Did I meet Sister Beatrice?'

'Yes. She's young too; you spoke to her last.'

'I remember. Give her my best wishes. It helped me, recalling the warmth you all showed me, after that incident at the Trade Mart!'

'We're all ashamed that that happened to you; it was disgusting.'

'Oh, don't worry about it! It made her feel better. She'd lost a son in Korea, I can understand her feelings . . . Look, Sister Agnes, you're busy and I'll get to the point: I'd like you to come to Washington for a few weeks, or maybe longer, as a researcher and adviser on moral questions. I need an intelligent, open-minded young Catholic, preferably a Southerner, and my instinct tells me you're the person I'm looking for. Will you do that?'

She waited for the panic to settle before answering. 'It's a great honour, but I'm very happy here, Mr President. I like my quiet life, and I like teaching. I think anyway you must have the wrong person. Sister Beatrice is much more intelligent and much more – thoughtful about moral questions.'

Almost aggressively so, she thought. That suicide poem, read to impressionable teenagers. And she wasn't the least concerned about parental complaints.

'You really think so?' the President asked.

'Yes.'

There was silence; he was about to change his mind; she didn't know whether to be glad or sorry. Sister Beatrice wasn't looking well, nor happy, it would be a terrific boost to her morale; how jealous she'd looked when Sister Bernadette had rushed in to say the President was on the phone *again*.

'She'd be the ideal person,' she added.

'I want *you*.'

Her heart leapt with joy, even as her agitation increased. His words seemed an echo of something, she didn't know of what. 'Oh! Then of course I'll come! If I can get permission.'

'You'll get permission.'

When Jack had rung off he sat rubbing his chin. He must be careful. He must see that she wasn't hurt.

He started to draw on hunting boots.

'We'll turn back,' Lyndon said. 'We'll try the other slope. You'd think the motherfuckers knew we were comin'.'

Jack turned in his tracks reluctantly. He wanted to see what lay beyond that clump of low cedars. He was quite happy that there were no deer on this particular hill. He turned his head for a backward look, and remembered Frost:

> Spending what onward impulse they still had
> In one last look the way they must not go . . .

He liked those lines. He liked the whole poem, about those two lovers who are climbing a mountain at dusk – seeing at the last moment an image of themselves in the form of a buck and a doe. A kind of spell in which the lovers feel the love of the earth for them. Jackie had first acquainted him with the poem, and then the old man had read it to them at a White House dinner.

He owed Jackie a lot. Jackie was real. Sometimes it seemed the more pain and sense of there being something missing, the more real and precious.

But he needed someone else. A spiritual presence. *Mostly* spiritual. He sensed a yearning in that nun's eyes, a warmth in her hand-clasp. He could imagine a long relationship with her, maybe as long as a year; yet he wasn't sure what he wanted from it. Well, he could teach her something of the world, and she could teach him something about the spirit. They were perhaps arriving at Love from opposite directions.

'We'll have to call it a day soon. Bird gave me strict orders we were to eat at one. Not that I give a shit about her orders, but we've got a mighty fine cook and I don't like offending her. Apart from which, Bird has a suspicion about what I was doin' in my study last night with the Roberts woman.' He glanced aside at his guest. 'You OK?'

'I'm fine, Lyndon.'

'You're not still worryin' about that old crone at the Trade Mart? Don't. Today she's a heroine in the right-wing press, with her boy killed in Korea and all; but tomorrow she's gonna be a lush who drove him to leave home at fifteen. We've got a dozen character witnesses, including a daughter and brother, talkin' their mouths off to the press right now. So have yourself a good time. I just wish the sport was better.'

Jack saw the animal first. It poised between a spur of the hill and a cluster of cedars.

'Take it,' Johnson whispered; 'shoot the sonofabitch.'

The buck, motionless, scarcely bigger than a rabbit, dark-brown and white-tailed, gazed at them unafraid. It would be impossible to miss. Lyndon would be hurt if he didn't bring home a kill. He didn't know why he felt squeamish; he would sit down to lunch in half an hour and devour venison with a hearty appetite.

He raised his rifle and looked through the telescopic sight. The eyes of the buck seemed to be directly on him. He aimed steadily between those brooding, innocent eyes, and imagined they were filled with love for him. And that he himself felt love for it.

This was foolishness. It was the effect of that poem, and you couldn't let poetry rule your life. He eased his finger against the trigger. He saw the tender, intimate eyes glaze instantly in death. God, he hated death. He fought it with all he knew; every time he got inside a warm pussy he was fighting it. He loathed it, much more than Communism. Still, this had to be done, for Lyndon's sake.

At the moment of firing he jerked the rifle up. The buck bounded away and vanished behind a hill.

Later that day, they were flying over Tennessee, the light outside beginning to fade. Jackie, who was resting, heard him come back into the bedroom and sensed him standing near the bed, troubled by something.

'Was that Bobby again?' she asked drowsily, her eyes closed.

'Yes.'

'More problems?'

'Nothing we can't handle.' No, he'd just heard something sad. Did she remember the nuns he'd spoken to in Dallas? Well, Powers had called their convent about some matter, and they were in a terrible state. 'Do you recall the last nun I shook hands with?'

'The pretty one?' Jackie murmured, her eyes closed still.

'No – she had some kind of facial disfigurement.'

'I don't remember; I wasn't really watching. Anyway, what about her?'

'She's had an accident; a bus ran her over, early this afternoon. She'll live, but will probably lose both her legs.'

Jackie lifted herself on an elbow, shocked. 'Oh, that's terrible!'

'It is!'

'You must write to her.'

'I'm going to.'

From his crouched-over standing position he moved to sit by the window. Coming round from the operation to find you were crippled for life: it was unbearable; he'd rather be dead. He'd invite her to join Sister Agnes in Washington for a while, when she felt better. Sister Agnes would be delayed; she'd want to stay with her friend. He would write to her too.

He gazed down at the sunset-tinted cumulus, as his thoughts drifted cloud-like between that tragedy and Bobby's news. The utter fragility of life. One moment you were in full vigour, and the next – you couldn't even say it was darkness or emptiness; there was no *you* to say it. There was just old Black Jack. There seemed no sense to it all.

So this was the real reason Bobby had sounded so depressed in his morning call. He hadn't wanted to say, then, because he was at the Johnsons'. That sounded a pretty weird reason; surely he didn't think . . .? But shit, Bobby was right, he was damned lucky! An alternative world would have slid smoothly into place, thanks to a high-velocity bullet. He tried to imagine the unimaginable. Well, there'd have been one helluva commotion. Jackie, poor girl, would have collapsed – that was one certain thing. And the kids! His stomach knotted.

You could only rejoice that for you it wasn't yet, that you were fully alive. He thought back to the lady at Fort Worth. Catherine. She'd tried to help engineer his death by persuading him not to use the bubble-top; but he couldn't bring himself to feel mad at her. She had a swell ass and she'd given it to him. And that other, unknown woman who'd *saved* his life; a lady who maybe didn't want to eat breakfast with two burly cops but it was the only seat: someone had just decided against more coffee and stood up. And they got talking because they liked her tits, and there was a lull, so she just happened to mention something odd she'd seen when driving through Dealey Plaza. And the cops weren't busy so they decided to check it out. The gunmen arrested ten minutes before they were due through. Jesus, that was close! That was as close as you could get unless you were in the Pacific with Jap bullets flying; or you were in hospital in a semi-coma and heard a priest giving you absolution. You were just a moment, a fleck of foam, a breath. But America stretched beneath you; some small town's glimmering lights. You were watching your wife sit up and comb her hair. You were riding home.

2

She was bearing the weight of his gross body on the museum's leather couch, his stubble rasping against her cheek. 'Do you believe me?' he grunted.

'Yes.'

'Do you forgive me?'

'Yes.'

'This ain't no rape, d'you hear? You ain't gonna run out and tell the cops you was raped. Because if you was to do that I'd blow your fuckin' head off.'

'You won't have to do that. I touched you.'

'Yes, you touched me. You're no fuckin' nun. Your sister's real cold, that Sister Beat, but you're different. I don't rape women no more. Anyway, I ain't screwin' you. I just got my fingers in your little pussy. Open your eyes and see – it's good!'

She opened her eyes and looked down. Her clothes were up round her waist and she could see his hand pumping between her bare thighs. It looked like a hand with only two fingers and a thumb. It hurt her but there was also a tingling feeling, not unpleasant.

'Did you really shoot him?'

'I shot him. I shot him good.'

The ripples started and she gasped, and chuckled. The replica blue Lincoln was spinning in the background. And then she was jerking awake, and she was in her room, pitch-black. Her heart was beating fast, her pelvic area throbbing, and the sheet tangled round her was drenched.

She lay quietly and her heart stilled little by little, the orgasm dying away. 'Oh Lord Jesus!' she murmured, her eyes tight shut, tears pressing out between the lids.

The tumult stilled further; she could feel her heart beating normally at last. But her mind was not calm. She sought words to still her mind; and she found in her memory the mysterious sentence, written by a medieval English mystic, that she had first wrestled with in the Saturday-morning study period after Kennedy's death. *Sin is Behovely, and all shall be well, and all manner of thing shall be well.* It had been incomprehensible then, even offensive. Everything, it seemed to say, was good; everything was for the best.

How could that be so? What would Dame Juliana have said if she'd lived today? The papers had been full of a gang-rape trial in New York. A jogger had been set upon by black kids in Central Park; after raping her they had beaten her until she was unrecognisable and left her for dead. They had thought it was fun. Thirty years after the dream that Kennedy and Martin Luther King had believed in, there were more black youths in prison than in college. Millions of young male blacks were dead from drugs or drug murders. That dream of her youth had also turned into nightmare.

Kennedy's eloquent words in Berlin had become greed for Deutschmarks. The dream of sexual freedom and women's rights had resulted in a holocaust of the unborn, unhappy children of broken homes, her nephew in a sexual death-row in LA.

But why look for evil outside of herself? That was a cop-out. What she'd dreamed of was as bad as any of the world's vast crimes. She'd even been aware of a perverted desire, those months ago in the museum. When he'd grasped her wrist. She'd been terrified he was going to make her touch his groin, where she was conscious of or imagined a bulge. Terrified – but also wanting him to, almost.

And what of Jackie? That girl who'd had the breakdown after watching the Zapruder film with her so many times? When she'd cried, and she'd held her to comfort her, her long fair hair brushing against her cheek, she'd felt a thrill go through her. She was sure she was not gay, yet she had trembled, she had trembled. Afterwards too, thinking back to it. Then, frightened, she had buried it. Until tonight. Until this.

She was ignorant in the only important area, herself. She had no self-knowledge. All this had been lurking for years and she never knew it. And it was too late for self-discovery.

Should she have chosen a normal life: boyfriends, husband, children? Maybe a normal sex-life would have helped her. Carnal knowledge they called it. But she might have discovered things about herself she wouldn't have been able to cope with. Just as she couldn't cope with this.

Switching on the lamp, she got out of bed, steadied herself, and went to the bookshelves. She would read those pages again. Maybe she'd missed something, all these years. The shelves were in shadow, but she knew by heart where the slim black book was, and she plucked it out. Hobbling back to her bed she sat down, and opened the book – rather, it fell open at the familiar page. The text was a blur, but she knew it was the right place because she could feel with her fingers the crinkly texture where her tears had fallen, that morning. She reached for her reading glasses and put them on.

She found she couldn't read the text. At first, shocked, she thought someone must have substituted a foreign-language copy, in an alien alphabet; for what she saw were lines of hieroglyphics. Then she thought it must be the wrong book. But no, it clearly wasn't: there were her pencil-marks, made that long-ago morning, but these too were unreadable. Her heart started to beat quickly, and she felt sick to the stomach. She couldn't read. She had forgotten how to read.

She went to the shelves again, and looked along the titles. It was the same. She only knew most of them because they were so familiar. She would not have been able to read even *War and Peace* on the spine if she had not known exactly where the paperback was, and its colour.

She panted, experiencing sheer panic. So much so that she

couldn't control her bladder and the urine was splashing on the floor before she could move. She could only crouch in her nightie and let it flow. Then she began to cry.

She got a towel and wiped up the puddle as best she could. As she did so she heard warring voices inside her head. You can't read. No shit. If only he'd let her learn English she'd be OK. Aren't you glad you were there? What if you hadn't been there? I'm just a patsy. They'll think I'm stupid; well, I'm not stupid, no sir. I'm just dyslexic.

After a while the voices died down. Her dream was by now almost forgotten; she was only aware of this terrifying illness that had come upon her in the night; something neurological, she supposed. A brain tumour?

She stumbled around in a tight circle, her hands clasped. What to do? What to do?

Her father had taught her to read. Jean had told her so. She herself had forgotten all about it. Had taught them both. Curled up with him in the big armchair in his study. The thought of her father made her yearn for that security, the tobacco smell that clung to his vest. Time, time was the real assassin; changing Marina Oswald into Mrs Porter, with three teenage children and a farm, a greenhouse, a flower garden. Changing her father into a wheezy old man; bringing this fearful cancer upon her.

Even blindness would be better; you could use braille. But not to be able to read – that was an unbearable punishment.

She was quite sure it was punishment, for all her sins. Kennedy's death had been the first stage of it. That jealousy she'd been carrying round, because her parents were vacationing with her sister . . . And that lust, when Kennedy pressed her hand . . . She'd been very wicked.

The first thing is to try to clear her head; stop herself trembling. She will look at something beautiful, something religious. Then, when she has stopped trembling, she will sit down and work out a course of action.

Sister Agnes walked to her desk and picked up an art book she'd been reading for her course on the Renaissance with the seniors. Titian's *Pietà*, it always comforted her with its deep spirituality. She found the page. On one side the reproduction, on the other – the baffling signs.

She gazed at the picture. Kennedy was almost naked, lying in the arms of Jackie – only for some reason she was wearing a scarf or shawl over her head instead of the pink pill-box hat. Standing near them was Rosemary Kennedy, her mouth open in a hysterical cry and her arm flung out. It was clearly she, though she'd been nowhere near Dallas, she had been and still was in a convent in Jefferson, Wisconsin. And the scene was too dark for Love Field; everybody knew the clouds and rains had cleared.

Overhead floated a winged child. Little Patrick Bouvier. Just two days old. The world held too much pain.

Her blurred eyes and mind cleared at the same moment. Now she was concentrating her gaze on the dying Christ. He'd absorbed her whole energy, used up her whole life, so that she was like a pre-school child again, unable to read the simplest words.

A tear splashed on Love Field.

'You prick! You fucking bastard!'

The obscenities rose out of some deep source within her, and gave her some relief. Picking up the Thanksgiving card she had bought, and her pen, she tried to write a short, comforting message for her parents, but she'd forgotten how to write. She pulled open the drawer again and took out a bottle of whisky. It was half full; Jean had left it in case her pain got real bad sometime. Well, the pain was real bad. Unscrewing the top she drank from the bottle; and went on drinking, standing before the open window, the sultry, heavy darkness. November had been exceptionally warm, with brilliant skies. She drew in the air with deep breaths. But oxygen was only a chance element thrown up by chaos.

Dizzy, she walked to the bed and picked up her bottle of painkillers. One of the voices started up: Hey, what the fuck are you doin'? You'll kill us all, you dumb cunt!

Oswald? No: her scalp prickled. Ferrie.

They were all inside her. Both assassins and victims. Even Marina, alienated, orphaned; even Tippit – she heard sometimes a rather childish voice that she knew was he. 'Who gives a shit about *me*?' he would say, sounding at the same time like a Texan cop and a small, desperately unhappy child. And Ferrie, unbelievably evil and depraved. A part of her mind. Even if he hadn't been like that in reality. Sister Beatrice, dear Sister Beatrice, had written of the assassination as drama. Well, there was no need for a stage; the drama had taken up residence in her, Sister Agnes's, mind, and every moment of her life was the moment between firing and impact.

She had the weird feeling they had been inside her even when she'd spoken to the President. And long before that. Perhaps everyone felt like it but kept it hidden. Well, for her it was no longer bearable.

She emptied the bottle out. It was going to be easy to die. Unless Ferrie or Oswald took her over and stopped her. She must hurry.

She swallowed one pill, then another, with water. She was feeling sick. She prayed she wouldn't vomit before the task was done. Some of the nuns and girls would miss her, but not for long. They would weep for a day and then she would be history.

3

Johnson, in the west wing of the White House, put down the phone, then pressed a buzzer. He spoke into an intercom: 'Ask the Senator to come in.'

He stood up, loosened his tie, and composed his face into an expression of intense sorrow, his features crumpling; already tired eyes became more swollen; without quite being able to weep he became an embodiment of tears. The grey sky outside the big window was not more melancholy.

The door opened and Senator Kennedy entered. Despite his neat and well-fed appearance, black tie and white shirt pigeoning over his buttoned jacket, it was easy to see he had not slept and was shattered, yet by comparison with Johnson he looked euphoric. Johnson lurched forward and threw his arms round him. 'Ted!' he said in a breaking voice. 'What can I say? Jack was like a brother to me too. We're gonna miss him so much.'

He stepped back at last, thought about asking him to sit down but decided not to. There was a lot to be done. 'You're flying up to Hyannis, Ted?'

'That's right. I have to tell Dad. They've been pretending all the TVs have broken down.'

'I don't envy you your task.'

'It's going to be – ' He stopped, unable to continue.

'How's your Mom takin' it?'

The Senator sighed. 'Oh, she's taking it as Mom always does. Her faith's like a rock.'

Johnson sighed. More a sob than a sigh. 'And your family's been through so much. Joe Junior, your sister Kathleen. Poor Rosemary. Now Jack, the worst blow of all. It's too much for one family.'

If there was anything he could do. Anything. He wouldn't keep him; he appreciated his looking in. And again if there was *anything* he could do. He took the Senator by the elbow, escorting him to the door. 'Ted, I need your support in the Senate more than Jack needed it. We'll get those bills through. I don't want this job, but I'll just have to do my best, for Jack's sake.' He pulled out a handkerchief and blew his nose. 'It's like a nightmare. Shit, we should be out huntin' together right now!'

The Senator looked at him sorrowfully. 'I guess Jack was the hunted, Mr President.'

'I guess he was. That rattlesnake – I'd like to personally break his friggin' neck.'

When his footsteps had faded, Johnson called through the door: 'I'll see Mr Hoover now. Rustle up some coffee for me and a glass of cowjuice for him.'

He returned to his chair, sat in it and tilted it back, his hands behind his head. He looked at a television screen, its sound turned off. Jackie and the kids kneeling before the catafalque. Hoover, black-tied, turtle-faced, entered the office. Johnson pulled himself upright and threw his arm out. 'Thanks for comin', Edgar! Take a seat!'

'Thank you, Mr President.'

Hoover sat erect, perfectly still, like a stone Pharaoh. He touched an impeccable white cuff. A secretary slipped in with coffee and milk. Hoover took a sip of milk and waited for Johnson to speak. He took his time, blowing on the hot coffee.

'Edgar, who's at the centre of the web?'

Hoover replied unemotionally and in a monotone, 'The Soviet Embassy staff think it was you, Mr President.'

Johnson considered this, drinking. 'And some of my people think it could have been you, Edgar.'

'I'm not smart enough, Mr President. Looking for the centre of the web is pointless. No President has been more detested. It's happened, that's all that matters; the important thing now is that it should be investigated thoroughly, subject to national security. Presumably you want the Bureau to carry out the investigation. I'd like to have seen it through myself, but I'm sure my successor, whoever he is, will do just as good a job.'

Johnson stood up and began to pace. 'I was hoping it could be concluded before you have to go out of office, Edgar.'

That might be so. But no one could guarantee that a successor would not rake over the ashes. 'Also, Mr President, as anyone would expect, given your long political career, you yourself have some enemies. Who have presented the Bureau with so-called evidence of malpractice.'

Such as what?

Election-rigging, taking bribes; even inducement to murder. Absurd accusations. He would have been able to bury them for the duration of this presidency, and perhaps permanently, if only he wasn't obliged by law to retire soon.

'We'll change that law. We're old friends. I know I can work with you, Edgar.'

'I shall be proud to serve a President of good character once more.'

Slumping in his chair again, running a hand over his hair, Johnson said tiredly: 'Tell me about Oswald.'

The further you went into Oswald, the less you knew. He might not even be the same Oswald who joined the Marines. It was impossible to say if he was right-wing or left-wing. There seemed to be several different Oswalds, appearing simultaneously in different places.

'So – a perfect patsy?'

That would be one interpretation. His Russian wife was another complication. She seemed straightforward, but in Moscow she'd visited an address where American turncoats were interrogated. The likelihood, however, was that Oswald acted without her knowledge, in consort with one or more other person.

But it was also perfectly possible, Hoover continued after a sip of milk, that Oswald was solely responsible. And if that were found to be the case it would be the best result. For the Kennedy family too. They wouldn't want the former President's private life dredged up out of the mud; and he had no wish to subject them to further suffering. The late President would be the first to say, Don't go into this thing too deeply.

Johnson nodded. 'I say amen to that, Edgar. But what about the doctors and nurses at Parkland? They all said it was a frontal shot.'

'They can change their minds. It was total chaos, and they were concentrating on trying to save his life.'

Johnson nodded, uncertain. 'And what about Oswald's trial? We can't control what's said at a trial.'

'That's a long way off. A lot can happen before then.'

Johnson gazed through the window at the murky light, then turned to stare at the TV. Hoover followed his gaze. They saw Mrs Kennedy, in a black coat, coming out after Mass, John and Caroline's hands in hers. 'The tragic queen,' Johnson said.

'I'm surprised she isn't still wearing the pink suit. That was in very bad taste; someone should have made her change.'

'We tried.' They saw Robert Kennedy come into view: stumbling a little, his eyes vacant. 'At least that little runt Bobby will be dancing to a different piper.'

'Who's Bobby?' Hoover responded, allowing himself a brief smile.

The smile vanishing, he continued. 'He won't be able to take the law into his own hands any more. Bundling Mr Marcello on to a plane for Guatemala, with only the clothes he had on, was a disgrace. You've heard he was acquitted?'

Johnson nodded.

'There's no case against him. Marcello's a businessman. If he went out of business so would Louisiana.' The Attorney General had been motivated by pure malice; and Hoover hoped the new President would step down the campaign against so-called organised crime. It didn't exist. It was all based on unfounded rumours. For instance, Marcello's so-called gambling and illicit betting interests in Texas: the same people who accused him of that were saying that fifty thousand a year from it went into Johnson's pocket. There was no limit to their malice.

'Scale the investigation down, Edgar,' Johnson said.

'Thank you.'

Johnson glanced at the TV monitor: Hoover followed his gaze. People pressing up against barriers, many weeping.

What had surprised him, Johnson said, was all this hysteria.

It was just shock; it would soon pass.

'No one believes I'm President, Edgar.' His face took on some of the earlier grief.

'They will.'

'Y'know, I hear those shots all the time. Even when I managed to get my head down on the pillow for a couple of hours, I heard them.'

Hoover nodded sympathetically. 'It must have been very unpleasant.'

'Unpleasant! Dammit, Edgar, it was a total screw-up! If they had to kill him, why the fuck didn't they use just one good sniper? We wouldn't've had to shit-ass around like incompetent hoods.'

With a lift of two plump ringed fingers Hoover deplored and forgave the obscenities. Then he was motionless again, his short thick neck seeming to withdraw deeper into his tight white collar. His eyelids gave a slow, saurian blink.

The Everglades, Johnson thought. Hoover belongs to the Everglades. Then the slow, heavy monotone started again.

'I know. That bothered me too. We can only guess. You've been enormously brave, Mr President. Here's a President of the United States, worshipped by liberals, and his corpse has been hauled around and cut open and tricked-up on his successor's orders, deprived of all dignity. The nation has been deceived. I actually woke up this morning in a sweat, thinking of your bravery. Would anyone understand the necessities of state that dictated your action? We both know the answer. So it follows it must never come out. Not in fifty years, not in a thousand. And that means it must *all* be buried. We've got to see it's put in a concrete overcoat and sunk. If there *were* conspirators, who could ask for more?'

'Jesus Christ.'

Controlling his distaste for the blasphemy, Hoover held the President's ravaged gaze for a while, then shifted his eyes to the screen. They were arriving at Love Field yet again; unable to broadcast normally, the TV companies were encouraging the hysteria with endless repeats of sentimental images like this one. Hoover wondered what Communist in the media had proposed banning all advertising until after the funeral.

4

She emerged first, blinking, into the bright, warm sunlight. Cameras caught them as they paused for a second. The distant crowd clapped and cheered, drowning the scatter of boos. With a wave and smile, they climbed down the ramp. Lyndon and Lady Bird stepped forward. 'Welcome to Dallas, Mr President!' Lyndon said, his hooded eyes twinkling. Their hands clasped.

'It's good to be here, Lyndon!'

'You're a goddamn liar!' Lyndon hissed under his breath. He grasped Jack by the elbow and propelled him towards the welcoming delegation, drawn up in a row. Just one friendly, welcoming face; the rest stony. But their faces broke into warmth as Connally, ignoring protocol, rushed up to them first, pumping hands. The faces became masks once more as Jack went along the line of light-suited, Stetsoned men; they greeted him courteously, coolly. The Mayoress stepped forward and presented Jackie with a bouquet of red roses. 'We want you to know Dallas is a friendly city. We're sure you're going to enjoy your visit.'

'These are wonderful! Thank you! I've had yellow roses all through Texas, these are the first red ones.'

'They go with your suit.'

'You're right! They're perfect.'

'Let's go meet the people,' Jack said to Lyndon; and they strode, carefully avoiding puddles, across the field. Security men trod in their wake, their eyes alert, darting about.

'It'll soon be over,' said Lyndon. 'You can relax at my ranch, do whatever you feel like. And in the morning, you and I are going hunting!'

'That'll be great,' Jack said, though his heart quailed.

'The sport's been real good this fall.'

The clapping became enthusiastic as they drew near; the boos and hisses increased in volume too. Someone at the rear was waving a Confederate flag. The hands were reaching out to grasp the President's, and Johnson stopped, hung back.

Jack went quickly along the line of eager, enraptured people, the embattled Democrats of Dallas. 'It feels good to be here.' 'Thank you!' 'Thank you for coming!' 'From Boston? Really? How do you like it here?' He was heading as quickly as possible towards a bunch of teenage boys who had been hissing. They fell into a sullen, embarrassed silence as he came up close. He offered his hand to each of them; reluctant at first, they shook his hand.

'What school are you from, boys?'

'Thomas Jefferson High.'

'Well, it's named after a very noble man. Don't you agree?'

A few of them nodded, looking doubtful. Yet they couldn't help feeling a little excited too. Talking to the President. Even if their parents and teachers told them he was a disgrace to the Presidency.

'Jefferson once said that a little rebelliousness can be a good thing. I agree with that. I guess you're playing hookie from school?'

They flushed, hung their heads.

'Well, that's OK by me,' he said, in that voice so much more clipped and laconic than theirs. 'You don't get to see a President all that often. Just remember the Presidency is greater than the incumbent. You might hate a particular President, and think he shouldn't hold that position, but you should respect the Presidency. It's good you question authority. But question *all* authority. Don't act out of prejudice; think for yourselves. Jefferson was a Southerner; but he despised slavery.'

Ignoring them then, he stretched over their heads to shake the hand of an old, gap-toothed Negro. The Negro called, above the crowd-noises, 'I have a dream!'

His back is hurting and the sun is burning down fiercely. But you have to go with such things. It won't be long; Jackie, separated from him by the red roses, is squirming in the plush seat, making her discomfort obvious, which irks him a little. She has put on her sunglasses; and, although the few people lurking along Lemmon Avenue seem to be staring through rather than at their President and First Lady, it's important that they see her and that she smiles.

'Take off your glasses, Jackie.'

He said the words without a break in his friendly wave, and as if he were saying, 'Isn't this terrific?' She removed them, held them in her pink-skirted lap. The lead-car, a white Ford containing the police chief and the sheriff, moved ahead quite quickly. They hadn't really expected any spectators on this first stretch, past a sprawl of ugly factories. Televisions, slacks, motor parts: this was where the American dream was being manufactured, he thought; but the faces of the workers who chewed gum and stared blankly didn't reflect that dream. Colourless lives.

Real Sippin' Whisky. Kwiksnax. Home of the Big Boy Hamburger.

A stretch with no spectators and she found relief for a few moments behind the sunglasses. Then there were a couple of gangling men in Stetsons, looking like extras in a western, lounging against a fence, and she had to remove the glasses again. She smiled; they stared through her, and one of them spat on the sidewalk. She didn't break her smile. She wished she could light a cigarette. An underpass gave a momentary blessed coolness.

'MR PRESIDENT, PLEASE STOP AND SHAKE OUR HANDS.'

'Let's stop, Bill!' he called to the driver; and Bill Greer brought the Lincoln to a halt. Governor Connally and his wife, who were in the jump-seats, glanced round, disconcerted.

244

Jack had bounded out and was engulfed by excited children. He was shaking their hands, ruffling hair, asking them where they went to school, which football teams they supported, did they know the name of their state governor – he was that man sitting there.

Agents clambered out and gently broke up the party. Jack climbed back in. 'Nice kids.'

Mrs Connally turned round again and said to him, 'That was a lovely gesture. They'll never forget it.'

5

The giant glass and steel columns of the city centre loomed ahead, close now. The groups of people were more frequent, friendlier, excited. The sun also seemed to be hotter; Jackie couldn't put her glasses on but occasionally she had to close her eyes, almost lulled asleep by the sun. She felt the heat burning through her layers of clothes. Her stockings stuck to her thighs. She longed to be out of them, out of her clothes, diving into a pool.

'Those nuns must be hotter than we are, and they're not complaining,' Jack said, nodding towards the cluster of people just ahead of them. 'Stop again, Bill.' He was out of the car almost before it had halted, and in among a small group of beaming, black-habited nuns. 'What convent are you from, sisters?'

'The Sacred Heart,' said a plump, rosy-cheeked old nun. Instead of taking his offered handshake she bent and kissed his hand. 'We pray for you, Mr President.'

'Thank you. I need your prayers.'

'We're so proud to have a Catholic President,' said a much younger nun. He turned his eyes to her. A shy, sweet, candid face; for a few moments, as they shook hands, their eyes met. Her gaze seemed to pierce right through him, to sense all his weaknesses, yet to forgive him everything. 'Do you pray for me too?' he asked.

'Oh, of course.' She blushed, dropped her eyelids.

'Then I can sleep easily.'

She opened her mouth to speak again, hesitated, then said, 'You taught my father how to sail a PT-boat!'

'Oh? What's his name?'

'Mason. Jerry Mason.'

Jack frowned, trying to recall. To help him she said, 'He was older than most, he'd been a teacher for several years in Atlanta before he volunteered for the Navy. He says you enjoyed his piano-playing.'

'I remember him! How's he doing?'

'He's fine.'

'Give him my best.'

She nodded, still smiling, her eyes still full on him; he was aware that she knew he didn't remember, yet was grateful for the courteous untruth in front of the others – to whom he now turned, a warm glance taking them all in. 'I am grateful to you, sisters.'

He pressed their hands and exchanged a few words with each.

There was a young nun who held back. Beautiful brown eyes peered out from her habit, but she had a terrible skin problem; perhaps a burn. He took her hand and drew her towards him. 'Is there one thing you think your government could do more about?' he asked.

Her eyelids lowered, avoiding his gaze. 'I think women have a hard time,' she whispered.

'I agree with you. We haven't done nearly enough for women . . . Where are you from?'

'Galveston.'

'I must go there on my next visit.'

After giving her hand a squeeze, he let go, waved to the nearby spectators, and went back to the car. As they moved off his eyes rested again briefly on the nun who was proud to have a Catholic President. She was staring at Jackie, smiling.

He kept the image of the young, pure nun as the motorcade moved forward again, bearing right and passing through Oak Lawn Park. A statue; dignified pose, beard: Robert E. Lee. He ought to refer to Lee at the Trade Mart. His nobility in the agonising problem of loyalty that he faced at the start of the Civil War. 'Though I love the Union and detest war, I cannot in all honour fight against my own people, my own blood.' So he took the fateful ride across the Long Bridge to Virginia. Yet never crossed the bridge into baseness and dishonour.

Lee, the finest spirit of American integrity. Lee and Lincoln in essence on the same side, as Lincoln recognised in his great speech of reconciliation over the Gettysburg dead. A hundred years ago, almost to the day. I don't apologise for quoting such famous words: 'Four score and seven years ago our fathers brought forth upon this continent a new nation conceived in liberty and dedicated to the proposition that "all men are created equal". Now we are engaged in a great civil war, testing whether that nation, or any nation so conceived and so dedicated, can long endure . . . In a larger sense we cannot dedicate – we cannot consecrate – we cannot hallow this ground. The brave men, living and dead, who struggled here have consecrated it far above our poor power to aid or detract . . .'

And then how about – In a sense we are still engaged in that civil war; there are still hatreds and divisions, there is still enslavement in our country . . . Lee. He should come back to Lee. He should say more about him. It would be a difficult speech.

The sidewalks were crowded now. People thought he looked preoccupied.

6

'But you're going to be OK, Tessa?'

Her mother was crying down the phone.

'I'm going to be fine. I'm just very tired, Mom; that's why my voice is slurred.'

'Are the nurses good to you?'

'They're wonderful. And the doctors. Parkland's a fine hospital. I'm surrounded by roses. Thank you for yours, they're beautiful – the best.'

'Oh, you've got them? I'm glad.' Sister Beatrice had been so kind to them; she was such a sweet lady. 'Thank God she heard your screams, Tessa!'

'Yes. God was good. Most of the sisters are too old and deaf to have heard. He saved me from my own stupidity, sleeping with the window open when I'm on the ground floor.'

But she didn't think it could have been the man who'd confessed to her at the museum preview. He'd been sincere. It might have been someone higher up, whom he'd told about it. It was bad that all that had come out in the press and on TV; she'd told no one but Sister Beatrice, and now the police.

'All that matters is you're safe. And they want you to come home with us, to recuperate. You're to have three months off. It'll be wonderful; Jean's coming home for Christmas – we'll be all together.' Sister Agnes heard her mother's voice, which had brightened a little, grow husky again. 'It'll be the first time in thirty years!'

'That would be good!'

'Sweetheart, your father's just coming . . .' Sister Agnes heard the thump of his wheelchair descending the hallway step. 'I'll hand you over to him.' She would call again in the morning, after church.

'OK, Mom. Goodbye. I love you.'

'I love you too.'

She heard her father's frail, shaky tones. She assured him she was all right. He asked her if she remembered what had happened yet. No, she remembered nothing. She'd felt a fool, not being able to give the police the least help. It was probably nature's mercy, he said, till she felt stronger. 'You're coming to us, honey; we've been in touch with Mother Inez and she agrees you should come home and have a good long rest and recuperation.'

'I know – Mom said. That'll be good.' Feeling the tears gather, she whispered, 'Dad, I can't read.'

'You *what*?'

'I can't read. They say it's an effect of the shock to my system, and that it'll come back. But what if it doesn't?' She choked up. 'I don't think I could live if I couldn't read. I'm trying hard to forgive whoever did this to me, but it would be hard if I can't read ever again.'

'You'll read again, honey,' he said. 'I'll teach you. I'll teach you again. You'll be readin' in no time. You were a quick reader, quicker than Jeannie. We'll start fresh over!' There was a chuckle with a sob in it.

'OK, we'll do that! I better go; I'm kinda tired. I love you, Dad.'

'Love you, sweetheart.'

She stretched to put down the receiver by her bed; closed her eyes, exhausted.

A buxom Mexican nurse came in with a glass of milk, and she was lifted up, her pillows plumped, to drink it. She picked up the fall issue of *November 22*, fresh off the press. Wedges of hieroglyphics, page after page. She looked at the pictures. There was a variation on the famous picture of the arrival at

Love: a print never before seen in public. She shivered. They were close; close.

A stout, sixtyish consultant, with a lantern jaw and fringes of red hair round a bald dome, comes in and sits for a while, chatting. The scan showed there was no organic damage; the reading problem would clear up as the shock receded. How terrible it was that someone should try to murder a frail nun! And, even worse if that was possible, trying to make it look like suicide. He despaired of America.

He'd never believed in a conspiracy before, but this was making him think. He'd worked on the President, had been with him from the moment he came in to the moment they put him in the casket. And he could vouch there'd been no entry wounds from the front. But whoever had killed him, they'd sure done right for America, in his view.

The phone rings again, and he pats her arm and leaves. The call is from Jean. She sounds torn between anxiety for Tessa and pleasure, since her attorney lover has got her half the house in Weston as well as the New York apartment, which she can sell because she's moving in with him.

Thanks for the roses, Sister Agnes says; they're beautiful. The first red roses I've had. Hearing a light knock on her door she covered the mouthpiece with her hand and called, in as strong a voice as she could manage, Come in. A familiar grey head, tousled like a mop, peeped round. The patient smiled a welcome and Sister Beatrice tiptoed to the bedside chair. 'I have to go,' Sister Agnes told Jean, ignoring her visitor's silent protestation that there was no hurry. 'Sister Beatrice has come to see me.' They said goodbye and she replaced the receiver. Her friend took the phone from her and placed it on the bedside table; then they hugged.

'You look so much better. I was worried sick, seeing you still in a coma yesterday.'

'I'm on the mend.'

'Thank God!' Her pale lips trembled, she was on the verge of tears. 'I don't think I have to tell you how much you mean to me?'

Sister Agnes took her gnarled hand. 'We go back a long way. You're closer to me than my own sister . . . And here, you've saved my life once again!'

No, she'd saved herself, Sister Beatrice said. By having the courage and strength to break free, just for a moment, and to scream for help, even though she was almost unconscious from the whisky and the drugs they'd been forcing down her. 'The nurse said you don't remember a thing?'

Sister Agnes shook her head.

'It's no wonder, my dear. The police found a stocking-mask down by the creek. Of course they don't know yet if it belonged to one of your attackers, but it almost certainly does.'

'How did you find me? How *was* I?'

'We pushed the door open and you were lying crumpled-up against it, in your nightie.'

'And you didn't see anybody?'

'Sister Elizabeth thought she saw a figure running off through the trees, but she's not sure. Your screams must have scared them off.'

Sister Agnes sighed. She remembered undressing for bed; that was all.

Thank God, her friend said, she hadn't been sexually abused. She'd been fearful of that, when the police told her about the other abuse.

Her eyes widened; her body tensed forward. 'What other abuse?'

'Haven't they told you? They found a towel soaked in urine. They think he – or they – urinated on the floor and made you get down on your hands and knees and wipe it up.'

'God forgive them.' Sister Agnes crossed herself.

'It's unforgivable, what was done to you. Even by God . . . I feel so terrible, sister' – she squeezed her hand – 'for having doubted you. I've been blind. You were right all along. Forgive me.'

'It's OK.' She laid her head back on the pillow, and sighed.

'You're tired, you must rest. I'll be back tomorrow.' They would miss her at the Thanksgiving dinner; yet they would have much to be thankful for. 'Everyone wants to come in and see you, when you're well enough. They send their thoughts and love.'

'Thank them for the lovely flowers.'

'I will. I brought some books and magazines.' She slid her hand into a shopping bag. 'You got your journal? I left it with the nurse for you – oh, and some peaches.'

'Thank you,' she whispered. Her eyes were shut. Sister Beatrice leaned over to kiss her on the forehead, then tiptoed out on squeaky sneakers.

Now, three floors up in Parkland Hospital, there is silence again. Sister Agnes listens to it.

She thinks about what the consultant said. No sign of front-entry. You could tell he was lying. He talked at me as if I was a moron.

Books. I can't even tell what their titles are. It's so difficult, surrounded by words in an unfamiliar alphabet. A kind of permafrost in my heart, a frozen-over Neva. Shirley's too. She loves me. I felt it when she kissed me on the brow.

It was good to fall asleep, knowing that she was loved.

She woke, feeling clearer-headed, and to a clear, dazingly blue sky outside. Twenty-seven years ago, it had been raining; Brenda Johnson was at this hour showing her the *Wanted For Treason* leaflet.

She always felt especially confused and strange when Thanksgiving fell on the anniversary day. And how weird it was that she was in Parkland. But that was thanks to the weirdness that her attacker or attackers had chosen just this week. She hadn't really given a thought to Kennedy all semester, since putting the fall issue to bed: until this week, when she'd been reminding her pupils of what had happened in their city. Pupils whose only interest in the Kennedys was that their lives had closely touched the life and perhaps death of a screen idol.

Maybe as it was Thanksgiving she wouldn't be bothered by the police today. She really could tell them no more. They were doubtful, as she was, it had anything to do with Wayne Hines, though they were trying to trace him. They thought he was just a loony. Why should those who felt threatened by his confession wait three months? Their theory, while they waited for forensic reports, was that someone felt she had some information as a result of being editor of *November 22*. Well, she could think of nothing.

A nurse came in with a breakfast tray, and Sister Agnes got out of bed to go to the bathroom. She didn't need any help walking; in fact there was freer movement and less pain than she'd felt for ages. A shock can do that, said the nurse; it can drive arthritis into remission. Wouldn't that be wonderful?

The nurse was new, a fill-in for regular nurses who were at home with their families; she didn't know about the patient's reading problem and she handed her a *Time* magazine, brought in by Sister Beatrice, to read while eating her cereal. After she'd gone, Sister Agnes tossed the magazine aside; but then she thought: How did I know it was *Time*? She dropped her spoon and grabbed at the magazine; but the four big symbols on the cover were unreadable. She sipped her juice, and wondered why there had been more relief than disappointment in the discovery.

She didn't want to read again, she decided. Not yet. It was good to be like a child. To enter again the Kingdom of Heaven, to be suffered to come unto Him, in innocence. To become a primitive, without written words. To rest. To be able to go home. To be blessedly free from sisters, for almost the first time in her life.

She would confess to Sister Beatrice today that she couldn't read, and her friend would read to her some of the messages of sympathy that lay on the bedside cabinet. There were a lot of cheques among them. Simply from yesterday's brief local newspaper and TV news items. There were reporters from all over the States clamouring to be allowed to interview her. Her heart quailed. Of course she would give the cheques to charity. Americans were very generous, as Marina Porter had said. A financial wizard, like Joseph Kennedy, could have founded an Oswald dynasty on the basis of the cheques that had poured in for Marina. In America, Sister Agnes reflected, the next best thing to being a rich and powerful man was to be the innocent wife of someone who'd killed a rich and powerful man. But it showed her country's heart was in the right place.

Her breakfast tray was removed, and she was left in silence and peace. She watched a vapour-trail across the azure. Time draws on, and she feels a prickle at her nape. He is close, so close. The cloud has thinned out and the sun burns through.

They are in sight; have drawn level; the car has stopped and he has bounded out, grinning broadly.

'We're so proud to have a Catholic President!'

'Do you pray for me too?'

The warm, tingling grasp; she feels it.

They have moved on, into downtown Dallas. She's walking back to the convent, measuring her pace to Sister Bernadette's hobble; everyone talking excitedly, except Sister Beatrice, who's very quiet these days.

She hears, in the Parkland room: You only live once, Sister Agnes; and even that's a fucking miracle! She was used to his vulgarities; there was no harm in them.

They can hear the cheers of the crowds, muffled by the skyscrapers. He won't be falling asleep alone.

Immediately after that thought, a sudden and violent revulsion. She gets out of bed and goes to the bathroom, washes her hands over and over. Yet still her hand is sullied by him. Grasping it so tight, willing it towards his groin. And worse than that. The pure effrontery, her thighs exposed; taking advantage of her pleasure that he was doing it to her and not any of the other sisters. He used her, as he had used all women. She's just an ornament for him, with her personable looks and shy smile and whispery complaisant voice. Sister Beatrice has been right about him all along. Weeping, as she dries her hands, she desperately wants her father's arms around her. Sitting down on her bed, she picks up *November 22*, finds the arrival of the Kennedys at Love Field, and rips it out.

They have entered Main Street and the reception is terrific. Astonishing. The crowds. The noise. The happy, welcoming faces. In this man-made canyon, the heat is even more savage, seeming to focus on the blue Lincoln as on a burning-glass. But Jackie is no longer so conscious of it; she is too caught up in the excitement of the vast crowds, too thrilled at being liked by all these people and she likes them back. It was a wonderful idea to hold the motorcade during the lunch-hour, allowing workers to come out and see them, or hang from windows. Through thousands of windows, stretching half-way up the skyscrapers, typists and office-workers can be seen, hanging out, white blouses and shirts, waving. For them there is a cool breeze, delightful after the airless heat of endless summer. It is a break from dull routine. They have no idea they have already become a part of history; that they will never forget this day; that the day will go on happening for the rest of their lives. They are simply enjoying themselves taking a look at their President and his beautiful, elegant wife, before returning to their peanut-butter sandwiches and Cokes and coffee.

The press of the crowds on the street is so great, spilling out on to the sidewalks, that the motorcade has slowed from thirty to a little over ten miles per hour.

'Keep looking to the left,' Jack reminds her. He is looking right. More than a million people will have seen him in Texas, and they will have seen Jackie too. Texas is going to be a cert next year. His gaze is drawn like a magnet to the smiling, adoring, white-bloused secretaries.

So many lovely women, all over the States. This is just one street in one city. It would be the same in every street in Dallas and every city and town in the country. Millions of white-bloused secretaries; and all, if given the chance, would respond to me. That girl there, hair in a braid, breasts thrust out – and such breasts! – would love to get laid. There's just so little time.

Nelly Connally. Attractive woman for her age, though no Jackie. I wonder if she lays around?

So much colour, drifting by. Red skirts, green dress, blue slacks. The flash of sunlight on that woman's gold bracelet.

They are about to turn off, turn right. He is a little surprised. He can see a sign saying 'Stemmons Freeway', and the underpass is straight ahead. Surely it would be easier, despite the traffic island facing them, to keep going? Not many people ahead, they could pick up speed. Still, these guys know what they're doing. Safer, I guess. It is actually pleasant, after the confined, compressed noise and heat of downtown Dallas, to emerge into a green plaza, Dealey Plaza, with shade-giving trees and a glimpse of pergolas and water. Jackie thinks of saying so – Isn't this nice? – but there is no time, she has to smile at a group of Post Office workers who wave frantically and call 'Jackie!'

The sidewalks are still crowded, though not so dense as on Main. There are workers from the County Records Building, the Dal-Tex building, and the Texas Book Depository, a dull-red, seven-storey building facing them at the end of the block. Jackie senses, although she has no idea what these buildings are, a quieter dignity about them; she would not be surprised to learn they contain books and documents. The onlookers seem more relaxed; they have been picnicking on the grass, many of them, and as soon as the motorcade has passed they will sprawl out again. They will carry the image of the President's boyish hair and eyes above the thickening neck, his warm smile; of Jackie's pink suit, pink pill-box hat and the curve of her dark hair, her eyes and her smile. They will never entirely lose the memory, though it will blur into a hundred other images of them, seen on TV, in newspapers and magazines as the years pass.

The police motor cyclists in the lead have to stop, one foot on the ground, as they manoeuvre their machines around the tight bend into the final section of Elm Street before the triple underpass. The car following, with the police chief and sheriff, slows almost to a halt as the turn is made. A Secret Service man thinks: This is actually against the rules, making such a sharp turn. But we're almost there, we're only five minutes late for lunch, I can do with a long cold beer.

A spectator says to his wife, 'Do you want to see a real live Secret Service man?' He points up to the sixth floor of the Book Depository, where a man is cradling a rifle, gazing out blankly.

The Lincoln makes the left turn, also slowing almost to a halt as it does so. Jackie can see the underpass, and thinks it will be cool there. Thank God.

To their right, past the last building, a grassy slope, and there are people standing and sitting on it. It's the best spot in all Dallas for seeing us, she thinks. It must be almost over; the sign saying 'Stemmons Freeway' suggests freedom, release. She is glad; it's been good, unexpectedly good, but I want that underpass.

A man raises and unfurls a black umbrella. What an odd thing to do, Jack thinks. He must be crazy. Well, let's just say he's eccentric. It's something an Englishman might do. Kick's husband, the perfect English aristocrat, I can see him raising his black brolly at Ascot. Summer of '39. The Nazis got him. Poor Kick, she thought she found happiness with someone else; and then the storm, the mountain. Mom hard-hearted, wouldn't forgive her for loving a divorcee. She can be terribly unforgiving.

Nelly Connally says, over her shoulder to Jackie, 'We're almost through, it's just the other side of that.' She points at the underpass.

That nun, though, really got to me. I'd like to have spent the rest of the day with her. Contact her, find out her name. Mason. Jerry Mason. I've got it! Wiry black hair, glasses. 'Teach', they called him. Reactions too slow for us, applied for transfer to education.

Sad about the other; she too has eyes that can pierce right through you; but doesn't care to use them. Has chosen a house with few mirrors. Poor Rosemary; what is she doing at this moment? I hope she's sitting out in the sun, or walking. She makes us all feel so guilty.

'Teach' Mason. Amazing what you forget, yet know all the time. There was some scandal, when his application was processed. That's right. Child-abuse. Had taught black kids to read using porno magazines. Fondling them, I guess. Claimed you had to gain their interest somehow.

Would have been lynched if they'd been white kids.

I think we made him a naval clerk.

Good pianist, though. *Yes sir, that's my baby!*

Could do with a long cold drink. Not long now.

Nelly looks over her shoulder at him, smiling. 'Well, Mr President, you can't say Dallas doesn't love you!'

The people on the grassy slope waving their arms, cheering.

'I sure can't!'

Nelly straightened in her seat. A plump woman in red, pushing forward, positive the President was smiling straight at her, hears a fire-cracker go off; and sees, just behind the Lincoln, a fiery spark hit the road. Kids! Whoever it is ought to be whupped.

Amid the glow of colours, a red dress, a mauve sweater, the blue sky, Jack felt a strange, unplaceable discomfort beneath his right shoulder that wasn't the normal ache. He moved his shoulder to get rid of it. I don't feel so good. It's hot. Something not right; should get out of here, get to Love Field.

He put his fists to his throat, the breath taken from him; then he heard himself say, My God, I'm hit! He was leaning towards Jackie, and the sky was wheeling. Was nestling against her breast, in a scent of perfume and roses. Her voice, muted, echoing: I love you, Jack! in tones not heard since Patrick Bouvier died.

Then he was outside himself, like Joe over the Channel, like Kick heading into the mountain: flying.

8

It is Sunday, midnight, sixty hours since the shots rang out in Dealey Plaza, yet for Jackie it's as if only seconds have elapsed; in fact, in a sense she and Jack have just left Love Field.

She has been told that Oswald is dead too, shot in Dallas police headquarters, but the news has hardly registered.

Fully dressed she lies curled up on a double bed in the silence of the White House. She reaches over to the empty space.

> . . . And yet there's One whose gently holding hands
> This universal falling can't fall through.

The poem Sorensen, weeping, handed to her, as she and the children turned away from the catafalque, and whose last lines she now whispers to herself, comforts her a little yet also tells her Jack is dead. He has gone from the world. Fate has chosen its path, and flown as straight as an arrow.

To come, only the muffled drums and the riderless black horse.

Later, still unable to contemplate sleep, she wanders out into the grounds. She gazes up through a tree's bare branches at the stars, cold and brilliant. She wonders where, in the vast cosmos, he is. Is it possible he is nowhere? She whispers his name. She is only aware of the silence. Then she hears a rifle shot, and as it echoes she sees a small deer, racing away through long grass, vanishing.